The Istanbul Agent

Jeffrey E. Seay

ISBN-13: 978-0692566510 (Jeffrey E. Seay)
ISBN-10: 0692566511

Cover Art by Christa Holland - Paper and Sage Design
Proofing and Edit by Julia Gibbs - JuliaProofreader

To Earl Seay - the man who saved my life.

CHAPTER ONE

May 15, 2005

Dr. James Bennet was a stand-out in the check-in line. Nearly all of the seventy or eighty people inching between the ribbon barriers were in jeans, shorts, knit pullovers or Hawaiian shirts. Sockless, sandaled feet supported holiday revelers waiting with tickets and passports in one hand, and pulling bags on rollers with the other.

A doctor of biophysics, quantum physics and mechanical engineering, Bennet had gone to the airport directly from his lab. At six foot four and a hundred and seventy-five, the all-nighter he'd pulled to get himself ready for his vacation made his already lanky form look gaunt.

The two-month-old patchy, red-brown and graying beard, sprouting below dark ringed hazel eyes, emphasized an emaciated visage. The thin wiry hair that crowned his melon-shaped dome hadn't had a visit by a comb or brush since he stopped shaving.

Aside from his fidgeting, a sour body odor seeped through his white, button-down cotton shirt and dark blue polyester suit. A smell common to meth tweakers that was making his new traveling companions uncomfortable.

His only luggage was a brown Sharo bag, of time-softened, distressed leather. The large flap with twin buckles concealed a homebuilt laptop, a number of USB flash drives, a toothbrush and a *Qur'an* in both Arabic and English text.

When he reached the counter, the young woman who accepted his travel documents had the good sense to assign him a seat at the back of the aircraft near the galley and toilets. Since Cancun seemed an odd destination for a man with such a dour countenance and motley appearance, she also flagged him as a passenger for TSA to be particularly mindful of. Two security officers dutifully searched his bag and patted him down at the security checkpoint.

The irony was the indignity he felt over being singled out. The humiliation of being groped, his belongings examined, and having to endure the few questions about the purpose of his trip incensed him. He'd somehow compartmentalized this ignominy from the fact that he was indeed about to betray his country and place millions of lives in peril.

It was a three-and-half-hour flight from Dulles to the Mexican resort town. Pleasant, to the extent the cabin attendants left him alone other than to bring a meal and a few snacks. He'd wrestled with the life choice he'd made only a few weeks prior. Once he'd accepted it intellectually, the emotional content in the decision became irrelevant.

Jimmy Bennet wasn't a Muslim. Sired by a pair of inveterate Presbyterians, he grew up in a Detroit suburb steeped in Calvinism and John Knox reformist Christianity. While he didn't consider himself religious, he espoused from time to time, the laboratory as his church; his altar an electron microscope.

If he had a bible, it was the *New York Times* or the *Washington Post*, delivered daily to his lab at the Biological

Technologies Office, a division of the Defense Advanced Research Projects Agency—referred to by those in the know as DARPA. He was reading the *Qur'an* to gain a better understanding of the oppressed people of Palestine and identify with those downtrodden by the Zionist state, Israel.

He believed what he read about the questionable morality of the Bush administration with its continued aggression in Iraq and Afghanistan; its silent acceptance of the atrocities of Israeli imperialism. He also became increasingly disgruntled with his own organization flatly rejecting several project proposals for bioengineering a number of new bacterial agents he'd developed.

The aerosol delivery schemes were beyond cutting edge. The modeling indicated penetration of all but the latest in level B encapsulated bio-hazard protective wear. An infected subject would become contagious within minutes of exposure.

The sweet spot, however, was after a few short hours from the aerosol release, the agent that hadn't been ingested would become inert, harmless. A mass casualty weapon, as effective as carpet bombing, without the attendant property damage.

He knew this was some good stuff and no one was willing to fund further research, let alone production and testing. It wasn't until he'd been contacted by a fellow sojourner in his rarefied field who had been placed on a limited distribution mailing list, that he saw an opportunity to further the science. Apparently, the man had access to sanitized versions of at least three published papers, and because of his own developing research in similar areas of bacterial agents and bio-toxin models, reached out.

The man's name was Randall Ian Hodges, with a company called Power Elite Computing, a subsidiary of a larger private conglomerate interested in financing global philanthropic enterprises. He could guarantee Jimmy the funding he needed but there was a catch: the good doctor would have to be willing to relocate to a facility in the Middle East, owned and operated by an entity unfriendly to the United States and committed to the destruction of Israel.

Doctor Jimmy was elated and terrified at the same time. He was going to be allowed to set things right; bring balance to the world he saw as upside down.

After clearing customs he found the driver he was told would be waiting. It was another twenty-five minutes, enveloped in cream leather in the backseat of a Phantom Drophead Coupé, before Jimmy stood in the lobby of the Live Aqua. A sweeping ten-story white and sea blue structure with terraced sides, it was an adults only, all-inclusive beach resort hotel. A third-world five star, it sat halfway down the strand on Boulevard Kukulcán.

A twenty-something Selma Hayek lookalike at the registration counter handed him a large manila envelope after she checked his passport, and then directed him to the elevators. The lobby was glass and marble with a large not-so-reflecting pool she smoothly guided him past.

"Dr. Bennet, we have you registered for three nights in our Aqua suite. I believe you'll enjoy it. It has its own terrace, jacuzzi, a well-stocked mini-bar, king-sized bed, Wi-Fi and full cable television."

Jimmy was beginning to crash and had difficulty focusing on the words forming through the petite woman's smiling lips. "Uh, yeah, thank you. Did you say three nights?"

"Yes, sir. By the way, your luggage arrived this morning. We had the floor steward hang the suits and formal attire in the closet; underwear and folded shirts are in the dresser."

"I'm sorry, what luggage?"

"Your luggage, sir. Three large suitcases and a steamer trunk. Quite a lot actually for only three nights, if you don't mind me saying, sir."

"No, no...I, uh, forgot about it." *There must be some kinda mistake...*

They rode the elevator to the fourth floor and using a card key the woman led him into the lodging. A two room affair, one was filled with an over-stuffed sofa, a couple of matching easy chairs and a mahogany veneered desk. A forty-inch TV hung from the wall.

The other space had a platform bed that Jimmy thought would sleep six comfortably. *All inclusive...* There was also a small gray settee, coffee table and breakfast nook with frameless windows on three sides. The bathroom was to the left as he walked into the room, separated only by white sheers. The toilet was in a little space that reminded him of a closet. *Water closet...go figure.*

The doctor may have been a true genius and consummate professional in designing nano death dealers but he didn't get out much. It wasn't that he didn't like people or seeing the world at large. On the contrary, he found people and human events, in general, intriguing. Unfortunately, he was utterly ill equipped to connect.

He could watch and listen but didn't have the patience or energy to dial down to a level that allowed him to interact. He had to memorize simple but acceptable responses to almost everything.

A perfect example were comments about the weather, which always seemed to be a conversation starter with many of the people he encountered. While mystified why anyone gave a shit if it was hot enough for him, he also discovered detailed meteorological explanations were definite show stoppers. *Yeah, boy...hot enough to fry an egg..uh-huh...*

Jimmy had learned to live with his ineradicable loneliness, which made his correspondence with someone like Randall Hodges particularly special. It wasn't often he came across a person who appeared to operate in the same time and space. Had he known how to put it in context, the encouragement Randy provided for Jimmy's new adventure would have been described by ordinary folks as peer pressure.

"Is the room to your satisfaction, sir?"

"Huh? Oh, uh, sure...it's nice, thanks." He could feel his anxiety suddenly grow. She wasn't leaving and he knew he was somehow missing the point.

"Doctor Bennet, we hope you'll enjoy your stay." She extended her hand and spread a sweet smile.

He took it reflexively and gave it a gentle squeeze. She, in turn, giggled at his confusion. A tip was an alien concept to a man who looked and smelled like a hermit.

As she spun to leave he remembered what he thought he was missing. "Ah, excuse me but you still have my passport."

She turned, still exhibiting her well-kept teeth. "Yes, sir. It's hotel policy to retain our guests' travel documents until after their stay."

She once again pointed out the menu of services, dining options and hotel-sponsored activities, finishing with a comment that sounded more like casual advice. "The staff here are well trained, friendly and attentive. Gratuities, while unnecessary, are greatly appreciated." With a parting bow, she was out the door.

Now embarrassed, he was about to chase her down the hallway with a few bills, when his attention landed on the manila envelope she'd presented to him at the reception desk. It was still cupped in his left hand.

Using a letter opener he found in the desk's center drawer, he slit the top seam and pulled out an aged passport, a cell phone and a folded piece of stationery with a waxed seal. Cracking the signet he unfolded the paper and read a welcoming letter that reminded him of the type of documentation a human resources department would provide a new employee.

Much to his surprise he learned he had a cover name: Jerome Francis Brody. The Canadian passport he'd pulled from the envelope had the name inscribed, accompanied by an old photo of a younger, beardless James Bennet. It also had dozens of stamps from various countries going back seven or eight years.

He grabbed a piece of hotel stationery, and using the Montblanc Meisterstück he carried in a plastic pocket protector, scribbled the name. When he compared it to the signature on the passport, it seemed to correlate that it would indeed look exactly the same.

The cell phone had a local number. The letter advised he'd be receiving a call on the mobile at eight pm, from an individual who would provide him additional information. He was then instructed to bathe and shave. A plastic bag on the bed was for the clothes on his back, his shoes included. An appointment for a haircut had also been made.

He checked his watch. The barber would be there in forty-five minutes. Jimmy, now Jerome, always appreciated structure. Although he appeared unkempt, he was hardly the absentminded professor. A schedule-driven anal retentive, Jerome Francis Brody had his orders. His mind was now free to ponder those subjects with which he was obsessed, as his body completed the directed tasks.

After a shower and a soak in the jacuzzi tube, a Mexican gentleman in white tunic arrived. He used clippers to give him a number two on the sides and back, and a seven on top. An Ivy League crew cut. He removed the beard with scissors and a straight razor.

Without the whiskers, Jerome had an angular face. His

long, thin nose had a dimple on the tip. Below it was a crooked nearly lipless mouth, and his chin was broad and square. His eyebrows, thick but trimmed short by the barber, were covered by a pair of round, rimless glasses.

When the cell phone rang at eight sharp, Jerome was sitting in a hand-wrapped wicker chair on the terrace. Dressed in white J. Crew chinos, a light blue Indian cotton button down with the sleeves rolled to the elbows and a pair of navy Aston Barlow canvas slip-ons, he pushed the green button.

"Hello?"

"Good evening, Dr. Brody. This is Control. I appreciate you've followed the instructions in the envelope I left for you."

The French accent with its quiet and low resonance tickled Jimmy's ear.

"I'm sorry, you said your name is Control?"

"That's how you will address me. It's somewhat formal, I know but it's easy to remember and good for your security and mine."

Jerome didn't argue. When it came to security, he'd toiled for the last several years through layers of procedural constructs and measures created to protect the projects he'd been involved with. It was expected. Even his initial correspondence with that fellow Randall Ian Hodges had to be maintained using terminology that wouldn't set off alarms with the key-word recognition software installed on DARPA servers.

When things got serious he changed venues. He went to a Starbucks for the free Wi-Fi, and using a laptop he'd built, communicated via a Secure Socket Layer and OpenPGP. It was basic, but safe and effective for a short period. The OpenPGP gave him the method encryption and the SSL provided the protocol for encrypting and decrypting data sent across direct internet connections.

assignments resulting in death and destruction. Circumstances not ordinarily associated with NCIS operations. No one argued the mission requirements weren't completed. Whether or not they were ultimately successful was another matter.

He'd hoped 2005 would be the beginning of a smooth downward slide to an uneventful retirement. A prospect he not only looked forward to, but aggressively pursued. Within six months of the turn of the half-decade Ruben had to weather a nasty internal investigation by the Inspector General's Office, called a 2B by NCIS, and found himself listed as persona non grata with the Malaysian and Chinese authorities.

He was lucky it only went that far. Both countries were unhappy with the apparent body count but the Chinese had the added insult of millions of dollars' worth of property damage and the defection of one of its People's Liberation Army officers.

Pack out for Ruben was a relatively simple process. While it had been years since he could stuff everything he owned in a duffle bag, a team of three could box his belongings and load it for shipment in less than two hours.

A bachelor with few prospects, he'd turned fifty-three during his last dust-up in China and was still knitting from a couple of bullet wounds and some dental work. He had his paperwork in hand for his final check-out when his boss, the Supervisory Special Agent for Counterintelligence at the NCIS Far East Field Office, ordered him to a half-day seminar on retirement planning. Ruben had a feeling the guy was trying to tell him something.

The four hours were divided into sections covering pay, insurance, taxes, social security, and a number of other mind-numbing topics. It felt like a series of eulogies for the nearly departed. Along with that he had to make time to work out the details with his partner Barry on how to manage his half-interest in the bar and live-house they owned in central Tokyo.

The plan was to return to the Land of the Rising Sun in two years, either as his swan song with the Service, or as a retiree. Barry expressed serious interest in a physical security and executive protection startup. They'd run it out of the bar. Ruben thought it sounded a bit clichéd but couldn't think of better place to spend his afternoons.

With a strategy mapped out, he boarded a chartered flight provided by the Air Mobility Command aboard the Naval Air Facility Atsugi, wondering how realistic a return to Japan could be for anything more than a short visit. Considering how things had been going recently, predicting even the obvious couldn't be trusted. As the cabin door closed, he turned the page.

The *chili relleno* at Fonda La Reforma was delicious, but always gave Henry heartburn. The chicken mole was his favorite, but taste aside, within a few hours of a sit down at the famous hole in the wall, he could strike blue flames that would cut like acetylene. He had a country team meeting that afternoon, and decided on the grilled chicken and avocado tacos.

Henry Dever had been in Mexico City for about four and half months. His transfer to the Latin American country had been a sudden one, and an odd assignment for the former Special Agent in Charge of the NCIS Singapore Field Office. Thanks to a highly touted but nearly blown operation earlier in the year, political expediency dictated a change in venue.

A graduate of the Field Training Course at Camp Peary, Henry was a CIA certified Case Officer. Trained in offensive intelligence collection tradecraft, he was already well known in the 'community' as an effective operator. He'd produced a couple of NCIS double agents ops in the run-up to the second Gulf War that turned more than a few heads.

However, it wasn't until he played host to Carver and his team earlier in the year, that his career plans began to unravel. Dever's role was to support their investigation into the deaths of three Special Agents and the disappearance of another, which occurred on his turf.

It was a messy week. While the identification of those responsible for the murders was heralded, the apparent vigilante justice that followed ruffled some feathers. A few righteously indignant climbers at Headquarters couldn't help exercising their intellect with terms like 'due process' and 'standards of conduct'. One of the brain trust even mentioned, with straight face, the lack of Posse Comitatus.

Henry figured things could have been worse. What saved their bacon was uncovering an espionage ring trying to infect Seventh Fleet systems with a really nasty piece of malware. In the process, they bagged two U.S. Embassy employees and confirmed the collusion of a now deceased husbanding agent.

There was also the embarrassment NCIS suffered over the suspected involvement of one of its own. That was marginally counterbalanced by the collaboration with the Singapore police in dismantling an organized crime syndicate.

The Inspector General's report capped its findings with a comment about the impropriety of placing a number of Special Agents and local law enforcement officers at risk both physically and professionally. While Carver took the primary hit, management felt it propitious when Henry's name popped up in a CIA communiqué.

The intelligence agency had requested an experienced foreign counterintelligence specialist to assist in its operations in Central and South America. For some reason Henry had been asked for specifically.

He was halfway through the fifteen-minute drive back to the Embassy, situated in the heart of the Mexican capital, when his cell phone rang. It was his admin support, Gladys, and while he didn't want to be bothered to pick up, he knew she'd continue to ring until he did.

"Hey, Gladys. Traffic is shit. Can it wait?"

She had a high, squeaky voice coupled with a Boston accent. "It can if you're on your way back to the office."

"Why, what's up?"

"You have a visitor from Virginia."

"Is he here for the country team meeting?"

"He didn't say, but he's in your office on the phone."

Dever had a couple of irons in the fire generating interest in DC but nothing had reached a point to generate a personal visit.

"What's his name?"

"It's good that you should ask. It's Arthur Sheppard. So maybe it'd be a good idea to put the pedal down."

Oh crap, what's this about? "Okay, let him know I'll be there in about ten minutes."

Dever remembered reading an announcement generated from CIA Headquarters that Arthur "Art" Sheppard, the Chief of Station in China had been promoted. He was now the Chief of the Near East and South Asia Division. While it was not the sole reason for Art's bump in salary, Henry knew the last shitstorm Carver was responsible for in China netted the new CNESA a couple of big 'at-a-boys at HQ.

Henry had also heard through the NCIS grapevine that Carver and Sheppard had some previous history. It had something to do with Carver's tour in Vietnam during the war, but didn't know the particulars. He hadn't had any contact with the big guy after the Singapore romp, and only bits and pieces about the

China mission came Henry's way during his regular Navy Yard bi-weeklies.

The Embassy was a five-story square structure, with columns of windows separated by framed white marble panels. The second floor was a mezzanine encased in glass with a terrace accessible from the cafeteria and small commissary. In the center of the complex was an open air patio—an architectural nod toward the traditional Mexican villa.

The main entrance was off of Avenida Paseo de La Reforma. Folks on foot, needing to visit consular affairs or U.S. citizen services, went through that entrance. The Embassy was built in the early 60's before concerns about offsets and vehicle barriers. Employee parking wasn't a consideration then and none was available.

Most Embassy staff continued to use the parking structure behind the Sheraton Maria Isabel Hotel and Towers, which he drove past. He then hung a right on a one way axis road called Eje 2 Pte.

At the next intersection, he made a right on another one way street called Rio Lerma and five hundred feet later jogged right again on Rio Danubio. A narrow avenue that separated the diplomatic mission from the Sheraton was the entrance to parking.

Hustling to the guard station, he was greeted by a Mexican national dressed in a black military style uniform with bloused boots and beret. Henry's face was known but the guard had him display his badge anyway.

Once inside and through the Marine checkpoint, he stepped into an empty elevator and rose to the fourth floor where he had a tiny office inside the CIA's space. Gladys Marquez, a barely five-foot bottle blonde with a bowling ball shape and matching short, tight perm, buzzed him through the entry. At the end of her extended hand were several yellow message slips she waved at him.

She said nothing as he pulled them from her grip but bobbed her head in the direction of his door. Flared nostrils and a tight brow delivered the alert.

He took a breath and moved forward. He may have only been on loan but the Agency was still writing his performance evaluations. Art Sheppard had the reputation for being draconian. While good operations officers loved the guy, everyone else not fitting that description had a tendency to hate his guts.

Henry's office was a seven-foot cube with a window just big enough to let in some light. In the time he'd been on station he hadn't done much decorating. The pictures he had lining his walls in Singapore were still in boxes crammed in a corner. The desk filled most of the room but it did have a couple of metal-framed chairs for visitors.

Without bothering to sit down, Henry flipped through his phone messages Gladys had handed him. The two men made eye contact when he walked across the threshold, but the dude in his chair was still on the NSA issued STU-III, talking softly into the handset. Dever noticed the key he'd left in the unit was turned to secure mode. *At least he's not using the desk as an ottoman.*

In his late-fifties, Art Sheppard was a welterweight at five foot nine. He wore a two-button cotton twill suit with a light blue and white plaid shirt; no tie. His white hair, combed straight back, was so thin Henry wondered why he didn't do the fashionable thing and go with a number one cut.

He had a round face with bushy eyebrows and hair sprouting on the edges of his ears. His jaw jutted from an underbite and the heavy lids on his small eyes gave him a squinty look.

Couple that with a half-inch vertical scar at the bridge of his nose, and Art had the appearance of being perpetually pissed off. Uncharacteristically conspicuous for a guy in his line of work.

When he laid the handset in its cradle he didn't get up. He locked on Henry with a stare that begged the question: *You got a problem with that?* He then nodded at one of the chairs in front of the desk.

"You know who I am?" He spoke with the kind of self-assurance that made the query rhetorical.

"Ah, Art Sheppard?" Henry's response sounded like code for 'fuck you'.

The smile was more of a smirk. "That's right and you're probably wondering what I'm doing here."

"It crossed my mind."

"Well, Hank, I understand you and Ruben Carver have a special bond. Not unlike the one I share with the man, although it's been over thirty years."

"He's a friend of mine. I've known him since my first day on the job. What's this about?"

"I'll get to that in a second." Sheppard paused for a heartbeat. "I've been through your file. You've got a good track record—impressive really. While you may think this is a punishment tour, considering your previous assignment, the folks at Headquarters are happy to have you here.

"You've got a knack for counterintelligence and apparently you've already started ticking some of the boxes the Agency has had on its sheet for this area of operation."

Dever said nothing. His elbows indented the thinly padded armrests as he sat back and crossed his legs. He knew Art was one of those guys who constantly assessed people in his domain. As long as Henry didn't break a sweat or get defensive, the prick would get to the point.

"Before I go on, I need to let you know I've conferred with your Director about this conversation and NCIS has expressed its support in what I'm about to tell you. It has to do with an operation I believe you're suited for."

Henry dropped his head a half-inch to the right. "I'm all ears but I'm guessing it's somehow gonna involve my good friend, since you brought him up."

"Aren't you the smart lad." He drummed his fingers on the desktop and said, "Hang on to that thought. I'll come back to it in a minute."

"What about the COS? Shouldn't he be included in this 'briefing'?"

Sheppard leaned forward with forearms on the desk and fingers interlocked. "Don't worry about him. He and I've already talked. You work for me now."

Istanbul was his kind of town. Yves Moreau, Algerian by birth, French by choice and the man Jerome Brody addressed as Control, lounged at a round, gingham-covered table set below a hundred-year-old oak.

He slowly sipped a Turkish coffee and sucked on an unfiltered Gauloise he'd screwed into a four-inch engraved ivory holder. He never got tired of the view from the outdoor cafe, named after Pierre Loti, a nineteenth century French naval officer and novelist. It sat on a hill overlooking the Golden Horn—the estuary that began at the point where the Bosphorus Strait met the Sea of Marmara.

At exactly six feet tall, his narrow shoulders and waist had an almost caricature quality in the over-tailored steel-gray sharkskin Givenchy two-button. A purple silk ascot with a paisley print adorned his neck and was fluffed with flourish under a black Chennai silk shirt. His black-hosed feet were tucked in a pair of hand sewn, Santoni suede loafers, the tassels curled from the humidity.

An excellent day. The light breeze ruffled his oiled, jet black hair, and as he smoothed it with a narrow-toothed comb, he thought about his teleconference a few hours

18

earlier. He'd been able to report a major breakthrough on Dr. Brody's research that put him at least six months ahead of schedule.

Testing had begun within a month of their arrival. As advertised, it had little or no effect on animals, but they'd recently tried it on a couple of street urchins. It was beautiful and terrifying. While there didn't seem to be any symptoms for at least forty-eight hours, when the bacterial agent did go toxic, the subjects were dead within an average work day.

The pathology reports weren't ready yet, but the visual results were amazing just the same. With constant praise, a shiny new and well accoutered bio-research laboratory, Control kept the nutty professor motivated and productive. A steady diet of the *New York Times* and *Washington Post* anti-Semitic op-eds, images from CNN and Al Jazeera, and an occasional crystal bump also helped.

As he slipped on a pair of Lanvin sunglasses over an aquiline nose, he reflected quietly on The Board's parting cautionary comments. Over the FBI's objections, the CIA had assumed jurisdiction in locating DARPA's missing scientist. Somehow they'd determined he was in Istanbul. A troubling fact that had The Board examining its operational security and communications infrastructure.

Even more concerning to the members of the organization, however, was the possibility the Agency was considering enlisting the aid of the Naval Criminal Investigative Service, and more particularly an individual Yves Moreau had never heard of. Someone named...Ruben Carver.

CHAPTER THREE

September 5, 2005 - Labor Day

In the seventeen years as a Special Agent with NCIS, Ruben calculated he spent less than thirty days at Headquarters. Without being too cynical he felt pretty good about it. As he rolled onto the Washington Navy Yard through the gate at N Street SE, he had a sneaking suspicion he wasn't going to break his personal best. Not when it came to his ass in a chair at the NCIS center of operations.

Assignments at the seat of government were fluid. What he was told when he left Yokosuka changed twice by the time he landed in Los Angeles. Since he had leave coming, and it didn't seem like anyone was in a hurry to have him sit at a desk, he decided to buy a car in LA and take two weeks to drive cross country.

A week later he was in Houston visiting his little brother, Claude, when he got the phone call. Jason Hartley, the GS-15 in charge of NCIS's global counterintelligence operations, referred to as Code 0022, had reached out to deliver the message personally. A manpower request had come from another agency for a special task force being developed, and while Hartley opposed it, the Director made the decision to assign Carver.

Not one to disappoint the man at the helm, he wanted Carver in his office immediately. After some pointed discussion, however, he made allowances for the family visit and drive time. Then the hurricane they called Katrina hit.

Ruben was a week overdue and knew there were a few folks on the fourth deck of the building on Sicard Street SE who were apparently wringing their hands over his late arrival. He didn't understand why it was so important he be the one to man a task force. The scars from a couple of bullet wounds he acquired on his last 'special' mission were still pink, for cryin' out loud. Besides, there were plenty of young Special Agents who lived for that shit.

It was a ten minute walk to the office from the parking structure. He didn't have a vehicle sticker yet, but because of the holiday, the lot was nearly empty. There was plenty of visitor parking near the entrance. He checked his watch: eight-thirty.

As he stepped out onto the concrete and threw the door closed, its solid sound was a self-satisfying affirmation. After commandeering a BMW 745i from a bad guy in Shanghai, during that same special mission, he decided life was too short not to indulge in his own ultimate driving machine.

He couldn't afford the 7 series but was able to stretch the budget to find himself tucked behind the wheel of an M3 Competition Package. The 2006 model had just been delivered to the dealers in LA, and with a phone call to USAA, he had his financing and insurance in thirty minutes.

The Interlagos Blue ragtop had over three hundred horses in a straight six under the hood. It could do zero to sixty in four-and-a-half seconds with the six-speed Getrag manual transmission. The top end was a hundred and fifty-five mph but with the electronic governor disconnected he could red-line it at one seventy.

While he didn't expect to be going that fast, it gave him testosteronal comfort knowing he could. The guy who said the love of a good woman was the most fulfilling experience of a man's life had obviously never sat on top of a great set of wheels.

Getting past the building's guard station took almost ten minutes. The uniformed security professionals behind the counter had him sign in and then dicked around making phone calls and searching through drawers trying to find his badge. He was eventually awarded with a visitor's pass delivered with pinched fingers.

He didn't bother with the elevator in the atrium. Instead, he took the stairs two at a time to the second deck where the lunch room and vending machines were located. After grabbing a large Styrofoam cup he half-filled with something resembling coffee, he proceeded to Hartley's office on the fourth deck.

Headquarters on Labor Day was quiet. Except for those pulling duty in the Multiple Threat Alert Center, or at workstations pounding out late paper, the building was abandoned. While it was generally bustling with a dichotomy of the semi-competent self-impressed and the truly brilliant shit-hot operators, Carver found the place in a constant state of renovation—while at the same time in perpetual need of a paint job and fresh carpet.

After being escorted into the counterintelligence space, he was greeted by a few Special Agents who were missing out on the family BBQ. CI activity overseas didn't stop in observance of a national day off. Ruben acknowledged a few and waved. Truth was, he either knew or knew about most of the men and women riding desks in the crappy confines of Code 0022.

Some were solid case officers overseeing a number of double agent or collection operations. Others, who'd opted for a quiet life of obscurity, were monitoring and analyzing various other activities worldwide.

When he got to Jason Hartley's cubbyhole, he found not only the CI global head, but two other men from his recent past: Henry Dever and Art Sheppard. They were huddled around a four-chair table in a dimly lit office, the walls of which didn't go all the way to the unfinished ceiling.

They didn't look up until he started talking. "I think you guys need to complain about the working conditions. Has this place ever been checked for asbestos? What a shithole."

With more than half his career at Headquarters, Hartley's sense of humor was reserved for only a very few people he trusted. Even then it was limited to benign wisecracks and Pollyanna jibes.

"We keep a jar for donations up at the admin station, asshole. It's about time you got here."

Hartley cut an imposing figure at six foot eight and nearly two hundred and fifty pounds. The jowly baby-face liked cream and sugar in his coffee, to go along with the ham and cheese omelet, pancakes and bacon every morning. Monster deli sandwiches piled with roast beef or pastrami were his general fare at lunch.

He also made a habit of stopping at Shooter's Sports Bar in Springfield on his way home three nights a week. The fried spring rolls, won tons and half-dozen Coronas were staple.

"You know these two guys, right?" Hartley waved a hammy index finger at his two guests.

Ruben did a reverse nod with wary eyes, and then shook hands with each man. Looking directly at Art Sheppard he said, "Task force, huh?"

"You can only say so much on an open line."

"Which one of you guys drew the short straw on sloppy seconds?"

Dever spoke through a grim smile. "Maybe we can get a dinner and movie in first."

"Now wait a minute, Carver." Hartley leaned back in his ergonomic chair, palms braced on the armrests. "The Agency here has the answer to the Headquarters tour you've been bitchin' about."

Ruben looked in Jason's direction but responded to all three. "I've been bent over a table enough times by this organization to spot the signals. My shoulder isn't the only thing still sore from the last operation."

Art spoke up. "Yeah, you definitely got your hands dirty in Shanghai, but that's your style isn't it?" Unlike Dever, Sheppard wasn't smiling. "What we've got for you this time isn't gonna be a walk in the park either, but before you choose not to participate, let me tell you what it's about and why you."

Fuck. Had they lied to him, Ruben would have felt justified in walking out. Now, he might as well have been stapled to the chair.

"All right. Let's hear it."

For the next thirty minutes Sheppard outlined the national security threat. He didn't dwell on the projects Dr. Bennet had been involved with, but rather focused on proposals the researcher submitted for funding consideration. It was no secret Bennet became increasingly unhappy as one requested enterprise after another was rejected.

Sanitized versions of his submissions, though, had been published in a number of scientific journals because they were, in fact, ground-breaking. They presented postulates with real potential for biomedical advances. The weaponized versions of the agents Bennet was developing through his modeling, however, breached a number of international agreements regarding WMD.

Sheppard emphasized that anyone with a background in bacterially derived toxin research and reading those published papers would certainly have been able to extrapolate a deadly purpose. With him gone missing, the logical fear was Bennet had been co-opted into completing his research. He could conceivably provide an active and deadly agent, with a delivery system the U.S. had no effective defense against.

Sheppard's chronicle of the details of the DARPA scientist's disappearance was clear with regard to his trip to Mexico. When he arrived, and how long he was scheduled to stay, had been well documented.

His room had been paid for out of an account opened in a Grand Cayman bank, seeded with cash for this single transaction. He arrived with nothing more than a leather satchel, but had what appeared to be an entire wardrobe waiting for him. Hotel staff advised he enjoyed a makeover the day he arrived, but no one remembered seeing him after that.

Agency analysts felt certain he wasn't dead and equally certain he hadn't been kidnapped. It was believed he left the resort the evening after his arrival, with a large French tour group returning to Paris. Hotel and airport security video confirmed this with images of a man fitting Bennet's description moving among the *bon chic bon genre*.

The capper for the analysts was, the gentleman they assumed to be Dr. James Bennet had in fact checked out of the resort. They also confirmed he was listed on the passenger manifest under his true name. He disappeared when he got to Paris.

As Carver listened to the rundown of the missing person slash possible defector scenario, he thought it was all very intriguing. A nice adventure for some young agent full of juice and derring-do. He didn't see why Art, or anyone else for that matter, would want him on this assignment.

The gray flecks at the temples, along with stiff joints,

muscle pain and longer recovery periods were signals in his mind it was time to take a seat on the bench.

"This is a great story, Art, but you haven't said anything that even comes close to a reason to bring me into this, let alone NCIS."

Sheppard looked at Dever and Hartley, both sitting and staring in a way that punctuated Carver's comment.

With Art's silence Ruben pursued the logical. "Correct me if I'm wrong but the newly formed National Clandestine Service is full of people trained for this kind of stuff. Right? I mean you've got operations officers with special skills like core collection and paramilitary training, not to mention area specialists and language talent. Fuck...your guys have got it totally goin' on. Plus you've got the kinda deep pockets that makes the FBI jealous. Whaddya need me for?"

Sheppard's brow puckered and his bottom lip popped out as he set his protruding jaw. "So you're saying you're not gonna to help me?"

"I'm not sayin' that. I'm *always* happy to find something that'll get me out of the office. I know it's my fault for not lettin' you get to the point. I'm assuming the job you've got is to go find and collect that poor misguided peripatetic prober, and bring his sorry ass home."

"That sums it up pretty well."

"So just tell me why you think I'm the right guy for the mission. China may have been good for you, but it not only kicked my ass, it also got me kicked out of the Far East."

"Okay, okay...cool your jets, cowboy. You aren't asking any questions I haven't already had to answer to my management and yours. The investigation into Bennet's disappearance revealed a few things that linked it to not only your China punch-up, but peripherally to your Singapore operation as well. He went missing on the first of June after what now appears to be a series of emails with Randall Ian Hodges. Does that ring a bell?"

"Oh, shit."

"Exactly. We pored over hundreds of emails Bennet had corresponding with other researchers interested in data related to his published works. While Hodges' correspondence was benign, the fact his name came up sent ripples through the Agency."

"You think The Board is behind this?"

"After you repatriated Ryan Henderson, part of his penance was to work for the NSA and help identify The Board's members and track their activities. For the most part they were successful, but we believe because of their connections at the seat of government they found out fairly quickly we were on to them. They changed their methods of communication, but not before we acquired some intel that suggested where Bennet might be located."

"Okay, I'm following."

"Ordinarily, we'd never shop an operation like this outside the Agency, however, when it comes to The Board, we've found ourselves sailing in a leaky ship. That's why I'm here. You've come up against this group twice this year and survived. You've put a major crimp in their modus operandi in the Far East and we want you to do it again. This time in the Near East."

Ruben remained motionless for a few seconds before he focused on Dever. "What's Henry's role?"

"He's your handler. If you run into a snag, he'll be sending in plays from the sideline. You're gonna be running solo on this one. There won't be anyone else privy to your movements. This is a CIA covert operation from the standpoint that my Headquarters will be funding it and we'll give you as much support as we can. You'll get whatever equipment you need and pretty much carte blanche on expenses. Just do me a favor and hang on to your receipts."

"Is there gonna be any other interested parties in this gig?"

"Whaddya mean?"

"Come on, Art. Who else knows about us misplacing a DARPA scientist? Who can I expect to try to crash the party?"

"We believe he's in Istanbul, so the Russians might know, quite possibly the Iranians and for sure the Israelis."

"Well, that's fuckin' great."

"Oh, and you might run into some of your Chinese pals. So, how 'bout it?"

"I'll give Henry a list of the stuff I want but it'll have to be sent via diplomatic pouch to the Embassy in Istanbul. You decide who should receive it. I also want one more person on the team—Ryan Henderson. Since he's the one who probably turned him, it's likely he knows Dr. James Bennet as well or better than anyone."

CHAPTER FOUR

The Lab

He pumped the pedals in rhythm with his state of mind. Dr. Jerome Brody's head had been in overdrive from almost the moment he'd arrived in the city that bridged the east with the west. He was initially disappointed about being in Istanbul. It was rarely displayed in the media as being down for the Palestinian struggle. It didn't take but two or three days, however, to have a mood shift.

As he rode his one-speed bike along a cut-stone paved walk, between marble edifices housing modern research facilities, libraries and classrooms, he began to believe if there was a heaven, this was it. It was a sense of tranquility he'd rarely experienced before, and it was now quickly disintegrating.

His lab was a leased space on the campus of Koç University, as was his faculty housing. A relatively new institute of higher education, Koç was located near a village in north Istanbul, called Rumeli Feneri. Carved out of the forest, on several hundred hectares, it overlooked the mouth of the Bosphorus as it opened to the Black Sea, from the European side of the city.

With the comforting feel of isolation, it was only forty-five minutes by university shuttle to the Grand Bazaar in the heart of west Istanbul. When Jerome questioned the logic of working in a place noted for its research and international scholastic achievement, Control's response was simple: "If you want to hide a tree, plant it in a forest."

As part of Dr. Brody's cover, he was plugged in as a visiting adjunct professor of biochemistry. For one hour, three days a week, he taught young, eager minds the secrets of life at the molecular level. The rest of the time he labored at developing more effective and economically efficient methods of destroying it.

His laboratory was, like so many on campus, strictly access-controlled. Unlike the others it had been kitted out by The Board. A twenty-five hundred square foot facility located in a sub-basement under the College of Engineering, it was shielded from the latest electromagnetic emissions detection and monitoring capabilities. Control used NSA TEMPEST standards provided by the good doctor when building the security infrastructure.

It was tricked out for microfluidics and microelectromechanical systems. A complete microfabrication facility with the emerging lab-on-a-chip technology, it also provided him with everything he needed for surgical, histological and molecular recombinant DNA techniques, as well as developmental, molecular and computational biology and neuroscience resources.

The three isolation rooms, a hooded autopsy table and incinerator, allowed him and his team of four to not only develop but test his handiwork on subjects without leaving their comfortable confines. Dr. Brody was able to limit his human interaction to his students and lab assistants—who called him Jerry—along with a daily video confab with Control.

He had had no complaints until the previous week.

One of his assistants, a thirty-two-year-old Croatian with a PhD in molecular genetics, didn't show up for work on Monday morning. Over a long weekend she'd gone shopping on the Asiatic side. After three days, her body was discovered in the bathtub of a cheap hotel room.

When the police came calling, Dr. Brody was informed through the university administration, the woman was apparently not Croatian but Israeli. While everyone had questions, the wheels had been sufficiently greased to keep his name out of any official inquiry. That did not, however, ease Jerome's mind. The woman had become something of a protégée and at her insistence his paramour.

Control had also gone off the grid and Brody, thinking the worst, believed the Algerian's body would be the next one found. By the weekend that fear was abated. Moreau contacted him and scheduled a face-to-face with a promise to provide details regarding the death of the doctor's first love.

As he rode across Koç Square past the main library, he saw Yves Moreau sitting in the shade of the clock tower, sipping coffee at a bistro table outside the student center. The doctor would have preferred meeting in the lab but for some reason Moreau had always insisted their one-on-ones be held elsewhere.

Jerome rolled up to the table and stomped on the rear pedal. The back tire locked and squealed, depositing ten inches of rubber skim on the stone inlay. He said nothing as he yanked his leg over the comfort-padded seat and jammed the kick-stand down with the heel of a gray Hush Puppy.

Storming the three feet to the seated, well-coiffed gentleman with slicked back hair and a bristled, pencil-thin mustache, Brody could barely contain himself. "*Where have you been?* What's going on? Medleva has been killed..."

Moreau sat with his legs crossed, a demitasse cup in his right hand as he waved his left at the chair on the other side of the table. "Please."

The quiet, calm intonation was disconcerting at first, but not to be put off, Jerome opened his mouth to continue his fulmination. At that point Control firmed up and ordered the doctor to sit down. "Jerome, get a hold of yourself. I know she was killed—murdered actually—in a rather horrific manner from what I understand. I'm looking into it."

"What does that mean, you're looking into it? Do you have any idea how important she was to the project?" Jerome couldn't remember the last time he cried. He wasn't sure he was even capable of shedding a tear, but his guts were in a knot. He didn't have the words to describe what he was feeling.

Sucking through the holder on a freshly lit cigarette, Control responded. "Nonsense. This is your project and you have other assistants. This woman was important to you because she took you to her bed. It's a shame your little head doesn't have the same IQ as your big head.

"Anyway, my concern is two-fold. I need to know how we missed she was Israeli. Her background investigation checked out. She had some excellent backstopping, which leads me to believe she was probably Israeli Intelligence Service—likely Shabak. That said, we have to assume the Jews are fully aware of what we've been up to.

"More than that, it was unlikely she could have withstood the treatment she received without giving up the program to whoever took her. I've taken the liberty of changing all the access codes and authorizations. If you've been to the lab this morning you already know this."

Dr. Brody wasn't sure how to respond. He was, in actuality, aware of almost nothing going on around him since he'd heard the report. Apparently, he was the only one who didn't realize his relationship, with the now deceased Medleva Jankovic, was evident to anyone who saw them together. As he watched Control's lips move, his mind slipped to the start.

The overnight flight from Cancun to Orly was barely a memory. He had a first class ticket, and with the exception of the hour he spent preparing a journal entry on the laptop, and jotting down a list of lab equipment, he must have slept most of the way—odd for the newly monikered Jerome Brody. Ordinarily, he could never get any deeper than a doze on an aircraft. The low hum and slight vibration wouldn't allow him to get past a sense of groggy inertia.

The trip to Istanbul was a different matter. Yves Moreau was waiting for him upon arrival in Paris. He wasted no time in escorting Jerome through the bustling airport and out the glassed exit to a car waiting at the curb. They left the luggage. It had been managed separately for delivery to the final destination.

Seemingly aware of the doctor's difficulty with small talk, Control kept the conversation limited to when, where, how and why. They drove straight north into the city for fifty-minutes during which time Jerome was advised exactly where they were going, how long it would take to get there, who they would meet, and approximately how long it would take before he could settle into his new environment.

The clarity with which the details were presented was as calming as fractal repetition. A salve to his psyche.

The list of the hardware and software he would need, he presented to Control on four airline logoed napkins. They were accepted without question. The assurance Jerome received that the orders for the equipment would go out that afternoon, along with a scheduled three week buildout for the laboratory, reaffirmed the validity of this divergent reality.

At Gare de l'Est, they boarded a train for a four day trip to the doctor's new home on the Bosphorus. It wasn't the fabled and recently rejuvenated Orient Express, but it did take him to Vienna, Budapest, through the Carpathian Mountains to Bucharest and into Istanbul. The history of the region spanning more than two millennia didn't escape him, and while filtered through the logic processor between his ears, the traitorous tour had taken on a romantic quality.

The university administration greeted him with nothing more than a warm smile and friendly handshake. Fanfare on his arrival had been purposefully squashed. He was stepping into the role of adjunct professor, taking the place of a fellow with the same name and general appearance.

Two days after he'd received the key to his well-accoutered on-campus apartment and his class schedule for the coming semester, he met the four lab assistants who would help him make some history of his own.

Each of them had been identified, vetted, assessed and recruited at the behest of The Board. They were introduced as ideologically sound, without any attendant fanaticism. Dr. Brody had been briefed that the The Board wanted believers, not terrorists.

What Jerome discovered regarding the three men—a Georgian with a doctorate in molecular biology, a Spanish medical doctor with an expertise in neurotoxin associated disorders, and an Indian from Mumbai with a genius for bioinformatics—was the surprising lack of sound ideology, or more specifically no ideology whatsoever.

Three individuals with no underlying or foundational belief systems strong enough to challenge their amoral drive in the 'pure' sciences. Jerome genuinely liked these guys. There were no uncomfortable justifications or rationalizations somehow connected to the good of mankind. Their brains didn't work that way.

When it came to human trials, the only thing they couldn't tolerate was leaving the lab to find subjects. They relied on their boss, Jerry, to manage those details. Clean-up, on the other hand, was no problem. They cleared the table, did the dishes and disposed of leftovers. A trio of fun-loving sociopaths, whose only disagreements erupted on poker night when they'd catch each other cheating.

Medleva Jankovic was a horse of different color. A genomics whiz by vocation, she was a passionate ideologue, constantly preaching the plight of the Palestinians and Chechens. Any group, for that matter, identified as being oppressed—which numbered, apparently, in the tens-of-millions—could be the focus of one of her daily litanies.

While her three lab partners found it exceedingly easy to ignore her diatribes, Jerome was smitten. Aside from the political polemics, Medleva had a way of making Jerome feel connected, interesting, even desirable.

The doctor could never abide people getting in his personal space, which he calculated once to be exactly one point three five meters square. However, once she started touching him, both mentally and physically, it became painful when she wasn't near him.

At five feet one inch and one hundred and thirty pounds, she had an earth mother figure, with heavy thighs and breasts. Her brain, with an IQ difficult to assess, was encased in a round crown, which supported a thick, kinky black mane. At least twenty inches long, it didn't fall to her shoulders but rather grew out in a frizzy mass that sagged from a part in the middle of her scalp.

She had a clear, burnished complexion, with cherubic cheeks that had a constant rosy glow. A large mouth with full, smooth lips covered even teeth, stained yellow from the Turkish blend tobacco she hand-rolled in licorice flavored Zig-zags.

Her nose——long, thin and slightly curved at the tip——was bookended by walnut-shaped eyes with coal black irises. They were capped by thick, arching eyebrows, plucked clean at the bridge of the Romanesque schnoz.

It wasn't kismet. She took charge of the relationship and guided him through the entire process. From suggestive innuendo regarding viral delivery systems and impregnated petri dishes, to touching during conversations, frequent dinner and drinks, and the inevitable first kiss. She managed everything and he went along for the ride, learning as he went.

When it came to coitus, Brody was never sure what all the fuss was about. His limited experience had him viewing it as an awkward, uncomfortable and smelly exchange that took more time to prep for, than the actual act.

Medleva, however, had a few psychological, physical and pharmaceutical tricks that catapulted Jerome through a range of physiological states that were both excruciating and sublime. With this zaftig woman at the helm, he discovered the difference between sexual intercourse and great sex.

The doctor was in love, in lust and apparently, in the minds of those around him, in a ludicrous state of adolescent infatuation. He wanted to make a life with the woman and had even contemplated marriage, envisioning the unthinkable: children.

While never a romantic, Jerome felt as if the woman had filled a big, empty space in his heart, which was now breaking. Yet, the grief over her death was being swallowed up by a morass of conflicting emotions.

Informed she was a complete fabrication and the

knowledge everything she confessed in their intimate sessions was a lie, was confirmation to Jerome that so-called normal human interaction was a mirage.

She'd played him for a fool and betrayed his trust. As he refocused on the words being quietly articulated by Control, the doctor could feel that place inside him, filled briefly by light, warmth and love for another, grow opaque. A cold void was quickly taking its place.

It was time for retribution.

"Dr. Brody——Jerome——are you listening to me?" Control had both feet on the cut-stone pavement, and sitting on the edge of his chair, leaned forward with both arms planted on the tabletop.

"I'm sorry...what?"

"I said: the project will have to be put on hold until I've reevaluated the integrity of the program, and confirm the results of the review with our benefactors."

"*No!* I want to get back to work today and I'll need another test subject this week. It should be a woman." ...*preferably Israeli.*

CHAPTER FIVE

The General Concern

Apprehension was a mild descriptor of Ruben's misgivings about the assignment. With the exception of an extended tour in Iraq, his operations were focused primarily in the Pacific Rim and China. He'd had some forays into India and Pakistan but they were, for the most part, connected to a situation in the Far East.

Ruben appreciated Art's position regarding the exigent circumstances surrounding his desire to use him. He even felt a little flattered, but the idea of a solo run into a decidedly foreign environment was bugging the aging Special Agent.

Earlier in the evening he and Dever met to poke around his concerns. They'd grabbed a table on the second floor of Madam's Organ, a jazz and blues bar in Adams Morgan. A place where Ruben liked to hang out when he was in town, sitting in occasionally with the house band.

Since Agency money was footing the bill, Carver had checked into the Hilton on Connecticut Avenue, near Dupont Circle and only a ten-minute walk to the watering hole. Aside from that convenience, he also liked the neighborhood. The area was the center for gender confusion in DC and as in many gay communities, it was easy to find a good breakfast joint. *Grandma's adage: if you wanna be gay, ya gotta have a good start on the day.*

Ruben leaned forward, the palms of his hands resting on the base of his martini glass. "I gotta tell ya, Henry, this gig could be my retirement—if ya know what I mean."

"Yeah, it's a little strange. The Agency's got to have some serious issues with intel leaks if Art thinks you're the solution to this problem."

Carver didn't know quite how to interpret the comment. He was glad his friend wasn't blowing sunshine up his ass. On the other hand, Dever made it sound like the Agency was making a big mistake by putting Ruben out front.

He sat back from his drink, and looking at no one in particular in the direction of the bar, yelled, *"Excuse me...has anyone see my walker?"*

"You know what I mean. It's not just your age. You've got back problems," Dever sat laughing, "and it would probably be a good idea to have an EMT on standby during your PRT. I mean, seriously, when was the last time you actually ran the mile-and-a-half? I bet you can't do a decent pushup or sit-up to save your life—literally. And from what I gathered from your last physical, you're not fully recovered from what happened in Shanghai..."

"You have my medical records?"

"Of course." A comment made in a tone suggesting an explanation was unnecessary. "You apparently have a couple of squishy ribs left over from the Malaysia mission, as well."

"Nah, I'm okay. It's not like that kinda shit didn't hurt before. I'm just taking longer to recover."

Dever nodded. "And that's the point. You should have turned Art down for this assignment."

"Yeah, well...I didn't. Anyway, it's not the pushin' and shovin' I'm concerned about so much. It's the location."

Henry listened without expression.

"I asked for Ryan Henderson for the cyber support and his background with Bennet, but we're gonna need someone who knows what's goin' on, on the ground. Who's our referent in Turkey?"

"I'm not sure. It was Adan Hanna. NCIS had him embedded with OSI aboard the Air Station at Izmir, but I'm not sure he can give you the kind of backup I think you're looking for."

"Why's that?"

"Do you know where Izmir is?"

Ruben shrugged a shoulder.

"It's three or four hundred kilometers southwest of Istanbul—on the Aegean Sea. It doesn't look that far on the map but apparently, on a good day, it's about a six-and-a-half hour drive to the city."

Ruben shook his head. "That's a problem, but only from the standpoint that Adan probably doesn't know Istanbul that well. At least not like someone living and working there. I wish I had time to wander around and get a sights and sounds feel for the place.

"Oh, well...let's see if I can get a set of TDY orders for Izmir. I'll make my way to Istanbul from there."

Ruben took a sip from his drink that had turned room temperature. Then continued, as if he was thinking aloud. "You should be able to come up with a legitimate scenario for temporary duty.

"An office inspection or ship-visit support would pass muster. Since it's not a PCS I wouldn't need NATO orders. It would cut the U.S. Embassy out of the process. Would we need any other approvals?"

Dever tilted his head, and said, "The OSI detachment commander will have to be given a heads up, which means the commander of the air wing will know you're in country. You can expect that guy to get nosey about your reason for being there."

Henry took a breath and continued. "You'll still need a visa. If you travel on a tourist passport, you can get a visa from Turkey's Ministry of Foreign Affairs on arrival. Otherwise, if you use your official passport, you'll have to submit a request here. It's a fast process, but at this point it's all about who knows you're going and when."

"Yeah, that's another issue. I've gone TDY in countries, where I didn't touch base with the Legal Attaché or the RSO when I arrived. Most of the time the Chief of Station had no interest. The difference, though, is they were aware of my presence. They approved my country clearance.

"Adan's local source network is gonna be important to me, though. Those people, depending on who they work for, have contacts at the U.S. Embassy and they'd bring my name up just to vet me. It wouldn't be long before our Director started getting buried in emails and phone calls from the Bureau and DSS wanting some answers."

Henry shifted in his chair, exhibiting what Ruben perceived as a hint of impatience. When he spoke, his voice echoed that restiveness. "That's not exactly who I was referring to..."

"If you're contemplating how soon the bad guys are gonna to find out about me, you can forget about it."

"Whaddya mean?"

"Think about it, Henry. Art didn't hold anything back. He told us who we're up against and why you and I were selected to the run the op. It's for sure he wasn't guessin' The Board is behind the scientist's departure. No...we have to plan around the notion they're already aware I'm coming."

Art Sheppard was behind the wheel of his Pontiac, heading south on the I-495. He had a three-story townhouse off of Telegraph Road in Alexandria he called home. He'd purchased it a few transfer cycles before and while it wasn't much, it was comfortable and affordable.

Back in the USA, the shit-for-salaries in the Agency could be a struggle for employees who'd gotten used to Uncle Sam's largess overseas. Their housing had been covered and a pay differential was allotted based on the U.S. dollar exchange rate. Depending on the country a person was stationed in, life could be pretty damn good.

It wasn't uncommon for a case officer, or anyone for that matter, to bury themselves in a mountain of debt, living beyond their state-side means. While there was no excuse for it, Art understood why a jackass like Aldrich Ames would commit espionage: he had to keep the ol' ball and chain happy. She had certain lifestyle expectations that were fueled by the deaths of a dozen good men working behind the iron current.

Paycheck notwithstanding, and the lousy traffic coming off the beltway to I-95 south, he was glad to be out of China. It may have been viewed as a high profile assignment at headquarters, but it felt like lockdown. The Ministry of State Security had him under such tight surveillance when he left embassy grounds, one colleague commented it looked like he had a protective service detail.

He had a fairly extensive NOC program, and it did produce some decent economic intelligence. Unfortunately, those case officers who were operating with non-official cover, sans diplomatic protection, produced little else.

If there was one thing Art hated, it was operations that couldn't be assessed as providing benefit to the intelligence collection effort, or value to U.S. national security. The platitudinous reporting about the Chinese stealing technology, hacking computers and infringing on patents and copyrights, drove him crazy. It was as monotonous and predictable as southern California weather.

The real action was elsewhere and thanks to Ruben Carver, Art was back in the fold in northern Virginia. In his mind, the missing DARPA scientist was another ripple in the wake of the NCIS China operation, and he wasn't going to miss the opportunity to, once again, ride that wave.

The communique of Dr. Bennet going missing and the subsequent analysis he'd been recruited by The Board, had been forwarded to Art as a courtesy—an FYI. He'd been kept in the info loop because much of what had been uncovered about the arcane coterie, aside from its identified members' legitimate business and altruistic endeavors, came on Art's watch.

It wasn't, however, in the secret agent's nature to sit on the sideline, and idly observe someone else move the ball down the field. Art knew the kind of juice he was enjoying at headquarters had a shelf life, and he wasted no time in leveraging his influence to take control of the situational response.

He'd gotten his boss's approval to retrieve or eliminate Bennet, and didn't want to spend too much time looking in-house for an asset to plug into the operation. The CIA had a number of successes in Turkey. The 1980 military coup, as an example, was a big win for the company. The expertise in destabilizing and overthrowing a country was a different skill set, however, than the one he needed.

A paramilitary operation would have the surgical precision, but it didn't benefit from an on-the-ground investigative prowess. He needed someone who could fly in, find the traitor, put the grabs on him and devise an extraction, without involving in-country CIA or military support.

He was aware Carver was hurting but the guy had talent. A natural born problem solver—smart, focused and effective.

He also had an incredible survival instinct, tempered in combat, and honed through years as a federal agent. It wasn't that Carver didn't consider his mortality. Art assumed the big lug worried about getting killed, just like anybody else.

The difference was Carver had the gift. He was cold as ice under fire. An intuitive tactician with only one thing on his mind during a fire-fight: how to kill the other guy. However, Art saw something else in the troop he believed went unnoticed by those obsessed with Carver's often heavy-handed approach to conflict resolution.

Sheppard viewed it as a kind of mental ambidexterity or cross dominate thinking. Carver had an eye on the end game before he acted. Within seconds he could build a strategy to reach a defined goal—the desired results already visualized—while almost simultaneously going tactical to get the job done.

Sheppard was certain all he had to do was point Carver in the right direction, provide him with the resources he wanted, be willing to overlook any concomitant collateral damage, and the dude would deliver. Fast.

When he pulled into his driveway, he punched the button on the garage door opener. As it rolled up with a rattle, he thought about the first time he laid eyes on the man.

CHAPTER SIX

Thanksgiving 1972

In November 1972, Lieutenant Arthur Sheppard was the leader of a Marine Corps weapons platoon assigned to what was left of a fire support base, or FSB, south of the demilitarized zone. It was located in the I Corps Tactical Zone, five kilometers from the Laos border, just north of Lang Vei.

The peace accord was on going in Paris, with heavy discussion about the importance of the size and shape of the table. The Vietnamese on both sides were downright testy when it came to seating arrangements.

The carpet bombing of the north had ceased and the Marine Corps air wings, flying out of Thailand, were getting ready to pack it in and go home.

U.S. forces had been steadily drawing down throughout all of the country's four military regions and the fighting, while still going on, was sporadic. Rifle squads conducting daytime patrols were mostly ARVN troops, and much of the nighttime sweeps and search and destroy missions had come to an end.

Lt. Sheppard's job was to support ARVN operations. The South Vietnamese forces, euphemistically called marines, had gotten their asses handed to them in the early spring, during the North Vietnam Army's 'Easter'

45

offensive. A division of devil dogs, in place at the time to train and advise, had to step in and counter the NVA's advance, allowing the Republic of Vietnam's forces to regroup and rest up from all the running they'd been doing.

After the battle for Hue city in May, the USMC mission in the Vietnam conflict was officially over, with the exception of advisory roles, of which the young lieutenant was apart. His weapons platoon consisted of a mortar section with crews manning a couple of 60mm tubes and an 81mm mounted on an armored personnel carrier; an M-60 machine gun section with three squads of two guns each; and an assault section armed with M-72 LAAW rockets.

The Vietnamese company his platoon was embedded with, manned three 105mm towed howitzers—the M102 variety—four .50 caliber machine guns, three squads of 81mm mortars and three rifle platoons.

For what it was worth, Sheppard felt the daily training sessions with the Vietnamese regulars began to sink in, but a futile effort nonetheless. They didn't exhibit the same fortitude or grit of their communist enemies. Those bastards were fighting for a cause.

The fire support base was a bare, brown spot on top of a hill in the middle of the jungle. It had been utilized by Marines, off and on, since '69 and the bunkers and trenches were deep and reinforced with sand bags, dirt-filled ammo cases and logs that had been cut and split from trees knocked down by bulldozers during construction. It had a hundred-meter radius and was surrounded by a six-foot berm, with layers of concertina wire.

On November 22nd, about two or three hours after sundown, the sounds of a fire-fight to the west, near the Xe Pone River on the Laos border, had every man at his defensive position. A check with the ARVN company commander confirmed no night time patrols had been scheduled and all other patrols out that day had checked in.

Although a country-wide ceasefire had been announced, the FSB had been harassed a few times a week by mortar fire, the occasional rocket-propelled grenade and small arms fire from the tree line. There were also sappers in the wire at night, setting off trip flares and claymore mines. It was almost a full moon that night, though, and visibility was good. Sappers wouldn't be coming around. It was apparent the battle at the river had nothing to do with the base.

The fighting was intense. Not only could it be heard, the muzzle flashes, explosions and flares lit up the sky above the jungle canopy. It continued fairly steadily until almost zero-three hundred. When it went silent, Sheppard figured the obvious: the insurgents were either dead, or ran out of ammo. If the later was the case then they may have gone hand-to-hand.

He had intel that his patch of dirt was surrounded by elements of the 9th and 24th regiments of the NVA 304th division, operating out of Laos. Whoever the VC were tangling with had apparently failed to get the memo about the ceasefire, which made him think it may have been a disgruntled Laotian contingent.

Except for the regular watch, he had his men stand down, with a plan to mount a patrol with an ARVN rifle squad after sunrise. At zero-six-thirty, about the time the guard at the perimeter pulled the wire back to let the squad out, two men dragging a third, stepped out of the tree line.

As he checked them with binoculars, the tiger stripe on their grimy jungle cammies were visible. Each man's face, hands and arms to the elbows, were covered in green and black grease stick. No helmets or flak jackets—they wore boonie hats, with towels draped around their necks and their field pants were rolled up rather than bloused in their boots.

He could tell the ARVN private on guard at the wire was giving them a ration of shit. Instead of trying the field phone to talk to the man on post, Sheppard yelled at one of his guys who was cleaning his rifle.

"Johnson...go get Doc out of his rack and you two come and meet me at the gate with a litter. Oh, and find the Gunny. I want him there, too. We have visitors."

The lieutenant knew these guys weren't Marines...*pro'bly Green Beret pussies or an Army Ranger LuRRP.*

When he got to the gate, he discerned why the ruff-puff was more than reticent about allowing entry. None of the men were wearing any rank or service insignia, no name tapes, nor patches.

The man on the right was six foot two or three and lean; maybe a hundred and seventy pounds soaking wet. He looked bigger from a distance because his jacket was open and baggy. The guy on the left was shorter by at least three inches but had some girth, mostly in the chest and shoulders.

The third man was completely limp. His arms draped over his compadres' shoulders, they had him braced by his web belt to drag him through the jungle.

The exchange between the tall, lanky troop and the gate guard was in Vietnamese. While it wasn't a shouting match, Sheppard could tell the conversation wasn't going anywhere either.

"You fellas need some help?"

The talking stopped and three pairs of eyes focused on the lieutenant. The guy on the right who was speaking the local lingo, now replied with a slight southern drawl. "Good mo'nin', Lieutenant..." The man looked down at Sheppard's name tape and then back to his face. "...Sheppud and thank you fo' askin'. I have a man, he'a,

48

who needs some medical attention."

"I've got a litter coming, but I'd like to know who you are. By the look of you, I already have a pretty good idea what you're doin' out here."

"Yes, sah, I have fo'gotten my mannas. I am Staff Sergeant Ruben Caava, United States A'my and these gentlemen are what is left of my squad. Corporal Wilson, standin', and the wounded man is PFC Grainja."

About that time the corpsman and two other Marines showed up, hauling a stretcher.

"Come aboard, Staff Sergeant...what was it...Carver?"

"Yes, sah."

"Doc, here, will take your wounded to the infirmary and the Gunny, there, will show you where to get some chow. We're on C-rats until base camp choppers bring in more provisions. As a matter of fact, if you're still with us this afternoon, we're supposed be receiving a Thanksgiving dinner, with fuckin' turkey and stuffing. Hell, we might even get a visit from a donut dolly. Who knows?"

"Well, sah...that sounds invitin'." Carver looked at the corpsman, as the Marines laid the injured man on the stretcher. The cornpone came off his voice as he articulated, "He's got multiple frag wounds, mainly in his legs. They somehow missed his arteries but I don't know about organs.

"The fact he's still with us is a good sign. Anyway, we used field dressings to cover what we could see, and injected him with a morphine syrette. I believe his will to live was revived when he found out his pecker was still intact."

There was some self-conscious chuckling as they started up the hill.

Sheppard asked, "How many men did you lose?"

"Seven."

"All killed?"

The lieutenant could feel Carver's eyes bore into him.

"They weren't interested in takin' prisoners. If you don't mind, lieutenant, I'd like to use your CP comms to get in touch with my boss. I'll let 'em know we need a dust-off."

"That's no problem, but once you've made contact and gotten yourself something to eat, I'd like a sitrep. We heard you out there last night. Your run and gun lasted several hours. We've got a mixed complement on this hill, that's mainly ARVN. My Marines and I are here in an advisory capacity. I'd like to get a better picture of what we're facing."

"It would be my pleasure, sir."

As they got to the top of the hill, Cpl. Wilson split off with the corpsman, and a couple of more Marines came out of a hootch to help with the litter. Carver continued on with Lt. Sheppard and the gunnery sergeant toward the command post.

"Sgt. Carver, I don't mean to be a rude host, but a long range reconnaissance patrol is supposed to avoid contact with the enemy," Sheppard probed.

"Yeah, well...someone musta stepped on a twig. Fact is, I believe we crashed a surprise party bein' arranged in your honor."

"Whaddya mean?" asked the Gunny.

"We'd gone over the fence, maybe two klicks into Laos, to confirm the suspected location of Charlie's 304th Division. On our way back we ran into a large group, maybe two companies, that had moved across the river and were setting up mortars, heavy machine guns—crew serviced weapons—along with sappers and rifle platoons.

"I believe the only reason any of my squad survived is because the gooks were more surprised to see us, than we were them. We started greasin' 'em before they could go defensive and you're right, lieutenant, we spent the night movin' and shootin'. When we ran out of ammo, we used their weapons we found layin' on the ground."

"You're saying you diverted an attack?" Sheppard could feel tension forming in his shoulders.

"Ya, sah." The country seeped back into Carver's voice. "Ya might say we upset the apple cart. At any rate, once they've finished lickin' their wounds and examine the bodies of my men, they'a be comin' fo' ya."

Sheppard sucked on a toothpick as he evaluated what the skinny sergeant was saying. Apparently, the young GI perceived some skepticism and continued.

"Look, lieutenant, we put a hurt on Mr. Charles last night, which had to make them rethink their strategy regarding your compound. Once they figure out my team was an anomaly, not connected to this firebase, they're gonna try again."

Sheppard led Carver into the CP and introduced him to the ARVN company commander. Once the situation was explained, Carver was allowed to contact his command and Sheppard started the prep for what he now believed would be a busy evening.

By sixteen hundred, the hot food canisters and what was left of the Thanksgiving meal was packed up and loaded on a helo for base camp. Several hours earlier, Carver's wounded man was medevac'd to the aid station, as the firebase started to batten down.

Personnel had walked the perimeter wire, resetting claymores and trip flares. The company commander, at Sheppard's request, doubled up on personnel in listening and observation posts.

Extra ammo was issued to each firing point and weapons and magazines were cleaned and tested. Deuce gear, from gas masks and earplugs to helmets and flak jackets were the uniform of the day.

Honey dippers lit the shitters as one of the final touches. Sheppard didn't want the area sprayed with urine and feces, if a head was hit with a motor round.

The ARVN troops stacked cases of high explosive, beehive and willie pete at the three howitzers, and the belt-fed crew served weapons were locked and loaded. Sheppard then called in coordinates for pre-defined fire missions on those locations pointed out by Carver from the night before.

He also confirmed he'd have fire support from the base camp's 155mm howitzers and air cover from the Huey gunships and Cobras. If he could put the quietus on a VC mortar, heavy machine gun and RPG barrage, they'd have a better chance of keeping the dinks from breaching the wire and getting inside the compound.

As a courtesy, the Gunny provided Wilson a half dozen thirty-round magazines for his Colt Commando and begrudgingly unassed three-hundred rounds of 7.62 for Carver's M14—a cutdown version with a short fiberglass stock, rubber buttplate and pistol grip.

Sheppard looked at his watch as he gnawed on the bone of a turkey leg: seventeen-o-five. He, the Gunny and Carver were lounging in olive drab canvassed beach chairs outside the lieutenant's hootch trying to enjoy the sunset. The senior NCO was sucking on a Chesterfield, as Carver nursed a warm can of Budweiser.

The lieutenant had watched Carver and Cpl. Wilson throughout the day, working with his platoon getting ready for contact with the enemy. Sheppard graduated from the Naval Academy a year before, with a degree in sociology. While he thought it would somehow make him a better leader, what it actually did was make him more conscious of personality types.

Boxing his two Army guests into a kind of Myers-Briggs or Jungian context, he decided they were a pair of natural killers. Neither one could have been more than twenty years old, but they both seemed to display the ability to waste the enemy with no more emotion or conscious regard than peeling a potato. He was glad they were there. He was equally glad they were leaving when the fight was over.

"Tell me again, Sgt. Carver, why your command didn't want you on that chopper with your man?"

"The CO advised they'd prefer getting a direct assessment of troop strength, armament, tactics and maybe a semblance of command and control. They don't want to wait for a report from the Corps." Carver's southern drawl had once again slipped away.

"Where are you from, Carver?"

"I'm from an Oklahoma oil field just south of Seminole, called Bowlegs. And before you ask, I enlisted on my seventh birthday. My dad drove me to the recruiter in Oklahoma City and signed the consent." Carver took a sip of his beer and showed no sign of elaborating.

Sheppard nodded, and without focusing on either of his current companions, said, "Gunny, I want everyone uptight, outta sight and in the groove. If you think a mad minute is in order, let me know, but I'd prefer to save the ammo. Just do what you can to keep everyone chilly. No drinking. As soon as the sun is down, the smoking lamp is also out and make sure the flashlights all have a red lens."

After an "aye-aye", the Gunny shoved off. The lieutenant then locked eyes with the staff sergeant. "I've got no job for you but if we find ourselves in the shit tonight, I'm confident you and Corporal Wilson will apply your skill sets to the situation. Only thing I want you to remember is whose platoon this is. That's why I want you and the Corporal to dig in with me. If you see something I don't, advise me. I'll redirect fire or move defensive positions. Clear?"

"Oorah..."

CHAPTER SEVEN

Broken Arrow

The listening posts outside the wire were on a two hour shift. By zero-one, they'd been relieved four times. The Gunny, along with two other squad leaders were in a constant state of motion tapping helmets, keeping the platoon alert. Sheppard had made several visits to the CP and was satisfied the ARVN company was sharp.

Carver had been playing rummy with Wilson but was up peering through a starlight scope, when Sheppard jumped into the trench next to him.

"You see movement?" The lieutenant was panting, as adrenaline began to take effect.

"Nope but there's a lot of fog rolling in. What's up?"

"Every listening post is reporting movement."

As he spoke, the ARVN company popped three flares which didn't do much but create a reflected glare through the haze. While the flares were still floating on their shoots, the NVA opened up with 82mm mortars. They'd zeroed on the perimeter wire and a number of bunkers and were firing for effect. Sheppard took command of the company after the first cannonade, when the CP and its occupants were destroyed.

Rocket-propelled grenades rained down inside the compound, as the mortar attack continued. A listening post still active also reported sappers climbing the berm at the perimeter.

Although hunkered down, the Marines returned fire. The 60mm and 81mm mortar men had moved positions after dark and the initial pounding from the VC was landing on empty pits. While the Marines were doing their best to repel the ground attack from the west, the FSB was being assaulted on all sides.

The 155mm howitzers at the base camp were definitely doing a number on Charlie's gun placements near the river, but Sheppard's redirect of fire on the north and east—where the sappers had breached the perimeter—had brought friendly fire danger close.

He tapped Carver's shoulder to follow him. They ran east toward one of the ARVN's 105mm cannons. Carver was shooting as they moved, dropping gooks at almost pointblank range. Even in the dark it wasn't too difficult telling the good guys from the bad. The sappers wore nothing but shorts and Ho Chi Minh sandals. A few had bandanas, but that was it.

As Sheppard got within twenty meters of the howitzer, he tripped and as he went down had the air knocked out of him as Carver landed on his back. Seconds later the earth moved. The blast, even with his earplugs, caused painful ringing and the heat wave, as it blew over him, scorched his skin.

The weight he'd felt on his back was suddenly gone, replaced by someone grabbing him under his armpit and pulling him to his feet. It was Carver. While he was still disoriented, the sound of the staff sergeant's voice was getting through.

"Come on, LT, we gotta move."

"Wait...the 105..."

"It's gone. We have to get back to the platoon." At that, Carver brought the muzzle up waist high and fired two rounds, dropping a naked interloper charging them with

a fixed bayonet.

"Let's go, lieutenant! We got ourselves a broken arrow!"

He gripped Sheppard's right arm above the elbow and pulled him to a sprint. Once his legs were pumping, Carver let him go. Moving around a bunker designated "21" they spotted the Gunny. He had an M79 in his hand and was directing fire inside the base with the 60mm mortars and M60 machine guns.

Just as they were going over the sandbags the lieutenant was hit. The bullet punctured his right buttock with the sensation of a white-hot sledgehammer. His muscles failed him and he collapsed.

"Fuck...I'm shot!"

Draped over the barrier and frozen in place, Carver and the Gunnery Sergeant grabbed Sheppard by his flak jacket and pulled him to cover.

"Hey, lieutenant, can you hear me?" Carver was yelling in his face. As his eyes cleared he nodded and pushed the ranger back a few inches.

He opened his mouth and flexed the masseter muscle to try and open his ears. "Gimme a sitrep."

"We are completely overrun and it looks like about a third of your men are down. Gunny is directing fire and keeping us alive but we need air support. I'll see if I can find a radio but you'll have to bring the gunships right down on top of us. I don't know how bad you're hit but can you move?"

Sheppard knew he didn't have a choice—he had to engage. He reached up and grabbed Carver's jacket collar.

"Get me on my feet. I'll be okay for a while...my ass is numb. Get me some comms."

"Okay, just a sec." Carver reached down and pulled the lieutenant's gas mask from its pouch. "The bullet went through the rubber but it looks okay. The VC are droppin' tear gas. I can smell it. They're also throwin' satchel charges——that's what took out the 105. You hang in there, LT...I'll find a radio. You just keep killing the bastards until I get back." Carver then turned and went over the sandbags.

From what he could see there were two M60s still operating, each with about a sixty-degree field of fire. Cpl. Wilson was on one of them. The barrels on both guns were glowing red as they sprayed bullets at the marauders; now no longer just naked sappers but regular NVA as well.

He somehow found his rifle in the dark and started picking targets. In the bedlam he wasn't sure he was actually hitting anyone. The Gunny hadn't stopped moving between firing points until a dink came at him with a fixed bayonet.

The Marine took a sliding step back, parrying the blade outside with the muzzle of the M79. In the same motion he stripped his K-bar from its sheath and with a hammer grip used his body weight to run the knife all the way through——stomach to backbone. The Gunny had to hold the body down with his boot to pull the blade free.

While it was only a few minutes before Carver returned, it felt like an hour. With the muzzle flashes, explosions and flares, Sheppard could see him moving across the field of fire. He had a radio slung over his left shoulder, and an M1911A1 in his right hand. The lieutenant watched the young troop kill four VC before he rolled over the sandbags and dropped into the trench.

"Here you go, LT!" Carver pried the radio off his shoulder and shoved it toward the lieutenant. "Gimme your rifle!"

Sheppard watched him tuck the pistol in a tanker style shoulder holster.

"What happened to yours?"

"It's over there." He jerked his head in a direction

behind him. "I couldn't clear a jam."

Grabbing the radio he handed the ranger his rifle and slapped two full magazines on a sandbag. He checked the frequency and keyed the handset after wiping blood off the mouth piece.

"Bravo 6...bravo 2 actual." He waited three or four seconds and tried again. Three more attempts and he connected.

"This is Bravo 6 actual. What's your status Bravo 2? Over." The voice was clipped, distant.

Yeah, what the fuck is my status? "Bravo 6, we've been overrun. Estimate a battalion size aggressor. We've redirected most of our fire inside the base. We need immediate air support on our position. Over."

"Bravo 2, we have gunships on standby. They'll be inbound in ten mikes. Get your people to cover. Do you copy? Over."

"Aye-aye. Bravo 2, out."

Sheppard dropped the handset and wiped his sticky hand on his flak jacket. He then slapped Carver on the shoulder.

"We need to get our men under cover in the center of the base. Tell the Gunny and then you need to spread the word to what's left of the ARVN. We have air support coming...now. You got that?"

Carver nodded and handed back the lieutenant's rifle. The image of the young Army ranger at that moment stayed with Sheppard the next thirty-three years. He was grinning.

The garage door was coming down as Sheppard stepped out of his car. He no longer had nightmares but certain sounds or smells still brought on flashbacks of that night. He couldn't tell how many gunships showed up. The Gunnery Sergeant had the radio by then and was in direct comms with the flight leader.

The choppers came in waves, however, using missiles, mini-guns and 20mm cannons to decimate the enemy. He didn't get any reports of friendly fire casualties but the noise went beyond description. Before shock and awe became a military doctrine, he witnessed it on top of that hill.

The platoon corpsmen had their hands full with dead or wounded at over seventy percent. As far as the hole in Sheppard's butt was concerned, Carver applied a field dressing and jabbed him with a morphine syrette. The Staff Sergeant then manned an M60, and with his teammate Wilson, continued to kill VC until it was clear they'd been repelled.

Sheppard was convinced they'd almost bought the farm. Had it not been the prep and the extraordinary valor of his fire teams they would have. He recommend the Gunny for the CMH and would have written Carver up for a decoration but he and Cpl. Wilson disappeared during the mop up.

He had no idea what happened to the man until he showed up at the U.S. Embassy in Beijing four months ago. He'd heard of the NCIS Special Agent's antics for a couple of years, but never made the connection.

After the flack from Carver's operation in Shanghai died down, Sheppard became privy to the audio surveillance the NSA acquired—at least temporarily—on The Board. He was now cognizant of two things: to the cabal, Carver was like a bad penny, but to him, the big guy was a good luck charm.

He had no delusions about The Board's knowledge the CIA had taken over the responsibility of reacquiring the misguided scientist. He'd also made sure to drop Carver's name to a few folks inside the Agency he considered as having suspect loyalties.

In his thinking, after what occurred in Southeast Asia and China, the idea of Carver being on the hunt would scare the shit out The Board's members. He counted on his belief that frightened folks made mistakes.

As he punched in the six digit code on the key pad to disable the alarm system, he turned his thoughts to the person sitting in the car parked three houses down. He wasn't sure why she posed a threat. It may have been the way she studied him through the rearview mirror of her Benz, as he pulled into his driveway.

The call she made on her cell phone, still watching him as he waited on the garage door to open, also annoyed him. There weren't any other cars on the street that he could see. If she was waiting for him, she was alone.

He could have been bullshitting himself—it happened once in a while. However, since he wasn't authorized to carry a concealed weapon and didn't like keeping one in the car, he was more comfortable entertaining an uninvited guest in his abode. It was better than being run down on the road.

Part of his home protection system was a loaded Mossberg 590A1 in the hall closet and a Glock 23 in the kitchen, master bedroom and basement laundry room.

He didn't view it as gun collecting. For him it was pragmatic. With the exception of the shotgun, having the same model pistol stationed around the townhouse allowed the advantage of ease of access, one type of ammo and interchangeable magazines.

Though the definite cool points in wielding a matching pair of those .40 caliber bad boys wasn't lost on him. He just didn't cotton to the notion of police involvement. Especially when popping caps in the ass of an intruder who wouldn't likely be associated with a run-of-the-mill home invasion. Someone like the woman he peeped sitting inside a Mercedes outside his house.

The first floor of the townhouse, coming out of the garage, had the laundry room and three-quarter bath to his left. In front of him was the rec room, typical for a two-time vet of divorce court.

It was crammed with a two-stool oak wet-bar, the shelving back-lit to display all his favorites; a pool table under a Dale Tiffany fixture, with the conspicuous word "Billiards" inlaid in colored glass; and a black leather over-stuffed sofa and chair combo parked in front of a fifty-inch LCD TV. Antique beer trays and 70s-vintage posters of the Doobie Brothers, Lynyrd Skynyrd, Taj Mahal and the Allman Brothers, adorned the walls.

The pistol was hanging from its trigger guard on a padded hook attached to the back of the washing machine. Tucking it in his waistband, he grabbed a bottle of appropriately aged Macallan from the bar, along with two dimpled tumblers. He then proceeded to the second floor where the kitchen, dining area and empty 'sunken' living room was located.

As he climbed the stairs, his tie came off and went into a coat pocket. He discovered early in his career that a necktie was an inviting handle—an expression from one of his heroes, Judo Gene Lebell. A silk tie could become a noose in a fight.

The kitchen had a breakfast nook table, from which he had an unobstructed view of both the front and back doors. Taking a seat in one of the four oak spindle chairs, he waited. Sheppard figured if the woman wanted to have a chat, she'd let herself in. After all, she knew he was home.

If the diplomatic plates on her German sedan were any indication, she'd be able to come through the door without breaking anything. He hadn't finished pouring their drinks before he heard her working on the lock.

He'd had a commercial Schlage mechanism installed on the doors, which had a pick-proof guarantee. While it probably took her longer than usual, the front door slid open before he could take his first sip.

In an obvious effort to exhibit her peaceful intent, she stood motionless for several seconds, silhouetted in the door frame. As she crossed the threshold, Sheppard could hear her six-inch black stiletto pumps clicking on his hardwood floor.

She wore a sleeveless black shift, and pigeon-toed, her model's gait made her hips sway like a lantern on an anchored yacht. Her head was motionless, though, as if it was floating, disconnected from the rest of her body.

Large, almond eyes—Sheppard decided looked hazel—sat below broad, carefully trimmed eyebrows. Her thin, angular face had plump, heart-shaped lips turned up in a Mona Lisa smile. The long, Semitic nose, narrow at the tip as it was at the bridge, was framed by round cheekbones. A brunette, her hair was thick and shiny parted in the middle and pulled back in a short ponytail.

Ten feet past the entrance she cooed, "Hello, Arthur, how very nice to see you again."

Oh, shit...

CHAPTER EIGHT

The Transition

A half-empty cup on the gingham-covered table sat ignored as Moreau reflected on current events. Exhaling a thin plume of gray smoke, he wasn't sure who he disliked more. The lighthearted, love-soaked Doc Jerry or the morose, vindictive and soul-charred wreck that took his place in the form of Doctor Jerome Brody. The Board was, of course, more concerned with the security of the program.

The word was out faster than they'd anticipated. Medleva's torture was not the work of the Americans, that certitude had him looking elsewhere. The Russians weren't above the kind of abuse meted out, but the condition of her body suggested something closer to home—a Muslim approach.

The Turks would have taken her someplace more clinical. She'd also have been kept alive as a political bargaining chip. This had more of a contract feel to it. Islamic for sure, and no doubt state sponsored, but these characters were purists.

Besides the pliers, pruning shears, paring knife and soldering iron the police found in the bathroom, there were obvious signs she'd been tied to the bed. Moreau perceived that was more for the Muslim brethren's comfort than hers. *Yes, well...everyone knows how difficult it is to concentrate on the work at hand when encumbered with an erection.*

Remembering the crime scene photos he'd gotten his hands on, they'd apparently rinsed off the blood, shit and piss in the tub, then dragged her to the bed. He mentally visualized the beating, rape and sodomy conducted in a fashion reserved for non-believers. The fact she was a Jew and a woman, made that type of humiliation even more appropriate in their minds.

The maltreatment went through several cycles before her heart gave out. More than likely, she provided all the information they wanted after they stripped her and showed her their toys. The activity afterward was, in their minds, inevitable, if not imperative.

Yves Moreau was the kind of Muslim westerners loved. A stylish moderate who believed in the true meaning of the Muslim faith of peace, love and understanding. For him it played out great at parties. What most people in the west didn't understand, at least not as intensely or clearly as the Israelis, was that radical Islam or extremist Muslims are misnomers. They're nothing more than true believers—purists.

He mused over the surety that a so-called moderate Muslim was akin to a backslidden Christian or jack Mormon. The Jews, though, had a term the Algerian thought was actually closer to the heart of the matter. It was *apikoros* and roughly translated meant: heretic freethinker. In the eyes of a true Muslim, a moderate—such as himself—didn't deserve to live any more than that Judah cunt they'd debased and slaughtered.

As much as he found Dr. Brody's insistence to carry on an aggravation, The Board's consensus was also to push forward. The operation was too big to move and the doctor's focused efforts were producing the desired results ahead of schedule and under budget.

For those now interested in obtaining the bioweapon the scientist developed, it couldn't be effectively managed without him. A situation which necessitated Dr. Brody's capture. It was that or suffer a truly horrific end trying to handle the stuff.

Yves didn't doubt the Americans' and Israelis' paramount stake was in acquiring the research documentation and data. Brody was secondary and probably better off dead.

After Moreau presented these opinions, The Board continued to believe his primary mission hadn't changed, only intensified. An understatement, in the Algerian's mind, analogous to describing a hand grenade as a firecracker.

The team in the basement of the School of Engineering was successful in weaponizing a truly horrific bio-engineered bacteria. They still had to develop a method for mass production, safe storage, delivery on target and subsequent containment in the event it didn't go inert in the amount of time advertised.

Once those requirements were achieved, he could throw a post-production party for the team on his barge in the Black Sea. After a well-deserved toast, they'd be weighted and thrown overboard. His problem was reaching that point.

Whether or not the people responsible for the kidnap and murder of the lab assistant had any intimation she was an Israeli became moot. The operation was under surveillance and the Jews weren't the only ones on to them.

So, along with the CIA and some infidel named Carver coming his way, there was probably Mossad or Shabak gunning for him, as well as some other, yet unidentified, group. The likely suspects being Turkey's MIT or Iran's VAJA. He didn't want to think about the

Russians or Chinese.

He tucked a ten euro note under his cup, and waving at the waiter, he walked past the tables lining the guard rail to make his descent through the terraced graveyard toward the Eyuk Sultan's Mosque. A pleasant walk for a troubled mind.

When he got to Eyuk Sultan Road, he hung a right. On a walkway paved in square flagstone, he headed for his ride on Hz.Halid Blvd.

He'd never seen an American stock car race, but from what he'd watched in movies and on television, he imagined it was similar to driving in Istanbul. It was the right of way of the horn and Allah's will. Knowledge of traffic laws were necessary to get a license. After that it was every man for himself.

Street parking for the most part was sketchy. Traffic cops towed vehicles seemingly at random and certain parts of the city had its "parking mafia"—*les ballot*—who extorted protection money to keep vandals away.

Rush hour wouldn't hit for another sixty minutes. While still heavy, traffic was flowing. He hadn't noticed anything out of the ordinary when he turned left on Hz.Halid. With tires screeching and horns blaring, everything seemed normal. His silver and black Bugatti Veyron, still intact, was sitting fifty meters south.

It was the eye contact with a particularly aggressive driver of a white, late model Mercedes Vito, an otherwise nondescript panel van, that alerted him. Drivers in this part of the world avoided eye contact—with everyone.

Moreau never moved around the city with a bodyguard. With the exception of his automobile, he stayed off the radar by staying low key. His source network was extensive and far reaching not only because it was well paid, it was also the hallmark of discretion.

No one ever got burned and he was left alone.

He was no mistaking a setup, though, especially on the street. He became an expert early in his youth on the effective smash and grab, and his use of vehicles like this one was his stock in trade.

Ordinarily, he would have stepped into a shop to throw off their timing, or walked out into traffic as a moving barrier. But he was curious. If this is what he thought it was, they'd come out the side door, taser and hood him, and get him into the van where they'd truss him up.

When the driver jerked the wheel to the curb and slammed on the brakes, Moreau was at the side of the van as the door slid open. Three men with balaclavas jumped to the sidewalk and seeing a man in a dark suit, dropped him with four taser barbs.

Yves was impressed. It was a well-executed attack. The two with tasers ejected the spent cartridges and holstered the appliances while the third hooded their victim. Then all three picked up the stunned man, cradled like a piece of timber, to move him to the vehicle.

It took less than five seconds and went down so flawlessly, the Algerian wasn't sure if it was actually meant for him. That was until they saw him and deduced they had their arms full of the wrong man.

Each hooded assailant was no less than two inches taller and had forty or fifty pounds on him. While they were quick on the takedown, they were slow on the uptake.

Still holding the beleaguered citizen, they glanced at each other deciding what to do. Moreau, while finding this amusing, held his arms away from his body, flexed his forearms and flicked his hands outward.

Two spring loaded six-inch knives on slide mechanisms attached to his arms above the wrists, flashed into play. He grabbed the hilts, and with another slight twist of his wrists, the guide rails retracted.

In a low fighting stance, right leg forward, he moved on the man closest to him. An easy choice not only for distance, the fellow had his back to him.

Moreau's blades were double-edged and razor-sharp, with a single blood channel on each. Using a saber grip with both hands, he executed four right-left jab and rips into the kidneys. As the first man went down, the sudden change in the distributed weight of the victim, pulled the other two off-balance.

The Algerian cross-stepped with his left leg and spun right. Then shuffle-stepped again, right leg forward, low and to the left of the second target. He jabbed his left knife in an upward motion, starting below the rib cage, puncturing a lung. As the man twisted to face him, swinging his left arm in an elbow strike, Yves slipped it with an outside-in bob and weave, and planted the right-hand knife in the man's liver.

The third assassin jumped back in the van before the man Dr. Brody called Control could get at him. Screaming, he pulled the balaclava from his head, apparently believing the driver would understand him better without the encumbrance.

Moreau got a good look at him and the driver. As they pulled into traffic, for what became a slow getaway, he decided to take a minute to examine the two men dying on the sidewalk.

Man, I fuckin' hate this place. Ruben hadn't worked in a crappier environment since his days as a boot agent at the Long Beach Naval Shipyard.

The fourth deck at NCIS headquarters had lousy lighting, poor ventilation and uneven plywood floors, with worn-out dingy gray indoor-outdoor carpet. The desks, chairs, cabinet safes and storage lockers, along with the waist-high cubicle dividers, came straight out of the U.S. Navy's shipboard supply catalog——the used furniture section.

It felt like spelunking as he made his way to his workstation that morning.

He checked his watch: nine-thirty am. Izmir was seven hours ahead and he used thumb-on-fingers to calculate the time in Turkey. An email to the referent went out from Hartley earlier, but as yet they hadn't received a reply.

He was still in the middle of checking in, and while he had a desk with a phone, other items such as a computer, safe, STUIII and clearances for other Codes in the building, would take a week or two. Life back in the States followed the age old adage: if the process seemed simple, you were doing something wrong.

After the few hours it took to get authorization to make an international call from his desk, Ruben, phone in hand, dialed the number he found for the Turkey referent.

The guy who answered simply stated: "NCIS."

"This is Ruben Carver. I'd like to speak with Special Agent Adan Hanna."

"Speaking."

"Yeah, Adan...I'm calling from headquarters. Do you remember me?"

"Sure."

"Did you see Jason Hartley's SIPRNet email? It went out around one pm your time today."

"Yes."

"Then...you understand I'll be traveling to Turkey shortly."

"Yes."

Ruben held the receiver away from his head for a couple of seconds, then banged it four or five times on his desktop. When he brought it back to his ear he asked, "Adan, you still there?"

"Yes, I'm still here...what the fuck was that?"

"I wasn't sure we had a clear connection, bud. I just transferred into headquarters this week, and so far, the only thing I've got is this telephone. I haven't seen Hartley's email to you, so I don't know how much he related to you about my assignment."

"Not much. Apparently, if I want details I have to do it from the skiff."

"Yeah, so…what's the problem, Adan?" Ruben was sensing some negative energy with regard to the OSI Sensitive Compartmented Information Facility.

"Just a second."

Ruben heard him put the handset down and then heard a door close.

"Okay, I'm back." Adan took a deep breath and let it out slow, then said, "I know you're coming but I don't want to discuss even the unclass stuff on this phone. Hartley indicated he wanted the operation strictly LIMDIS but if I tell the OSI DetCo, which would be the proper protocol, since I essentially work for him, he'd be obligated to tell the squadron commander.

"That prick can be a real nosy, insinuating SOB. He wants to have the final word on any country clearance, notwithstanding the approvals from the embassy, and he'd demand a full briefing on your mission."

"Yeah, well, that's not gonna happen."

"Uh-huh. Okay, let me give you another number to call. It's not secure. It's my personal cell phone. I've got some ideas we can bounce around that don't need to be discussed over a secure line. You ready to copy?"

Ruben pulled a pen from his shirt pocket and opened the wirebound steno pad he found that morning rooting around in cabinets. "Yeah, I'm ready."

After jotting the number, Ruben agree to call back in an hour. He understood Adan's hesitance to open up. The years he spent in Misawa, Japan dealing with Air

Force commands, and some of the idiosyncrasies of the OSI detachment he was assigned to in Iraq, had him sympathizing with the Turkey referent.

Dever wasn't in the office. According to admin support he went to Langley and wouldn't be around for most of the day. Ruben would have touched base with Hartley but he was off currying favor with someone in the front office. From what Ruben had heard, Jason was a keen adept when it came to rim jobs.

It was one of the slowest hours he'd spent in quite a while.

He picked up on the second ring. "Adan Hanna."

"It's Ruben. Are you in a position to talk?"

"Yeah, I'm taking a walk. The battery on this phone won't last long so I'll get down to it. You don't want to come here...not to Izmir. The Turkish government, which in reality is the military, doesn't officially recognize NCIS or OSI.

"While I have solid relationships with people here that could be very helpful, it really depends on what you need. Don't expect any support from the three letter agencies at the embassy. The MIT, Turkey's National Intelligence Organization, is completely off limits to us."

Ruben didn't feel ready to interject a comment, being more intent on waiting for a suggested solution.

"Anyway, it's hard for me to explain in a few minutes what the environment is like that would be helpful. Except, maybe, that what you experienced in Iraq isn't what you're going to find here. If you want a down and dirty on the culture, get a book on Mustafa Kemal Atatürk, the first president of the Republic of Turkey. The concept of Kemalism will probably give you all you need to know."

Ruben still wasn't hearing what he needed to know and finally jumped in. "That's interesting, Adan, but I need to get in the country. Getting a visa for official travel would entail creating a cover story and the hassle of acquiring a country clearance. It sounds like I should travel on a tourist passport. Anyway, we need to meet— and more to the point—you need to be available to help."

There was dead air for a few seconds, then, "Travel directly to Istanbul on a tourist passport. Send me your itinerary on SIPRNet and get me some TDY orders for anywhere that won't raise any eyebrows here."

"Good. I'll be in touch." Ruben used his index finger to push the lever on the cradle. The next order of business was on a slip of paper he'd received when he walked through the door that morning. Lifting his finger he got a dial tone, and he punched in a number with a Maryland area code.

A familiar voice answered. "Ryan Henderson, this is a non-secure line."

CHAPTER NINE

Another Wrinkle

"I've got some bad news and some not so bad news."

Sheppard had gathered the small team in Jason Hartley's office. The inclusion of Ryan Henderson, who slouched in a desk chair, legs extended right ankle over left, with hands cradling his cranium, had been acceptable to Art.

Ruben noticed the computer and social engineering genius had let his sandy brown hair grow. He had a three centimeter butch cut, with a matching beard. Faded designer jeans, Teva Kimtah sandals and an orange tie-dye T-shirt, with a Grateful Dead logo, completed the image.

As he turned his attention back to Art, who was perched on the edge of Jason's desk, Ruben noticed a red discoloration peeking up above the man's white starched collar. It could have been a bruise but Ruben knew a hickey when he saw one. *I wonder how much he paid for that?*

He hadn't mentioned to the CIA honcho his conversation with Adan Hanna. He wasn't sure he wanted to. The inclusion of the Turkey referent in the mix would add another body to the logistical support Art wanted to keep to a minimum. Ruben figured it was no use getting the former lieutenant's panties in a wad. At least not yet.

Sheppard continued. "Ten days ago, a forensic toxicologist working as a research assistant at Koç University in Istanbul was found butchered in a hotel room in Kadıköy."

Art's pronunciation of the Istanbul suburb as *kadthikay*, suggested to Ruben he'd been told about the murder rather than finding it in his stack of morning intel reports. When that minor epiphany popped in his head, he looked again at the love bite on Art's neck. *I wonder if this is supposed to be the bad news...*

"The woman had been working with our missing scientist, and was apparently in a relationship that went further than mere academic collaboration."

"You tryin' to say she was workin' hard for that 'A'?" Dever wasn't sniggering, exactly.

Art ignored the remark and moved on. "According to our new source of information, Dr. James Bennet is going by Jerome Brody, a popular adjunct professor at Koç University.

"He's also got a subterranean, industrial-sized laboratory, where he's developing some particularly lethal cocktails. His team is working on weaponizing a bio-toxin that will take this form of WMD to a whole new level."

Ruben shifted in his chair but kept his mouth shut. Ryan, however, was motionless when he asked, "What's the not so bad news?"

"That was it.

"The bad news is we've got competition and you can lay money they're a lot closer to getting their hands on the stuff than we are. My initial intention was to keep this operation small and let Carver figure it out as he went. Dever would provide the operational support and handle comms, which is still in the plan, and I would be available to sweep up any mess."

The "but" was more pronounced than a Kardashian sister's ass and Ruben started getting fidgety. He thought it might have been a good time to brief the activity he'd already been engaged in, which included Adan Hanna and his source network, the TDY orders and the unofficial travel. He decided, however, to keep his trap shut after Art's next revelation.

"The dead research assistant was a Shin Bet asset. While the case officer who ran her is convinced her cover was not blown until after the body was found, it's believed someone put the grabs on her because of her connection to Bennet."

Before Art could elaborate, Dever chimed in. "That would mean, some other group, besides the Israelis, had an idea of what was going on. Bennet and his team musta been under surveillance for a while."

"Yeah, that's right," Art answered, nodding, then said, "That's why I've accepted an offer to partner up with one of your counterparts at Shin Bet. We have to put the kibosh on The Board's plan to further destabilize the region—if in fact, that's their endgame—and bring the wayward savant home.

"It's imperative we do that before someone else attempts a snatch." Art shifted his gaze to Ruben. "If you can't pull him out of there, you'll have to make sure no one else can. There's also one other issue."

Ruben crossed his arms and while convinced he'd already parsed the final part of Art's mission requirement, remained silent.

"You'll have to collect all the data on his research you can, destroy what you can't and deal with the other lab assistants."

Carver ruminated on the term "deal" as everyone now peered at him. "Art, you don't need me for this. This is the kinda mission a SpecOps team is used for. The quintessential SEAL intel collection op: drop in quiet, kill everyone and search the bodies."

"Not so," Art began. "We believe the reason Bennet hasn't already been nabbed and his research stolen is because of where he's located. A university setting wouldn't seem that secure but a raid on a university, especially this one, would create an international furor. We can't be seen using that kind of hammer.

"If anybody else did, they'd be at the top of NATO's hit list, not to mention the Turk's. That's why this was always a one man operation. Now it's a two person set-up."

Oh, no...no way. "You want to come again? What do you mean two *person* set-up?"

"You'll be working with the Shin Bet case officer who brought all this to my attention. Her name is Rivka Levitan."

The smile with his beady eyes and jutting jaw reminded Ruben of a cartoon ogre.

"Don't sweat it, Carver. You'll like her. She can be very...persuasive."

Brody derived a certain amount of pleasure watching Control's reaction when he came to the lab. It was similar to the discomfort those with an aversion to flying exhibited——elevated heart rate and blood pressure, along with profuse sweating and nervous agitation.

In the beginning, ratcheting Moreau's anxiety, was good-humored fun. Talk of unusual levels of contaminants escaping the laboratory's air filters and toxic transfer of biological material could visibly put him off his lunch. It was great for a laugh.

Medleva may have taught Brody how to tell a joke, rather than being its butt, but that jocularity came to an end when she did. The doctor's mockery of Control, while thinly veiled, was an example of his bitter contempt for people in general.

When Control came in that afternoon, it was once again to discuss security, the expense ledger and the difficulty in finding an open-air test site. Brody was impressed with Moreau's apparent total lack of empathy for the subjects in the lab, but his inability to locate a small, statistically insignificant hamlet for delivery trials had become nettling.

As he watched the Spaniard and Georgian tip the body of a young, Eastern European woman into the incinerator, he queried Control. "Since you can't find me a larger venue, do you think it possible to provide a *cavia porcellus* not addicted to some form of narcotic or alcohol?"

Moreau shook his head. "I've explained to you already, simply grabbing people off the street is too risky. A vendor provides our stock, who, I might add, is raising prices based on how many you're going through each week."

Brody jerked a look at the wiry snail eater and cogitating a second responded, "Yeah? What about the animals that took Medleva? They almost got you, too. They didn't think it was too risky."

Control parried with his own piercing glance. "A different story. They're not looking for a steady supply. For now, they just want you and your brainchild."

While Moreau's tension when it came to this lab visit was the same as any other, his cool demeanor during the conversation set Jerome back on his heels a bit. "Who are these people?"

"Frankly, I don't know, yet. I want to say jihadists considering the treatment of your girlfriend..."

"Don't call her that."

"...considering the treatment of your *research assistant*. How they know about us, however, is more troubling. The Americans and Israelis are certainly not their source. I have a scheduled call with our benefactors later today. They may have some information that will shed some light on our predicament."

Jerome only nodded. While his sour indignation and newly acquired misogyny were genuine, there were two factors in this theater of the absurd he refrained from sharing with Control.

He didn't need any new test subjects. He and the boys had begun to enjoy witnessing their handiwork and couldn't get enough of the show. From outward appearance the deaths seemed peaceful but the sheets from the electroencephalogram and the electrocardiogram indicated extreme distress. Their subjects were in agony.

The only complaint the team had was the speed in which it was over. Like a cocaine junkie doing a line every fifteen minutes to keep the high, the lab rats needed live bodies to tend to their jones.

The second little secret, Jerome kept exclusively to himself. He liked to think of it as his insurance policy——his get-out-of-jail-free card. He had a vaccine… of sorts.

At twenty yards, Moreau spoke a quiet command into his key fob. The small trunk lid on the front of his Bugatti Veyron released and rose on two thin hydraulic lifters. He didn't approach the car until the cover was fully extended.

The vehicle had an after-market RF jammer installed, along with detectors for explosives trace and tracking devices. Compared to every other aspect of his low key and modest lifestyle, the car was a rare indulgence.

As he described it to The Board, it was a Volkswagen that could outrun anything on the road. He'd driven it off the factory floor, four months before full production began.

It was a mobile office that managed stop-and-go city

traffic, as well as blistering highway speeds that surpassed Formula One racers. It had a forty-gallon, factory-installed gas tank, that allowed sustained speeds well in excess of two hundred mph for more than thirty minutes.

After he was satisfied no one had been tampering with his baby, he pulled the door and slipped behind the wheel. The ignition was coded to and activated by his voice. Responding to specific commands, the vehicle did two things: the sixteen cylinders rumbled to life and a section of the center console popped open.

An eight-inch LCD display appeared with a ten-digit keypad below it. An eight-digit pin for secure video conferencing was required. Once accepted, the call was initiated by a voice command——like everything else in the sports car.

"Good afternoon, Monsieur Moreau. The Board hopes you're faring well under the circumstances." There was a slight echo over the secure connection. It occurred most frequently when the communication took place while driving, which was almost always.

"I'm fine, thank you. Before I proceed with my briefing, is there any information you or any of the other members can provide regarding the circumstances to which you've so kindly referred?" Not a particularly obsequious fellow, he expected the sarcasm to be taken in the spirit in which it was presented.

"Hmm, yes, well..."

The odd, circumspect non-response, generated Moreau's next question in a statement. Since the video in the conferences were always one-way, the Algerian couldn't discern the complement of The Board. He was, therefore, gender-specific, based on the person speaking to him. "Messieurs, I have already alluded to the issues around the compromise of our operation here. You have been very direct concerning the Americans. The individual named Ruben Carver, to be specific. That was appreciated, but as yet has failed to unfold.

"However, answers regarding the Israeli lab assistant, who eluded your background check, her demise at the hands of an unknown group, and the attempt on my life, have gone unanswered.

"I'm sure you can understand my concern that essentially resonates around two probabilities. One, you have no fucking clue what is going on, which makes my trust in your capabilities and promises extended, increasingly suspect.

"And two, you have elected not to share information in your possession that affects me and your project directly." Moreau took a breath as he turned on to Rumeli Feneri Cd toward central Istanbul.

"Honestly, gentlemen, I hope it's number two. The first assumption, especially with such a revered and esteemed group such as yourselves, would suggest a monumental incompetence the world will never encounter again. And I say that because after what I've seen in that laboratory you've so generously financed, there may not be a world left after it's been unleashed."

There was soft buzzing over the connection indicating he'd been put on mute.

"M. Moreau, we have a consensus within The Board to share with you, at least in part, a larger view of our operational plan. Your job has been to keep the scientists, and very specifically Dr. Brody, on track.

"Apparently that has been much easier than we anticipated. Dr. Brody seems to be more than sufficiently self-motivated. Your previous briefings and the video feeds we have of the activity in the laboratory show strong signs of project completion for phases one and two. The third phase involving the development of a stable and safe method of transport and effective delivery systems should begin."

Moreau, still waiting for the punchline, felt compelled to interject an observation. "Excuse me, but you do understand the man has gone completely psycho? Self-motivation, as you describe it, means out of control in my book. You need to realize the man may very well start picking his own targets."

"We are aware of Dr. Brody's current state of mind. We leave it to you to manage his temperament. As for the Americans and Israelis, The Board has been the entity responsible for generating the impression of other state-sponsored interest, which you, to your credit, have been able to evade."

This news floored Moreau, causing him to slam on the brakes and veer to the shoulder out of streaming traffic. "*What?*"

"Calm yourself, Monsieur. While currently troublesome for you, it is a necessary diversion for those we view as your true threat.

"Now, please pay attention. The Board has been seeking the venue Dr. Brody requested for your large target testing. This, along with the phase three development and implementation, must transpire with as little hindrance as possible.

"We therefore need time, which we believe can be purchased by pitting the other perceived state-sponsored interests against each other. It's much better for you that Carver and whoever else he enlists to assist him, is occupied with the competition, rather than you."

For the wannabe Frenchman, events had suddenly gone outré. "Is there anything else I need to know?"

"Maintain the course." The connection was then terminated.

CHAPTER TEN

September 15, 2005

The overbooked flight was delayed two hours out of Dulles, causing Ruben to miss his connecting flight from Paris. The eight-hour transatlantic, with cranky flight attendants, cramped seating, lousy food and a flatulent Turk in the middle seat—who was up every thirty minutes to use the head—had put the Special Agent in a raw mood.

New federal policy prohibited government employees from using frequent flyer miles to upgrade into business class. All travel was to be conducted in economy. It had something to do with the notion of fairness.

Ruben was convinced the more the system was changed to make things fair, the more people got pissed and tried to game it. *I'd like someone to show me where fairness is in the natural order of things.*

The wall of apathy at L'Aéroport Charles de Gaulle didn't improve his mental state. The enervating seven hours he spent on standby was capped by another security check; the likes of which should have included a cuddle and some pillow talk.

The Atatürk International Airport in Istanbul at midnight was a mad house, with several flights arriving at once. Unorganized and disagreeable staff made little

83

effort to direct disembarking, worn-out travelers. Those lost or confused, looking for connecting flights or luggage retrieval, were treated with gruff verbal cuffing. *Somebody forgot to put out the welcome mat.*

Passport Control had hours-long, winding queues with uniformed personnel at each station asking questions in Turkish. The displeasure was evident on their faces when the individual standing in front of them didn't answer in kind.

After another hour waiting for the luggage to slide onto the carousel, the Customs official took his time flipping through Ruben's passport, studying his declaration as if '*nothing to declare*' had a deeper, more sinister meaning.

When he finally walked into the main arrivals terminal, at almost three am, he was struck once again by what appeared to be a universal equivalent. He could have been standing in the Bradley terminal at LAX or terminal one at Narita. While he was tired—after nearly twenty-hours on the road—he concluded the experience was utterly unremarkable.

Business travel on aviation mass transit reminded him of bad relationships: uncomfortable and inconvenient. It often took him places he didn't want to go, to do things he didn't want to do. He found the very act of moving long distances in cramped confinement was the perfect anecdote to wanderlust.

Since the metro service didn't extend to the area around his hotel, at least not directly, the self-flagellation would continue with a cab ride. As he rolled his grungy soft-shell Samsonite toward the exit, he spotted Adan waiting for him.

He hadn't changed much since the last time Ruben had seen him. It'd been almost nine years. They served together in San Diego. Adan was a boot agent, while Ruben was coming from his first tour in Japan.

As they approached each other, Ruben could see the country referent had filled out his trousers with some additional tonnage. His short cropped hair had gone salt and pepper, which must have spread to his beard. The heavy shadow Ruben remembered on the younger, clean shaven Adan, had lightened a few shades.

At five-eight, his eastern Mediterranean heritage was on display in the olive skin, hazel eyes and clear, even features. A good looking guy, with a quiet, unobtrusive presence, you'd have no problem introducing to your sister.

As they shook hands and patted each other on the back, Ruben was comforted with the standard query. "Hey, man, how was the trip?"

He blew out some air and advised, "Average."

"That bad, huh?"

"Yeah, pretty fucked up. Did you notice anyone in the terminal we should be concerned about?"

"Not really. Look around...the place is packed. Everyone is waiting for someone. How about you? Anyone suspicious on the plane?"

"Yeah, maybe. Hard to say. By the way, I'm glad you got my message about the flight delay. Did you wait long?"

"Nah, about thirty minutes. I knew Immigration and Customs would be a bitch so I took my time. Anyway, let's go. I used the valet service in the carpark—a no-no with the budget bandits back at headquarters."

Ten minutes later Ruben was in the passenger seat of Adan's Fiat rental. A four cylinder, five-speed stick that was peppy off the light and good in traffic. Ruben's fatigue had him wired, but lucid thought was evasive. He sat silent while Adan jammed through the gears merging onto Rauf Orbay Cd—the main road heading north along the Marmara coastline.

Over the last ten days, he'd been subjected to a

complete physical, a lifestyle polygraph examination and a psych eval. Even though the mission objectives were compartmentalized with briefings on a strict, need-to-know basis, the CIA still had boxes to check before Ruben could be launched.

He was able to enjoy a few extra days sitting in with the band at Madam's Organ, while Art did battle with a pencil pusher or two over the results of the physical and psychological assessments. That whole borderline sociopathy thing was a real toe-stubber for some folks. He spent little time musing on the matter. *The fact is: ya gotta be crazy to do this shit.*

Dever had already been in country for a week, with a desk at the consulate. His cover was to assist on a counterintelligence operation NCIS was going to attempt in Syria. It was valid to the extent there actually was a CI op in the works by an agent in Naples.

With his consular status, he'd been able to bring over Ruben's tool kit, which included among other things, his ASP folding baton, the Recon 1 tactical knife and his photographer's vest with the level 3A Kevlar inserts. The H&K USP .45 tactical, along with its suppressor and green dot laser site arrived in the diplomatic mail.

As Ruben scratched at the spot below his elbow where he'd been injected with a subcutaneous RFID transponder, he wondered when he was going to make contact with the Shin Bet officer. Art had gone quiet on the matter but assured him, as they drove to the airport twenty-five hours earlier, she'd meet him in the ancient city.

Traffic was sparse as Rauf Orbay Cd turned into Kennedy Cd, still heading north along the coast. The four-banger made little noise at a hundred klicks an hour and Ruben's system began to wind down as his head bobbed in a nod.

He was dreaming in a half slumber about a naked,

bald Chinese broad with a long, swaying Fu Man Chu mustache, when Adan backhanded him on the thigh.

Not quite fully awake, he peered, bleary-eyed at the guy behind the wheel. "What is it?"

"There's a motorcycle behind us. Maybe nothing, but he's stayed at the same distance whether I speed up or slow down."

Ruben took a gander behind but could only make out the single headlight shimmering from road vibration.

"Whaddya think?" Adan's voice was steady but quizzical.

"I think if he's following us, that's all he's doing. What I'm wondering about is the car coming up behind him. He's fuckin' flyin'."

At the instant Adan checked his rearview, the speeding vehicle pulled to the left of the two-wheeler in what looked like a passing move. As the right front fender went even with the rear tire of the motorcycle, the car jerked right, pitting the bike.

Instead of knocking it to the right shoulder, the crotch rocket remained upright, whipping perpendicular to the road. The stunned rider had the throttle open and with the rear wheel still spinning the bike shot left across two lanes into oncoming traffic, where it was immediately hit by a five-ton produce truck.

The whole event couldn't have taken more than three seconds from the time the biker was tapped until he became a hood ornament.

"*Holy shit*, did you see that?"

Considering it a rhetorical question, Ruben uttered, "Welcome to fucking Istanbul." Then glancing at his new partner, asked, "You wouldn't happen to have a firearm, wouldja?"

Jerome sat in the dark, staring at the laptop monitor. Until recently, he'd never had much trouble sleeping,

Jeffrey Seay

unless he was tweaking. When his head hit the pillow and he closed his eyes, the cerebrum went into slumber mode. It was akin to activating a switch between his ears.

After the Medleva revelation, insomnia set in. What had once been a reflexive process, was now a willful exercise to shut his brain down.

The love-hate conundrum had him warring with himself, nonstop. He wanted retribution. In that he was resolute. Where to lay the cross-hairs was his poser.

He had the antibiotic for the Zionist infection but those who took it upon themselves to relieve him of the only happiness he'd ever enjoyed, had also lost their privilege to live.

There was something about the email Jerome was re-reading that seemed vaguely familiar. Couched phrases, diction—he was familiar with the sender, or at least the writing style. He didn't, however, recognize the name, Moses Horwitz.

The doctor didn't have a problem with Jews, per se. It was the rotten Israelis that needed to be brought down. He'd made the distinction between the Jew and the Zionist early in his study of the New York Times. He considered it ironic at first that many of the obviously anti-Israeli op-eds were penned by the circumcised.

It came to his attention that many who hailed from the remaining two-and-half tribes, shared his belief in the plight of the Palestinian refugees and decried Ariel Sharon and the Likud regime. There was particular concern over the regenerating popularity for Bibi Netanyahu.

When he ran a trace on the email header it was even more puzzling that, while it bounced back through dozens of servers, it ended inauspiciously on the doorstep of a German neo-Nazi group in Hamburg. It was, in Jerome's mind, digital tongue-in-cheek.

This fellow knew where he was located; had a basic

understanding of what he was doing; and was unambiguous with regard to who Jerome was working for. However, it wasn't the depth of Horwitz's understanding he found interesting. It was the total lack of any judgmental editorializing.

The email advised with certainty, once the breakout capability was established, with all phases of his research and testing completed, The Board would abscond with the product—*there's that word again*—and terminate their association, with prejudice.

The email's only advice was to destroy any active cultures, wipe his hard drives, take only the research he could carry on a thumb drive and run. A good suggestion, to be sure, but Jerome, already divining his temporal state of affairs, had another course of action plotted.

When he was finished, the Middle East would be a clean slate and the rest of the countries of the world would be too busy minding their own respective business do anything about it.

Sheppard was still in his office when the secure line he had installed for the Istanbul operation, now codenamed Toxic Leverage, began to ring. He checked his watch: ten forty-five pm. He'd expected Dever to check in earlier with Carver's status but he was aware of the flight delays.

As he picked up the handset he also gripped the handle of a white, twelve-ounce ceramic cup, with a USMC logo. It was half full of coffee he'd poured in three hours before. With his head wrapped around the mission, and its myriad possible contretemps, he barely noticed the cold, acrid taste.

He answered with a nondescript, "Hello." The line was virtually untraceable to Virginia. If anyone tried, the routing number ended at the Cowboy Club fax machine in Sedona, Arizona.

"Hello, luv." The greeting came out as a low purr, with what he thought was a subtle posh accent reminiscent of Helen Mirren.

Art's autonomic response to the woman's voice was almost always the same: a warm, tingling sensation six inches below his navel that spread to his rectum. He couldn't get off a call without the persistent effect causing tell-tale pecker tracks staining his trousers. It was worse when they had a face-to-face. *I fuckin' hate bein' that bitch's bitch.*

"What happened?" Art couldn't hide the sudden dichotomous mix of irritation and attraction etching his voice.

"Why do you always assume there's something wrong?" The purr had changed to a specious pout.

"Aside from the fact whenever you contact me I want a Valium and a shot of Wild Turkey? It's got to be close to four o'clock in the morning in Istanbul—which is where you said you'd be. I don't b'lieve you're callin' me 'cause you couldn't sleep. So, what happened? Did you make contact with Carver?"

"In a manner of speaking. Although it wasn't actually Carver with whom I made contact. The canary trap you set at your headquarters seems to have paid off. He was followed out of the airport by a rather saturnine fellow on a motorcycle."

"Did you ID him?"

"Not yet, but I don't really care who he is. I'm more interested in who comes looking for him."

"What about Carver? Is he still in play?"

"He's fine, Arthur. He's at his hotel and tucked in. Oh, by the way...did you know he has someone working with him?"

"Of course. I told you we've got a guy we pulled from the NSA, who's still here in DC. He's Carver's IT go-to. Henry Dever's the handler and was plugged in at the

Consulate, there, a week ago."

"I'm not talking about them. The man I'm referring to looked more local. The way they greeted each other at the airport, however, suggested a long term association. They knew each other. I thought you told me Carver's experience in the region was limited to a tour in Iraq."

"It is. I don't know who you're talkin' about, but if Carver's picked up a hitchhiker, just go with the flow. The man is a free-range cowboy, and while he can be unorthodox and unpredictable, the shit he gets into is nothing but predictable.

"Anyway, when are you gonna introduce yourself to the man? The clock is tickin' on this thing."

"Soon, Arthur, but never rush a lady getting ready for a party. Even one she has to crash."

CHAPTER ELEVEN
Rough Start

Spreadeagled, belly down, he'd tried to occupy as much of the king-sized bed his six-foot three-inch, two-hundred and twenty-pound frame could manage. The banging on the door brought him around. With his face buried in a down pillow, he popped one eye open to look at the clock. It read five past twelve. He couldn't tell if that was am or pm.

He'd been dreaming of the naked, hairless Chinese woman again. This time she'd been playing a harmonica and singing Freddie King's *I'm Tore Down*. At some point, the harp morphed into a meat clever and smiling she said, "I'm hungry."

When he dragged himself to a sitting position, feet on the floor, the hard-on registered. *How novel.*

Whoever was in the hallway was still beating on the door. He figured it must be someone he knew. A bad guy wouldn't have bothered.

"Okay, I'm up! Just a sec..."

He'd closed the blackout curtains before he hit the rack and the room was pitch black. Fumbling around the table where the clock was glowing red, he found the lamp. After a few tries with a loose knob, the bulb flashed to life.

Slow getting up, his lower back was stiff, but he wasn't as sore as he thought he'd be. He grabbed the boxers dangling off a chair where he'd thrown them. He tried pulling them on as he hopped to the door, but tripped and fell headfirst into the solid wood portal. *That's a fuckin' wakeup call...Goddamn.*

The voice coming through the barrier was unmistakable. It was Henry Dever.

"Hey, Rube, you okay?"

Ruben didn't answer. Rubbing his noggin with his left hand, he threw the stopper free with his right, twisted the handle and tugged the door open.

The squinty-eyed and pained expression must have looked amusing to Dever as he stepped out of the hall.

With his mouth turned up on one side, he said, "Hey there, home slice...you gonna make it?" He was schlepping a black carry-on that he dropped on the ottoman at the foot of the bed.

Ruben was now flaccid, which he figured was a good thing. *Don't want to give my man here the wrong idea.* It was, however, replaced with bladder pressure that required immediate attention. Holding up an index finger, he headed to the bathroom. As he peed, he ripped a loud, moist fart and coughed up a wad of phlegm he deposited in the toilet.

Finished, he was able to communicate and yelling over the running faucet, said, "Open the curtains, I'll be out in a minute."

He stripped the plastic cover off a one-inch square piece of yellow something or other he assumed was soap, and scrubbed his hands and face. After he gargled some water, he peered at his reflection: bloodshot eyes, accentuated with soft bags. His two-day old stubble would have looked nouveau chic on a guy twenty years younger, but it only made him look like he felt: ragged and out of focus.

With a mental shrug he tossed the hand towel on the counter and walked out of the bathroom scratching his crotch. The room was flooded with early afternoon light, reflecting off stark white walls and furniture, highlighted with gold accents.

There was an arching, padded, gold lamé headboard; a round recessed ceiling light, encircled by a geometric swirl pattern; and gold lamé upholstery on all the furniture. After a quick scan, Ruben considered asking Henry to close the curtains.

Before wrestling into the pants and shirt he'd worn the day before, he picked up the phone on the nightstand and punched the button with the outline of a tiny knife and fork stenciled above it. Without asking Dever, Ruben ordered the continental breakfast for two, along with an extra pot of coffee.

Plopping into a wood-framed armchair, that could probably be found in an Alibaba catalog, he regarded his friend sitting in front of him. Dever had his laptop perched on his knees, trying to get a Wi-Fi signal.

After another couple of seconds Ruben asked, "Have you talked to Adan this morning?"

"Yeah, I did, and I got a call from Art as well. Apparently, he wasn't aware Adan was on the team."

"Any issues?"

"No. He just wanted to remind me he doesn't like surprises. He found out about Adan from the Shin Bet officer, who's supposed to be working with us."

"And...how did she know?"

"She's apparently the one who took out the motorcycle Adan is now trying to run down information about."

"Has he had any success?"

"We'll see. He's supposed to leave me an update in a drop box we've created. This place has Internet, right?"

"Fuck if I know. Wait a minute." Ruben got up and

looked around a wall table, he concluded was a small desk. A postcard written in English was propped against a hot water jug. "Wi-Fi Available. Contact the Front Desk for ID and Password".

Fifteen minutes later, Henry had his connection and was looking at the message Adan had left. His contact at the municipal police, known as the General Directorate of Security, wasn't immediately forthcoming. He wanted to know why the NCIS agent had an interest in a traffic accident, or more specifically *that* traffic accident.

From what Dever read, no emphasis added, Adan didn't bullshit the guy. He told him the truth. He was a witness to what happened, and while he believed he was being followed by the motorcyclist, was hoping to get some background.

Ruben figured, from his own experience with local law enforcement agencies, there was a lot more to the conversation than Adan let on in his report. The info that was provided didn't seemingly help much, though. The dead man had no identification and while his age was estimated at mid-thirties, they had little else to go on.

There were no hits on his fingerprints and what was left of his teeth didn't shed any light. Facial recognition through Interpol was unlikely. The bones in his face had shattered, an eye had been knocked out of its socket and the nose had spread like soft cheese on a warm bagel.

"What about the motorcycle?" Ruben asked.

"It had been reported stolen that evening."

"Anything about marks, scars or tattoos?"

"Nothing in this report but I'll shoot Adan a note and ask him to check. Are you thinkin' about Sonny Xú?" Henry had referred to a Chinese gangster and murder-for-hire specialist Ruben ran up against a few times, earlier in the year.

All the made guys in his organization sported a unique tattoo on their right forearms.

Henry then opined, "The guy who probably knows about Sonny's current state of affairs would be Art. You turned that chinkster over to the CIA in Shanghai last June, right?"

"Yeah..." Ruben was noncommittal. While he made a conscious decision not to get all neurotic, the possibility of the Chinaman coming after him to settle a few scores had crossed his mind on occasion.

He flicked that piece of lint off his shoulder with, "There's no harm in askin'. Anyway, let's go over quickly what we do know."

Henry gave him a puzzled expression. "We don't know anything."

"Sure we do. We know a lot. The guy was on a stolen bike. He had no ID. He's not in the system: no prints. While we can't rule out he wasn't a townie, he had some interest in me and Adan." Ruben took a breath. "Then there's the little matter of the dude getting the bug-on-a-windshield treatment from Art's girlfriend. That's got to tell us what her opinion of the situation was."

Henry leaned back and glanced up at the ceiling. "I'm trackin' but I'm not there yet. Where are you goin' with this?"

"The Board knows I'm here and just like they did in Singapore and Shanghai, they're gonna try to distract and attack; do anything they can to keep me away from the doctor. I was able to upset their apple cart in the Far East but they've got the home field advantage here.

"That's why I've got Adan helpin' me on this. With him we get some local support. Where's he stayin', by the way? Here?"

"No. His new bride's got family in Istanbul. They kinda weird-out on him if he doesn't stay with them when he's in town."

"Well, we're gonna have to keep him out of the line of fire, then. The dickwads who went to work on that lab assistant wouldn't have any compunction against going after Adan's in-laws—if they find out about 'em.

"Oh, and speakin' of Art's girlfriend, when is she supposed to come around? That stunt last night was a little too coy...if ya know what I mean."

Henry twitched his brow, shrugged a shoulder and his mouth curled up on one side again. Ruben was about to react to his boy's expression when there was a knock at the door and a voice announced: "Room service!"

After six or seven strides, Carver was at the door yanking it open. Seeing the woman with the food cart, he calculated there wasn't enough room at the entrance to hold the door and let her pass. She had to manage it while following him in.

"Would you like me to uncover the plates for you?"

The accent grabbed Ruben's attention. It wasn't London posh. He thought it sounded more like England's southern shore; Sussex county, probably Brighton. He nodded at her offer and looked her over.

She had a soft golden complexion, with large round cheekbones and full, heart-shaped lips. Her almond eyes could have been light blue or hazel, and the thick, burgundy hair, pulled back in a tight, short ponytail, had amazing luster.

Zero makeup, she wore a navy blue, cotton pant suit; a white, collarless blouse, buttoned at her neck; and a pair of short-heeled, black pumps.

Ruben had difficulty taking his eyes off her, as she lifted the lids from the plates. An appetizing fare of hard crusted sourdough rolls, soft cheeses, cold beef sausage, soft boiled eggs and pots of tea and coffee. He barely noticed.

Dever must have discerned Ruben's rapt mien, as he whispered, "Oh, brother." And fishing around in a pocket he retrieved twenty lira that he handed the woman.

In the only Turkish he managed to learn in a week, he said, "*Teşekkür ederim*."

With a hint of a smile, she waved it off and answered, "That's not necessary, luv, but aren't you sweet just the same. You must be married." Then redirecting to Ruben, sans the smile, uttered in an arid tone, "And you must be Carver."

The men's responses were immediate and identical. They began to chuckle. Carver folded his arms across his chest and wiggled his bare toes, while Dever scratched the age-formed, poker chip-sized bald spot on his crown.

"Officer Levitan?" Ruben asked.

"That's right."

He extended his hand. "Nice to meet you...I think."

She gripped it, applying firm pressure and with more of a jerk than a shake, answered, "Likewise."

Rivka Levitan was not Israeli by birth. Her father was a diamond merchant in Brighton, where she was born and raised. She loved England's southern coast and while the water temperature was always too cold for anything other than wading along the beach, it had, most days, what the rest of the island state found rare: bright, sunny skies.

Her parents were Haredi, and observed tenets of segregation, both secular and gender. That said, her father had a keen knowledge of Jewish history in the laic world. As Rivka labored over the Talmud, Totti poured into her the chronicle of Jews in the modern wilderness. An instruction that went beyond what even her brothers were receiving in the Yeshiva.

Jews like Rivka's father had been bouncing around England, off and on, since the Norman Conquest in the late ninth century. William the Conqueror imported Jewish merchants from France's upper Normandy for the purpose of filling his new treasury with coin. Until then, feudal lords had been allowed to pay their dues in kind, with tithes coming from the fruit of the land.

It was difficult, however, to maintain an army and navy when the coffers were loaded with grain, poultry and pork. The king could feed them but couldn't pay or outfit them, nor buy weapons, build ships or negotiate contracts for foreign trade.

Even then, Jews had the reputation, if allowed to move into a region, of accumulating wealth faster than rats produced litters. They soon controlled the economy, much to the chagrin of the indigenous population.

William I counted on this stereotype to hold true and scattered his Semitic minions throughout the country, embedding them with the landed gentry.

While the status of the Jews wasn't officially chartered until Henry I, it was understood their possessions belonged to the king. As usual, however, even with that bit of Chancery magic, and two hundred years of unfettered fortune, things went sideways for the descendants of Abraham.

They forgot the reason for their prosperity lay within the largess of their royal benefactors. When they pushed back on the demands from the Crown, and ignored the calls for tribute, the age-old anti-Semitic persecution began. By the late thirteenth century, every Jew that could be found was rounded up and sent packing with nothing but what they could carry on their backs.

When they were allowed back in by Oliver Cromwell, four hundred years later, all was not necessarily forgiven; however, they wasted no time taking up where they left off. Rivka enjoyed the revelation that with the return of the children of Abraham, the divine blessing followed. The British Isle soon became the British Empire.

It also seemed to her, when looking at the record of God's chosen, He didn't like it when they allowed themselves to get too comfortable around the goyim and shiksa. She perceived that nothing brought them back to Him faster than hard luck and trouble.

It took the lives of six million and the hand of the devil's own for the reformation of the State of Israel.

Rivka was a Jew, no doubt, but it wasn't until three events—the Munich massacre, Golda Meir's interview with Edman Newman, and the Yom Kippur War—occurring in close succession between September 1972 and October 1973, that cemented her *Jewishness*. The moral imperative that went with her birthright.

There was no sense of purpose or fulfillment of God's plan on earth by staying in Brighton and indulging in Talmudic masturbation. Over the tearful objections of her mother and the quiet blessing of Totti, she went home to the land. It was December 1973. She was three days into her eighteenth year.

CHAPTER TWELVE
Moving Forward

The text came as Moreau lay on the *göbektaşı*, the raised marble platform that covered the heating source in the center of the hot room. His hands were slippery with sweat as he punched in a reply.

"Currently occupied with a pressing matter. Will be in touch in ninety minutes."

The Board didn't indicate why they wanted an unscheduled meeting, but there was no sign of urgency in their text.

Since the Pierre Loti Cafe was off the menu for the time being, he found the Çemberlitaş Hamamı, one of the oldest Turkish baths in Istanbul, an acceptable alternative where he could mull over current events.

The police were still looking for a man of his description in connection with the stabbing deaths of two people near the Eyüp Sultan Mosque. The news sources didn't identify the individuals and Yves knew they never would.

The Algerian was always partial to western euphemisms. In this case, the Council of Forensic Medicine, Turkey's coroner's office and expert witness on things technical and medical, had a couple of John Does in the freezer.

Thinking back on those two, he'd only had a couple of minutes to examine the bodies. They weren't black, Far East Asian or northern European. He wasn't generally given to racial slurs, considering his own mixed breeding, but since he had to guess, he figured Eastern European —grimy white.

Made in EU was printed on their clothing tabs. For Moreau, as a discerning shopper and one time smuggler, that could mean sweatshops in Albania or Macedonia. Still nothing particularly useful except the material was cheap and worn—Balkan knockoffs of more expensive Euro fashions.

What made him decide who he was dealing with, from a purely ethnic perspective, were the military issue boots, a style popular in the countries northwest of Turkey; a bone handle jackknife, with *Bursa* stamped on the blade; and a machine pistol jammed in a shoulder holster—an M84, the Yugoslavian version of the Czech Skorpian vz. 61.

From Moreau's experience, the two men he left for dead smacked of Serbian mafia. The most base and ruthless murder-for-hire and kidnap-for-ransom villains he'd ever come across. Even the Russians steered clear of those cretins.

He'd also spotted an odd, circular tattoo on the right forearm of one of the gutted. The mech was in a tank top and except for the fresh ink, which looked like a tong sign, there were no other marks.

It was enough, however, to make him push the sleeve up on the right arm of the second bleeder and espied the same small scribble. New enough to still be scabbed over.

Men like this often had their life stories engraved on their skin. Especially if they'd spent time incarcerated. That was, unless, they were believers in Islam. Tats for strict Muslims were taboo.

The reasons for the prohibition was never clear to the

Algerian. He'd heard in his youth it had something to with debasing the human form. Changing the body for vanity's sake was considered haram—forbidden by Islamic law. For whatever reason, he himself refrained. It was, he supposed, the permanence that bothered him.

He could only assume the desperadoes he left on the sidewalk allowed themselves to be marked because they didn't considered it vain. He let his imagination drift. *Maybe it was a symbol of membership—an assassins' order...or some such drivel.*

Eyes closed and flat on his back, breathing the sauna's moist air, he tried to picture the face of the third man who retreated back to the van. He seemed more Eurasian, and Moreau knew he'd recognize him if he saw him again.

As he tried to recall an image of each man, in what he now believed to be a diverse band of cutthroats, he recollected what The Board said. They were creating the appearance of other state-sponsored interest. *The Board wants a patsy.*

Moreau liked the public bath but preferred self-service to the standard wash and massage by a male masseuse. The feeling of vulnerability was anathema. As he moved to a basin next to the wall, to begin a loofah scrub, he pondered The Board's motive around establishing a scapegoat.

He wondered if that hallowed crowd were only interested in the appearance of evil, rather than actually financing what had the potential of being a global killer. Yves wasn't exactly sure what he'd signed on for, but was confident it wasn't that.

He could see the benefit The Board would derive from a last-second thwarting of a terrorist's use of a WMD. It would go a long way in furthering their role in influencing sanctions against countries viewed by the world community as sponsors of terrorism.

Trade concessions and commodity markets would shift and prices on energy-based products would jump. Depending on the sanctioned country or countries, there could be negative ripple effects on arms proliferation controls, food production for export, construction material and international aid overall.

It was a way for The Board to increase its sway in global politics and policy. A step closer to its autocratic goal of directing socio-political and cultural evolution. It could manipulate the balance of power, while masking it entirely by a thin veneer of democratic process. *Une bonne affaire en effet.*

However, there were two big, ugly gorillas in the room, threatening The Board's global urban renewal plan: the Americans and Israelis. They knew The Board absconded with the DARPA scientist, along with his lethal bag of tricks.

It wasn't like they were going to be thrown off the scent through sleight of hand. Moreau couldn't feature how his benefactors would convince anyone some sovereign enemy of Liberty was to blame for the use of a super bio-toxin.

Then there was the matter of the new hired guns. They had no idea they were being used to draw fire away from the lab. A stopgap measure until the Algerian could move the doctor's chemistry set to the field. He didn't know how many men were in the crew but they were already down two and hadn't even met the real enemy yet.

At the rate they were going there wouldn't be any of them left to plant evidence of a malevolent state-sponsored conspiracy.

He poured hot water over his head and shoulders using a gallon-sized, wood slat bucket. As the soap rinsed away, so did his concerns over the issues he'd spent musing over the last hour. Yves knew Dr. Brody had started developing his own agenda. While he didn't know what it entailed, he was dead certain it did not match The Board's.

With that in mind, the Algerian began contemplating his escape plan. As he strolled out of the hot room, heading for the jacuzzi and a long soak, he was aware that in the end, he would be the one to put the doctor down.

Just because he didn't like working with women, didn't in anyway diminish his fondness for the opposite sex. Ruben would never be described as a philogynist, in the woman-on-a-pedestal-as-the-highest-form-of-humanity, kind of guy, but he did tend to groove in the presence of a charming female.

On the B-side of that single—ever since Shanghai—a strong, confident woman, with an obvious pernicious bent, had him involuntarily adjusting his jock. A subconscious confirmation he still had a pair. When he met Rivka, he felt a sudden compulsion to excuse himself and visually inspect the area in the bathroom mirror. *You may not be "the" man, but you're man enough.*

It didn't take him long, though, to size up his new acquaintance. She seemed to possess the casual countenance of someone who considered her gender a fortunate incidental. While a feminist 'tude may not have been an exhibited character trait, femininity was definitely a tool of her trade.

Ruben sensed having a nice rack below hazel eyes was as much a weapon as the Jericho 941 he assumed was causing the tell-tale bulge in her fitted blazer. He figured it wouldn't take long to get past the distraction of the package and establish an arm's length professional relationship—or so he hoped.

Ruben glanced at Henry and spotted the same

assessing regard. His partner had seen enough crap in his forty-two years not to be easily impressed. Knowing Dever, he probably couldn't decide whether he should buy her a box of chocolates or ask her to arm wrestle.

Apparently picking up the vibe radiating off the two men, Rivka gave a conciliating smile. "Relax, gentlemen. I'm not here to add to your PTSD."

Not entirely stupefied, Ruben responded, "I'm sorry?"

"You're casualties of your country's vagina warriors...no?"

Oh, man, I already like her. Please do not fuck this up. "Yeah, well...we've been told we'll survive as long as we shut up and color." Ruben remembered he was hungry and pointing at the food cart asked, "Would you like to join us?"

"Aren't you a dear. I could murder a coffee about now."

Ruben pulled the chair from the desk and drug it across the thin, gold octagon and x-patterned pile. He placed it at to the round two-chair table, situated under the small picture window, where he and Dever had been sitting.

She sat, legs crossed, holding in both hands a cup she'd taken from the beverage set on the desk. Without actually focusing on Ruben, she said, "I assume you spotted that motorcycle following you from the airport."

"Yeah, and I assume you're the one responsible for making him a grease spot on the truck's grill."

The corners of Rivka's mouth ascended a fraction as she pursed her lips. "How deliciously descriptive. Yes, that was my doing."

"Were you alone?"

"No. Like you, I have an associate on long-term assignment in country. However, any assistance he provides is somewhat limited. He has other mission requirements and I don't want to blow his cover."

"Well, since you were following him, following us, can you tell us anything about him?"

"Not much really, at least not about him specifically. My interest last night was in you and the bloke you met at the airport. It was my understanding you'd be operating solo, with the support of Special Agent Dever, here."

Dever shifted in his chair when he heard his name. "Call me Henry."

She nodded with a smile. "Thank you, luv. It does work better for me, if we can keep things on an informal basis. It allows me to pretend we're friends." She returned her gaze to Carver and asked, "Shall I call you Ruben? I rather fancy that name. I'm sure you understand why."

"Sure, why not. Let's be friends. The man with me last night is an NCIS Special Agent working out of a joint-use airbase in Izmir. Since your guy is going to be mostly unavailable, SA Hanna has a solid network of sources both in the public and private sectors. If we need a quick getaway, he's got the juice to make that happen.

"So what about the guy on the motorcycle?"

She tapped the cup with a nail. "He wasn't interested in Special Agent...what was his name?"

"Hanna."

"He wasn't interested in Special Agent Hanna. He was in the terminal when we arrived and as soon as he spotted you, he began the tail. We didn't detect movement from any other parties. The man was on his own."

"Okay, but why'd you take him out?"

"The motorcycle was unregistered, at least to the extent it had no plates. We considered the possibility he could have been MIT, but there have been no indications the Turks know about you or your mission.

"We didn't want to follow the bugger all night, so we

gave him a little tap. To be straight, we wanted him in the hospital. He'd be more likely to have his mates come 'round there, than at the morgue. Unfortunately, we weren't at all jammy in that regard."

Ruben wiped off a drop of yogurt sauce snared in his stubble, then advised, "From what Hanna could glean from his source at the Coroner's office the guy is undocumented. The pancake action made any photo ID impossible and unless the Counsel for Forensic Medicine wants to pick his teeth out of the pavement, we're outta luck with dental.

"I'm gonna ask Hanna to try and get a description of the body."

Rivka nodded her approval but apprised, "We've been able to acquire a few photos of the corpse. There's not really anything that sticks out," she paused, reflecting, "except for a single tattoo on the right forearm."

Carver and Dever looked at each other as Rivka provided a description of the small mark.

"It took a few hours but a hit in our tattoo database gave us a clue. I received an update just before I knocked on your door. It's not a tong sign, really, but it is used by an organized crime group operating out of the Far East.

"This is the first time we've seen any indication they've spread this far." Rivka caught Ruben's eye. "You were stationed in Japan. Did you ever encounter a similar mark?"

Ruben had no idea where to begin. He bobbed his head once and declared, *mezzo piano*, "Yep."

Rivka helped herself to more coffee and peeled a half-inch off a sourdough roll as she listened to Carver detail his experience with Xú Bao-Zhi, or the more familiar Sonny Xú to those who knew him outside China. Until an operation Carver was involved with, several months before, drove the gangster out of Singapore, the extent of his business interests were wide spread throughout Asia.

When his gambling, prostitution, narcotics and extortion rackets collapsed, he escaped to China and away from any possibility of extradition. He maintained, however, a side enterprise he conducted on a smaller but much more international scale. Rent-a-killers that had begun to net him a tidy profit, along with a growing reputation among satisfied customers.

The Shin Bet officer sipped at her tepid beverage, engrossed in Ruben's rundown of events. It was his blithe delivery, however, that clued her into the man's state of mind. She could see he hadn't fully recovered from the apparent trauma of his last few missions.

She'd observed this before with veterans of Yamas, Israel's version of the U.S. 1st Special Forces Operational Detachment-Delta or Delta Force——active counter-terrorism operators. Tough, dedicated professionals, with skill sets in close quarters combat, hostage rescue, high value target extraction, and other specialized operations that often involved target elimination.

Too many months under the gun, without enough time to heal up and recharge the batteries, turned them sour. They didn't get sloppy. They got weary. The edge started to come off. They looked left when they should have looked right; took the easy route instead of the best. Operations that should have been routine became fraught with difficulty because of obvious miscalculation.

She didn't know this American other than the assurances she'd received from Arthur. She was surprised by his age and wondered if that was the true center of her concern. He was, however, smooth without being glib; charming without being urbane; and concise and economical without being facile. That was appealing. *Maybe I'm wrong about him. We'll see.*

A discussion about her asset, Medleva, was critical but

she didn't want to get into it at this meeting. Although, the information Medleva passed about the DARPA scientist and his research would play heavily in the strategy to extract the man.

There was an aspect of this joint operation she felt the need to keep to herself. Rivka suspected whoever kidnapped and tortured the woman did so, not to pull information about the research in the lab, but to find out how much intel had already been passed to her handler.

The Shin Bet intelligence collection effort didn't surface any indication the word was out about the scientist. She'd factored the odds her own people were wrong in this regard at close to zero. The probability anyone knew about Rivka's asset was even less.

She was certain someone with access to Shin Bet source files gave Medleva up to the group Arthur referred to as The Board.

CHAPTER THIRTEEN
A New Problem

Moreau checked in with Brody before he pointed his car northwest on the 0-3, leaving Istanbul behind for a few hours. As usual, the doctor was otherwise engaged, and alternated between expressing aggravation at the interruption, and his nagging demand for an outdoor venue for testing.

Yves was now on the phone with Brody twice a day. The calls weren't necessary for progress reports. The bioweapon was ready. The holdups, according to the scientist, continued to be safe out-of-lab handling and a method of aerosol delivery.

It was the delay in those two aspects of the project that generated his suspicions about the doctor's own surreptitious scheme. Moreau felt compelled to verify the doctor's whereabouts and activities during the day.

Brody had developed a method to weaponize an agent from a cyanobacteria. It had a gestation period similar to the common cold but unlike the rhinovirus, an individual became contagious within minutes of infection.

Once ingested, it produced a neurotoxin that would release in forty-eight hours and within eight hours after that, compete paralysis occurred—the death knell. Control had witnessed its effect. A virulent microbial, toxic to humans only and capable of defeating biosafety level C gear. *De trop théâtre du grotesque.*

The money-shot for The Board, in this obscene effort, came in less than a day of the agent's deployment. It went inert after exposure to ultraviolet light for more than three hours. Land and livestock were unaffected.

With the genius to create the weapon and manage it safely in the laboratory, Moreau was confident the doctor was stalling on product delivery. An assumption that gave him little comfort.

There was no longer a moral compass at work—the doctor was devoid of conscience. Without it, his indignation lost its focus. Instead of a rifle with a scope, he'd turned into a bomb without a timer. *They should have let me deal with that woman.*

As he spoke the commands to activate the car's cellular system, he pondered whether or not to articulate his concern. Since this session had been initiated by his employers, he expected what they had to say would affect his disclosure.

"You're late, M. Moreau. Is there a problem?"

Still tinny in resonance, the person answering the call was new to the Algerian. Once again, The Board's complement was a mystery.

"My apologies. I was having some difficulty in getting connected, but be that as it may, I believe I should ask you the same question. Your request for a meeting was unexpected."

Moreau pulled a fresh pack of Gauloises from the glove compartment. He hadn't had a smoke that day and was itching for one. Traffic was heavy through the city, and the stop-and-go allowed him to take his hands from the wheel long enough to unravel the wrapper and peel away the corner foil.

He didn't bother with the holder. After tamping a fag free, he moistened the tobacco on the filterless cylinder with the tip of his tongue before securing it between his lips. He'd pushed the car lighter forward during the process and when it popped ready, glowing red, he lit up.

He slid the window down a few inches and the blue-gray cloud slipped into the breeze. The road noise would be another irritant for those listening over the encrypted connection. Control didn't care. The contentious bug up his butt was making him irritable.

A familiar voice responded. "We felt it prudent to let you know the NCIS Special Agent, Ruben Carver has arrived in Istanbul."

"From our last conversation, I understood you were handling Monsieur Carver. Has that changed?"

"No. Nothing has changed in that regard. You should also be aware the Israelis have sent someone as well: a Shin Bet officer—Medleva Jankovic's handler."

Merde. "How do you plan on managing that?"

"The officer's name is Rivka Levitan. Like Carver she's a formidable, seasoned counter-terrorism specialist. For us, we're fortunate in not having to fight these forces on two fronts. They're working together."

"Messieurs, I appreciate the heads up, but please be aware, I'm not hearing anything at this point that fills me with confidence. If the three characters I encountered are any indication of what you think is a going to be a 'diversion' for the two you've described, you'll need to think again."

There was dead air for several seconds before the reply. "Our decision to retain this specific outfit had nothing to do with the survivability of its personnel. On the contrary, we anticipate a high mortality. We count on it.

"We obtained validation for our plan when you handled, rather deftly I might add, what we were assured were the band's best in the region. While we admittedly ran the risk of losing you as our Control in Istanbul, you also successfully corroborated our faith in you to see this project through to fruition."

The comment answered a question that had been percolating since their last telcon. What was now bouncing between his ears was how this would make a difference. "I'm sorry, but I believe I'm missing something. This doesn't seem to change anything."

Even with the metallic tone, the strained patience was evident in the response. "The deaths of Carver and Levitan would result in considerable backlash. The countries they represent would be forced to provide an explanation that a simple disavowal would not satisfy.

"On the other hand, Carver's well documented tenacity and aggressive manner of case closer, will have him and his co-conspirator Levitan, sitting in a Turkish jail for days, if not weeks. Who's going to believe an adjunct professor at one of Turkey's most prestigious universities is manufacturing a WMD? By the time anyone bothers to make the inquiry you'll be long gone. Does that clarify our approach?"

It was Moreau's turn to have a moment of silence. The logic from a single perspective was sound. It would, in fact, buy him time. What it did not take into account was the nutty professor and his three stooges.

The Algerian had to find out what the doctor was brewing. He'd come to the conclusion The Board wasn't paying him enough to ride out the shitstorm broiling on the horizon. As Control, he had to reel Brody in and join in his madness, if only to give it direction.

While his employers had presented a good case, Moreau's own experience told him their machinations were suspect. In the end, he'd be the one to dispose of not only Jerome Brody, but also this Ruben Carver fellow and his *Juif copain*.

"Oui, Messieurs. Everything is becoming *très clair*...very clear."

* * *

Control stayed on 0-3 toward Edirne, a small, ancient city near the borders of Greece and Bulgaria. Located in the heart of the Thrace wine country, the lush green of terraced vines, visible for miles, usually played easy on his mind. Not today.

There was a cafe along the Saraçlar Caddesi, a white, square stone and brick pedestrian plaza in the center of town, that served an excellent cabernet sauvignon. Along with a platter of olives, cheeses and fresh baked bread, he'd at least display the image of a contented tourist.

He'd made an appointment with a former associate with whom he hoped he was still on good terms. Pushing the pedal until the needle on the speedometer ticked past a hundred and eighty kph, he contemplated the concept of employment for life. It may have been a utopian constant for the statist intellectual, but where he came from, it had an *or else* connected to it.

Conceived during the middle years of the Algerian war for independence, Moreau had little memory of his parents. He'd been given a history of his father by one his friends. A man who would ultimately take charge of Yves and raise him as his own.

His father was Harki, a Muslim loyalist who had served in the French Army in North Africa and Europe during World War II. A teenager at the time, he'd fought his way through Sicily, up the boot of Italy, participated in the liberation of France and continued to kill Germans until he was wounded at the gates of the Fatherland. He went home to Algeria with a medal on his chest and a limp he could never quite shake.

When the war for independence broke out in 1954, Yves' father transitioned from the French regular army to the auxiliaries. Committed to French Algeria, he fought the rebels of the Front de Libération Nationale with vigor.

There was no mistake on his part. He understood the grievance of the nationalists. In truth, Yves' paterfamilias had little regard for the Pied-Noirs—Algerians with European or Jewish roots. They were the minority by almost eighty percent. The only people in the land who held the designation of Algerian, enjoying the privileges and entitlements of French citizens.

As a Muslim, he'd refused apostasy and like those who wore the fez was denied citizenship, property ownership and education. Discrimination under French rule, in what was described by many scholars as colonial apartheid, was his lot in life.

Neither bitter, nor a gambler, he didn't bother to calculate the minuscule odds of success of the Muslim *intifada*. He was, after all, a soldier and ultimately pragmatic. The strength lay in the quantity and quality of the French guns and the training of its legions.

He also concluded Sharia law wouldn't improve his family's freedom of choice or standard of living. He may have loved Allah but he hated Islamic dictates and he had no problem with the seeming contradiction.

As he predicted, the French won every engagement against the smaller, more ill-equipped FLN. What he hadn't factored into his reasoning and wouldn't have believed, even if he was aware, had to do with the power of the left in France.

The leverage it brought to bear in the press, through the tactical use of incendiary rhetoric, helped turn the tide for the beleaguered nationalists. Opposition to the war in Algeria grew rapidly, but while the wicked grand colon and the oppression of the autochthonous, were the progressives' pet peeves, there was another, greater facet.

Much of the support to sue for peace came as a result of France already having its *grand cul* handed to it in Vietnam. Anti-colonial sentiment may have been rampant but it didn't come close to the humiliation felt over the loss in Southeast Asia. The fear of embarrassment on the world stage, of another Dien Bien Phu, resonated around Paris.

President De Gaulle, under this pressure of negative public opinion, acquiesced. With majority approval of the National Assembly in De Gaulle's Fifth Republic, the Algerians were granted their independence in July 1962.

That was all the history of the conflict Yves cared to learn. His last and most vivid recollection of his parents was the evening a FLN lynch mob came to visit. They forced him to watch as they strung his father up in the rafters and gang raped his mother—a celebration of righteous retribution.

She was a beautiful, round Berber woman, barely out of her teens, when they flayed her with the kitchen knives his father had sharpened that morning.

They left the hysterical kid sitting in a corner, forgotten, as they wandered into the street in search of other homes to exercise jihad. As long as they could get it up, they hadn't finished executing Allah's will.

The cheese plate sat untouched as Moreau rolled the half-empty wine glass between his palms. He didn't often scrape back the layers of his memory that far. He still had the occasional dream of those who beget him, but he couldn't consciously remember what they looked like unless he put them in context.

A regrettable state, since it was the context he wished to forget.

The reason for the stroll down memory lane walked through the door exactly fifteen minutes late: a thick-bodied Corsican that had more than five inches and seventy pounds on the Algerian.

He had a dimpled, vertical scar that ran from his temple, a few centimeters from his left eye, to his jawline.

117

An injury that severed nerves and muscle tissue, causing the left side of his face to have a noticeable droop. His nose, a lumpy mass, squatted above crooked, pudgy lips, set in a permanent frown.

Collocated with a visage that made babies cry, was a black Barsolino wide-brimmed fedora resting above slicked-back, thinning ringlets in a *Just For Men* dark brown. The Savile Row suit was a three-button, charcoal gray platinum wool. His conservative starched black, Egyptian cotton shirt and matching silk tie, were offset by a pair of Cerruti high-gloss, alligator shit-kickers.

Yves always admired this villain's sense of style.

As the big ugly got closer, his voice a husky purl from a lifetime of cigarettes, said, "Musa, you fucking sand nigger, what the fuck do you want?"

The two men had grown up together on the back streets of Marseille and this prick was the only person who ever called Yves by his given name. He was, in fact, the only one who knew it.

"I want to fuck your sister in the ass. Are you two still an item?"

It took a few seconds to get past the requisite stare down, then they had their laugh, embraced and kissed each other on the cheeks.

"Okay, squirt, I'm here. Who do you want me to kill?"

When Dever followed Rivka out the door, he left the small suitcase on the ottoman. The plan was to have Adan drive Ruben and Rivka to Koç University that afternoon but it was getting late. The clock next to the bed read 15:17.

Adan had already walked the campus, checking each building, all the laboratory facilities he could find, and sat in on two of Professor Jerome Brody's classes. Ruben expected Rivka to have questions for Special Agent Hanna on the drive out. He would.

After checking the contents of Henry's goody bag, he went back in the bathroom, lay in the tub and let the hot shower pelt him for ten minutes. The gunshot wound to his right trapezius had healed, but it took time to warm his shoulders up when he first got out of bed.

With a fresh shave and clean clothes, he slipped on the shoulder holster. Henry had been thoughtful enough to bring Carver his gear. The .45, with all its accouterments, had become Carver's weapon of choice after the Singapore mission nine months earlier.

He checked the three magazines he'd filled with +P Grizzly Xtreme and confirmed he had two more unopened boxes of the ammo in the suitcase. Before seating a magazine in the well, he field-stripped the pistol to its component parts and examined each.

Satisfied, he had the gun together in seconds. He dropped a round in the chamber, released the slide, decocked the hammer and shoved a magazine home. Hearing it snap in, he tamped the bottom of the grip with the palm of his left hand. *Just to be sure.*

NCIS got its knickers in a twist when agents carried sidearms not chambered for 9mm parabellum. All the fussing and hand-wringing about weapon quals and liability issues, ammo requisitions and training requirements was tiresome. One of his favorite arguments out of headquarters for a standard carry sidearm had to do with sharing ammo during a firefight. *Pfff...like that was gonna happen.*

He'd always believed the issue pistol, a Sig Sauer P226, was a fine gun. It shot straight and was dependable. He simply preferred a bigger bullet, and the only time Ruben could see himself accepting ammo from another agent was when that agent wasn't in any condition to use it. If that was the case, he'd also secure the agent's weapon, along with his creds.

Ready to leave, he put on the vest, adjusted the holster

for better concealment and tapped his pockets for wallet and badge. As he remembered to retrieve his tactical folding knife, taped inside the suitcase, his BlackBerry buzzed. *Fuckin' hold your horses.*

Thinking it was Adan he answered, "I'm on my way."

"Well, that's good because you better be."

It wasn't the voice he'd expected. "Ryan?"

"Yeah, listen, I got a reply back from your boy there in Istanbul."

"I'm listening."

"From what I can tell he's about to jump the reservation. I forwarded his message to Dever and Sheppard, you can talk to them to confirm. But trust me, I think you've got a guy who's ready to go postal on a massive scale. I mean any day."

"Did he tell you the target?"

"He wasn't specific, although I got the distinct impression it was targets—plural."

"Ryan, that's not tellin' me anything."

"The guy was on rant...okay? All I can say is, if you don't get to him soon, then you'll be able to find him by following the trail of the sick and dying."

CHAPTER FOURTEEN

Prepping for the Road

Two innocuous eight-ounce cans of men's deodorant spray sat in the cabinet below Jerome Brody's bathroom sink. He hadn't actually lied to Control. The problems of mass production in the weaponized form, along with storage and handling procedures did persist, from a certain point of view.

The cyanobacteria they'd synthesized for the agent was modified to reduce the risk of an accidental infection in the lab. Jerome thought of it as a natural vaccine. While the weapon was more deadly than the saxitoxin it was designed to emulate, they'd engineered it with a genome specific immunity.

He and Medleva may have been the only ones who knew of the modification but all the members of the team had been protected. In fact, anyone who shared the distinct genetic markers they built the agent around, would likely survive an outbreak.

It was also Medleva who expressed reservations about turning the agent over to a less than omniscient group of money-grubbing capitalists. As much as he wanted to discredit the woman's sincerity regarding social justice, there were aspects of her arguments he continued to view with merit. This was one of them.

There was no guarantee The Board would do the right thing when selecting the recipients of Jerome's bacterial treasure. If released directly into an international hub, the resulting pandemic would make humanity an endangered species.

He looked at his watch. Control would call soon. The last contact for the day always occurred close to Asr prayer, in the late afternoon. The team rarely worked at night anymore, other than to take shifts to care for the dying.

The doctor left the lab early after setting the timer. It was poker night for the boys and they'd be breaking out the cards and chips by five pm. They'd have a beer keg wrapped with a few liquid nitrogen coils and a couple of frozen pizzas in the dry heat sterilizer.

He had a sudden pang of what he analyzed to be guilt, over the best course of action. He determined the feelings were irrelevant, though, and consciously scrubbed away the emotional stain.

The night before, he'd disconnected the audible alarms in the lab, hoping the CCTV throughout the space wasn't actively monitored. He'd constructed three glass trays of hydrogen cyanide, which were placed in the ventilation shafts. Each tray had a timed charge attached to shatter the containers and disperse the poison.

The laboratory security systems, detecting the hazard, would go into shutdown mode. The doors would be sealed and no venting would occur until after the filters had cleared the air.

While this was going on, the lab's fail-safe system would engage and all cultures would be exposed to direct UV beams and then laser fried. Stored bacterial agent, in aerosol form, would be similarly destroyed.

To complete the going-out-of-business process, the hard drives on the thin client servers were also timed to wipe. Since print material was burned at the end of each day, as part of the clear desk policy they'd established as a team, Brody was sanguine about the final condition of the laboratory.

He would make his mark in history alone.

When Ruben stepped out of the elevator into the small, cluttered lobby he spotted Adan. He wasn't alone. Rivka was next to him, speaking in his ear. Carver thought she must have approached him cold. Adan had the harassed expression of a man trying to ignore an LA panhandler. *Man, this woman really loves to push buttons. If she has brothers, she pro'bly made 'em cry.*

They were no more than ten feet away, yet getting to them required some jockeying around a number of ornate, gold-framed sofas and chairs, along with their ottoman coffee and end tables. More concerned about who might be waiting for him when he checked in, he hadn't registered the heavy, purple brocade curtains, black and gold globe chandeliers and assorted candelabras. *What's the name of this place again?*

As he stepped closer, he said, "Great, you two've met. Who's driving?"

Without looking at Rivka, Adan jabbed an index finger in her direction. "Who's this?"

Not the least bit surprised, Carver introduced the Israeli. "This is Rivka Levitan." He stopped short and looked around to confirm an empty room. "She's our Shin Bet counterpart on this caper."

Ruben shifted his gaze six inches and eyeing his new comrade-in-arms, was about to make an apparently unnecessary introduction of Adan, when she cut him off. "I'm sorry, luv. I should have waited for you but I couldn't resist." Then, as if the country referent weren't in the room, she added, "He's cute. Can he shoot?"

Oh, brother. "You're lucky he hasn't shot you. If you

keep fuckin' around he just might." Glancing back at Adan, he asked, "So, you're drivin'?"

"Yeah, let's go."

As they turned in unison toward the exit, Rivka snaked her arm inside Ruben's vest and around his waist. She snuggled into his side, gripping his holster. "Blimey, what a stonker. I'll show you mine, if you show me yours."

Carver twisted out of the embrace, inducing the mental image of an aunt who came to visit when he was kid. She'd pinch his cheeks, lifting him to his toes, so she could plant sloppy, lipstick-laden kisses all over his face. *Fuckin' hell...*

Rivka propped the sassy hand on a hip as she strode to the door. In the same parched timbre he'd heard earlier, she declared, "You're such a big, strong bloke...I feel safer already."

The apartment phone rang at five forty-five pm. Doctor Brody had been busy for the last hour with online banking transactions, and packing clothes and accessories he'd recently acquired from Eddie Bauer. It was going into a cycling backpack he'd also picked up from a catalogue.

So focused on what he was doing, he was startled by the sound. When he answered it was Control.

"Doctor Brody, why is your mobile turned off?"

"Huh? What?"

"Why have you switched off your cell phone?"

"I didn't...I don't know..."

"Doctor Brody, are you all right?"

"Yes, I'm fine. I'm sorry. I must have forgotten to put the phone on the charger."

"I don't ever recall it coming off the charger. What's going on?"

"It's nothing really. The team have their poker night

this evening and I left early. You know, I don't see my mobile where I usually keep it. I must have left it in the lab." This wasn't a lie. As he ordered his thoughts, a picture of his phone in its charging cradle floated up. Though he also remembered he'd turned it off the night before.

"Well, I'm only calling to see if there are any changes in status. I suppose it doesn't matter until an outdoor test environment has been selected, but you understand we need a solution in place for those aspects of the program still outstanding."

Brody was only half listening. He'd logged into the laboratory's CCTV feed, counting down from the clock display on his laptop. He could see the three men standing in the lab canteen drinking their libations from a set of beaker mugs.

Jerome was pleased to see the camaraderie. He couldn't help reflecting on what great guys they were and thought he might actually miss them. When the university clock tower chimed at six, he'd watch them die.

"Hello...Doctor Brody, are you there?"

"Yes, I'm here. Is there anything else you want to discuss? I'm rather busy."

"We need to have our weekly face-to-face. How about tomorrow morning...say nine am, at the tables outside the student union?"

"Sounds perfect. Would you order me one of those fancy lattes they serve?"

Moreau was no longer worried. He'd blown past that anxiety marker ten kilometers ago——about the time his conversation began with Jerome. He was now approaching horrified.

What rang that bell for Control was what he didn't hear in the scientist's voice: a missing element that had become a constant in the man's personality. The agitation was gone.

The psychological hallmark of someone committed to suicide, or something equally self-indulgent, was a peaceful state of mind. He'd witnessed it, back in the day.

He'd sat for three days in that house. The first day the smell of shit and piss, exacerbated by July heat, filled the small space. Flies began to swarm and settle on the two forms he no longer identified as his parents.

There was food and water, but by the second day, another more pungent odor began to grow that was sweet, but...not. It was similar to the smell of half-eaten rats his father often raked from under the porch. He'd proudly proclaim the cats were on the job and the boy dismissed it as a positive, watching the carcasses burn.

This was different. The stench made his stomach roil, and by day three, it permeated everything. While fear had been the shackling force that kept him in the house, the miasma of the rotting bodies pushed him toward the door.

He wasn't old enough to consider dying, even with death manifest. His trepidation came from being alone. With a potato in his pocket he opened the door and crossed the threshold. A bold move for a five-year-old.

Within minutes several neighbors, who had done their best to ignore the obvious, came out of their homes. The terror of the roving gangs, saluting independence the few nights before, had been experienced by all. However, the putrefaction of human flesh wafting into the road demanded attention.

That day the remains were planted, without the customary Muslim supplication and washing. Had the boy been older, he'd have been relegated to the streets, but a woman in the neighborhood who had recently lost a child took him in. That's where he stayed, without uttering a word, for two years.

By day he suffered the cloying arms of that bruised soul. At night, came the assailing hands of her husband. The satisfaction the man couldn't derive from his grieving woman, he took from the pretty little boy.

The morning she made her decision was another vivid memory for him. He'd awoken, bruised and barely able to walk. She bathed him and anointed his rectum and penis with a salve she'd always kept on hand for herself.

It was the only time he'd heard her sing. She beamed with joy as she fixed breakfast and tidied his clothes. Then, an hour before midday prayer, she handed him a folded stack of French francs and a piece of paper with a name and an address.

She held his arms at his side and kissed him on the mouth. She then instructed him on what bus to ride, and who he could safely ask for directions if he got lost. Finished, she told him to be a good boy and left him sitting at the table. She was at peace.

When her husband came home for his afternoon meal he found her hanging in their bedroom. Musa hadn't gone to the bus stop. He'd found a place to hide and wait.

He waited as the burial rights—those denied to his parents—were performed. He continued to wait until the man returned from the cemetery. There was no sense of loss, no grief or mourning. He thought only of his father raking the half-eaten rats from under the porch.

Two hours after the lights went out, he tiptoed barefoot through the house, and with a knife he'd taken from the kitchen, cut the man's throat as he slept.

His eyes popped open, with mouth agape. As he struggled to breathe—his life pouring out of him—Musa leaned next to his ear, and whispered, "The cats are on the job."

* * *

Once Adan merged into traffic, picking his way north through the city, he didn't wait for questions. "It's gonna take at least an hour to get there. If we're lucky, we won't get stuck behind a stalled bus. Drivers have been known to stop for prayer.

"The campus is out in the boonies, but it's on top of a hill with a great view of the Bosphorus and the Black Sea. It's laid out in an 'S' pattern and divided into two sections. A parking lot and the buildings with the classrooms, research facilities, admin offices, shit like that, are on the north end.

"At the far end of that section is also a fifty-meter pool, a soccer field and helo pad. That should tell you somethin' about the school's trustees and moneyed supporters. The university was established less than twenty years ago and moved into brand new digs in 2000.

"It's considered a pretty good school. The donor pool has got have some seriously deep pockets.

"Anyway, student and faculty housing, which is probably where our guy is living, is in the south campus."

"Any idea where Bennet's lab is located?" Ruben asked.

"I couldn't tell from walkin' the campus, but we did get some information from Ryan Henderson. Turns out the NSA tracks the sales of the type of equipment and lab supplies that would be used in Bennet's operation.

"The engineering school at Koç had a ton of the stuff delivered about four months ago."

Rivka, lounging in back, leaned forward placing her forearms on the backs of the front bucket-seats. "The laboratory is in the basement of that college. According to Medleva, the place is over seven hundred square meters and when it came to equipment, it was the finest facility she'd ever worked in.

"She told me when Bennet arrived he'd already completed the bulk of his research. Apparently, it was really brilliant, off-the-charts sort of stuff. All they had to do was modify the bacteria to make the agent safer to manage in the lab.

"They had it in an aerosol form in a matter of weeks. It was difficult to keep her there once they started the human testing."

Ruben's head swiveled left. "Yeah, I bet. I heard some more bad news from Ryan today. He thinks Bennet's melting down. Whatever the agenda The Board had for this guy, he's now shit-canned it for his own game plan. Did your asset indicate a target?"

"Of course. It was Israel. In this part of the world, when aren't we the target? Medleva was supposed to bring me a sample of the agent and the research data. She was running surveillance detection on a new route when she was taken."

Ruben shook his head. "What a minute. I don't get it. How'd you get Medleva in that lab? She had to've been spotted and vetted long before The Board got their hands on Bennet."

"Please...we've got scientists everywhere. Medleva was the luck of the draw. I recruited her when she was still in high school. It didn't take much to adjust birth records, dummy up a family history and school transcripts. It was Chechnya after all.

"Because I picked her up young, most of what attracted The Board to the woman was actually true. She was a political activist with a police record. When they approached her, we had no idea it had anything to do with this DARPA scientist. It could have been anyone."

Ruben chewed on what she said for a second. "Okay, so that's why you think someone on your end dimed her out."

"That's right."

"Why would someone with access to your source files have any interest in your country's destruction? Kinda counter-intuitive, don'tcha think?"

Rivka answered with a distant voice. "It's a pickle, I'll give you that. But it's the only explanation I have.

"She was in too deep to be burned over some clerical error. Besides, she had Bennet by the gonads, literally. The man may be a genius when it comes to bimolecular engineering, but with a woman he was a marionette."

"You had her sleeping with him?"

"It was her idea. I let it develop."

Carver didn't have a clue what was going on in Rivka's head. He'd betrayed an asset's trust from time to time in the past. It came with the territory. He also tried to give the impression he could do it without conscience, but everybody knew that was bullshit.

Unless this Shin Bet officer was a kosher Machiavelli, she had to have reacted to the loss of her asset more than she was letting on.

His shoulders began to tighten as nervous tension worked its way down his neck. "So what do you want out of this?"

"I want the person who set her up."

CHAPTER FIFTEEN
On the Run

The speed limit on Turkey's highways was a hundred and twenty kph. After his chat with the doctor, Moreau pressed the accelerator another centimeter. He couldn't sustain the speed once he entered Istanbul traffic but twenty minutes at twice the posted *hız limiti*, cut an hour off his total travel time.

His recollection of Algiers' sun-bleached streets rolled into his mind's eye as he stared at the road in front of him. Anticipation and patience were natural attributes the Algerian had relied on since his first kill. His inclination being to watch and wait.

He'd wandered for weeks, competing with stray animals and other abandoned children for anything he could find to eat. The homeless tended to congregate for safety and they scavenged in packs.

He could spot groups casing markets, the elderly and women on their own. When they'd strike, there was a brief but unfailing period of pandemonium.

For some reason shop owners always gave chase and the window of opportunity invariably opened. Musa could gather enough to last a few days.

To keep what he took, he had the kitchen knife. He never threatened—it was a waste of time. He found it quicker and easier, in a confrontation with the desperate, to draw blood.

While he couldn't read the scribble on the scrap of paper the woman gave him, he carried it carefully folded in a pocket. A talisman that would eventually lead him home—the instinct to watch and wait.

The university parking lot was nearly empty when he pulled in and he didn't bother with the decorum of selecting a slot. He was in a hurry. As he unfolded from his mobile office, he smoothed a lapel and tapped the wallet he carried in the inside right breast pocket.

It's where he still carried that slip of paper. Through the years of education and training, he'd concluded the woman who wrote the name and address was, herself, barely literate. Yet, it reminded him of where he came from and allowed him to maintain perspective. He was a killer by necessity, not choice or enjoyment.

His legs were on autopilot as he went looking for Brody. He sorted through the different monologues he'd use to try to reach what was left of the scientist's rational mind. A futile effort, no doubt. Moreau was fully aware the doctor's head was now ruled by a skewed logic. There was no more ordered extrapolation—no more what-ifs. Brody had made a decision, and was at peace with it.

The Board wouldn't be happy, but he figured it wouldn't take the cabal long to find a suitable replacement to carry the project forward. *It's time to remove the doctor from his own equation.*

The cans of his special deodorant had been segregated into side pockets on the pack, with the lids taped down to prevent accidental discharge. Brody had an hour before the sun would set and with the pack on his back he pushed his new hybrid bike, a Giant Innova, out the door.

He had a map of all the hiking and bike trails and had selected a well-worn dirt road, grated from the rear of the fitness center. It extended directly north to a holiday retreat called the Golden Beach Club—two dozen cedar slat bungalows dotted along a hillside overlooking the Marmarçik cove.

It was a downhill glide for six kilometers. He was through the resort's arching gate and at the main building by seven pm, dropping a hundred and fifty Turkish lira on the counter for a one night stay. From what he could tell, the place had no direct Internet connection. With cash and his faculty ID, he was in for the evening, without leaving a footprint.

When the trio arrived at Koç University, they could hear the clock tower chiming the hour. The sun was on the horizon, and orange and gold reflected off the white marble buildings. It would have been worth admiring, if it wasn't for the silver and black Bugatti Veyron conspicuously occupying two parking slots.

Ruben wasn't the only one checking out the high-end Volkswagen. Rivka also gave it a once over, but her interest in the luxury sports car wasn't the same as Ruben's. Her expression didn't suggest a covetous desire. It seemed more like apprehension.

Stepping onto the pavement, Ruben jabbed a finger in the direction of the Bugatti. "Now, there's a car for the masses."

Rivka responded with a roll of her shoulder, as she adjusted her holster with an elbow on the outside of her blazer. "I know that car."

The comment made Ruben blink. His new best friend was holding back again, and the nervous tension in his neck returned. "Is there somethin' you're not tellin' me?"

"I'm not sure. It could be a nothing. Just a run-about for one of the oil rich, but Medleva described a man

Brody met every week, who drove a Bugatti."

Ruben's cognition kicked in as if a piece of a puzzle fell in place. In Shanghai, Ryan Henderson, a hacker extraordinaire, was used by The Board to steal U.S. military critical technologies. His handler was a Chinese femme fatale, named Qu. Ryan referred to her designation as Control.

At the time, Ruben thought it sounded a little hokey, but notwithstanding the hackneyed nom de guerre, he was still having recurring nightmares featuring the dragon lady.

Months before that encounter, he was in Malaysia working a murder case with espionage underpinnings. A U.S. Embassy employee was being manipulated by the enigmatic camarilla to infect Seventh Fleet warships with a computer virus.

His Control was unknown, even to him, until he became too much of a risk. The handler turned out to be the Regional Security Manager. Like Qu, that cheese-dick nearly sent Ruben into early retirement.

He peered at Rivka, aggravated this possibility didn't occur to him when he was in DC. "You said she described him?"

"He won't look like a student or staff."

Ruben scratched an eyebrow, as they continued toward the main campus. "Fuck...we should've expected this."

Adan stopped and turned. "What does that mean?"

"We may have another complication." Ruben paused to think. "We knew this was never gonna be a simple smash and grab. Otherwise, Art would have sent in his cavalry.

"That said, if my recent unpleasantness with The Board will out, there's more to this dude than good taste in cars. He's gonna be one bad mo-fo and he might have friends."

Ruben reached up and laid a hand on Adan's shoulder. "I need you to do me a favor. I want you to wait at the car."

"What?" Adan shook his head.

"Look, pal...if the next twenty minutes turns to shit, I don't want you involved. It's better you stay clean and healthy. We can't afford to have a situation that jeopardizes your source network and our ride outta here."

Ruben could see the gears turning behind Adan's eyeballs.

"I've got a camera kit in the trunk. If the owner of that shows up,"—it was Adan's turn to bob his head at the sports car that had consumed their attention—"I'll try to get some photos."

"Good. One more thing. Call Dever and let him know what we're up to and ask him if Art's been in contact with Sonny Xú."

"Who?"

"No, it's Xú—Sonny Xú. Henry'll know what it's about."

Carver glanced at Rivka and back to Adan. "Where's the engineering building?"

The elevator to the basement level was shut down and his card key for the door to the stairwell didn't work. Within seconds a cold sweat formed like condensate on his forehead and soaked through his shirt at the pits.

It caught him by surprise as he braced himself with a hand on the wall. Panic was a new experience for Moreau.

He understood what a lockdown meant. He was there when the security systems were installed and had a full briefing on what would happen if a biohazard alert went into effect.

Since the audible alarms didn't activate, he assumed

Brody had tampered with them. It made any further attempt to get inside even less desirable.

He took a deep breath and spun on a heel. He needed to get back to his car and access the laboratory's CCTV records for the last several hours.

He'd already gone to Brody's campus residence and other than the absent doctor, noted only one thing missing—the brand new bicycle.

He'd contact the Board once he'd confirmed Brody was in the wind. They'd be able to track the doctor's movement by ATM or credit card usage. If he'd found another way to finance his field trip, Moreau would need other help. While his reconnection with his Corsican family was tenuous at best, they were the only ones he trusted.

Thirty seconds later he came face to face with what he now considered the least of his problems.

It took five minutes to reach the College of Engineering's main entrance. Ruben and Rivka had walked at a crisp pace, scanning assumed fields of fire as they went. She was to his right and looked front and right. He had the left.

As they stood on the wide, cut-stone walkway, scrutinizing the building for other entry points, Ruben couldn't help but notice how square everything appeared. The hip roof, with its orange terracotta tile, was the only exception. There wasn't a curve, or rounded edge anywhere. *It looks like a jail.*

He glanced at Rivka. "Have you ever been here?"

"Once, with a tour group. I haven't been in this building."

The campus lights began to glow and looking around they saw students and faculty coming and going throughout the quad.

Nearly everyone had backpacks or briefcases. A broad

spectrum that ranged from sleeved tattoos, piercings and over-styled 'dos, to taped geek-frames and pocket protectors, yet no one seemed out of place. From the pictures Ruben had seen of the scientist, he'd be a perfect fit in the environment.

"I see two other exits. How about you?"

Rivka nodded and pointing at the portico under a two-meter rectangular sign declaring the school, said, "Shall we?"

As they passed through to a narrow cloister, with glass doors in front of them, a hinged section of the wall, twenty feet to their left opened. Apart from the visible portal seams, anyone not knowing it was there would have missed it.

When Ruben saw the man who stepped out, he stopped in his tracks, and gave a Rivka a light squeeze on her wrist. *Holy shit, where's Morticia?*

"You did say the chump wouldn't look like student or faculty. Check out Gomez Addams at your nine."

"Who?"

"Never mind. Come on—he knows we're here. We might as well get acquainted."

Before she had a chance to respond, Carver started walking—trying to cop nonchalance, in his just-out-for-a-stroll gait. *This is not the place to throw down.* To his relief, Rivka was at his side in two strides, slipping her hand inside his arm, resting it above the crook of his elbow.

They watched as the man pulled a filterless cigarette from a blue pack, screwed it into a white holder and lit it with an ST Dupont. With his weight on his left foot, he tucked his left hand into his pants pocket. Smoke curled from his nostrils, after a leisurely draw from the holder.

At a distance of six feet, he pointed the lit end in their direction and opened the dialogue. "M. Carver and Mademoiselle...Levitan, is it?"

Rivka bobbed her head a fraction. "You have us at a

disadvantage, luv. Who might you be?"

"Ah, *oui*. How charming! You secret agents always give me the goose bumps. You may call me Control."

Carver's head drooped right as he examined the man. He didn't detect any sign of a sidearm, although considered the alternatives. What struck him, though, were the sweat droplets and wet hair at the man's temples. "Seems we caught you at a bad time. How's that control workin' out for ya?"

"How perceptive."

Ruben watched the masseter muscles contract as Control paused before continuing.

"There has been an event in what I'm certain you've already ascertained is a laboratory. Whether it was by design or accident I haven't, as yet, determined. The facility is currently locked down."

Oh, shit. "Is James Bennet in there?"

"The man you are referring to is known here as Jerome Brody. Again, I'm sure you already know this. *N'est-ce pas?* To answer your question would require going inside, and even if we could it's a dangerous proposition."

"If he's not in there, is he carrying the toxin?"

"M. Carver, you need to stop asking questions you already know the answers to. And understand this, I'm prepared to answer only one question you might, or most likely Mlle. Levitan, would have." Control's gaze fell on Rivka.

"Did you kill her?"

"No, mademoiselle. I had nothing to do with that. It's not my style. In fact, I didn't find out until recently she worked for you. I offer you my condolences.

"Now, shall we get down to what you Americans refer to as the *brass tacks*."

Ruben slowly nodded his head, regaining eye contact with the apparent Frog. "Let's."

"Whether or not Jerome Brody is a victim in the basement of this building, the product and all his research data belong to me, or more precisely, to my employers."

Ruben began to interrupt and was cut off. "Tut, tut. I know your argument and as valid as it may be, I will be the one to retrieve the doctor. Once I get what I want, you can have him or what's left of him."

"That doesn't work for us, does it, darlin'?" Rubin glanced at Rivka.

"No, luv, it doesn't."

Control pulled the still burning butt from the holder, dropped it on the walk and crushed it under his leather sole. "Well, you do not disappoint. I enjoy a contest with a great deal at stake. Know this: the odds, they are stacked against you. You won't survive.

"As for the doctor, I once told him he was on the cusp of greatness. I believe the expression should be infamy.

"Au revoir, *mes amis*. I have business to attend to. Please, don't bother to follow." Control dropped the holder in his coat pocket, did an about face and strode away without looking back.

CHAPTER SIXTEEN

Putting the Pieces Together

When the two got back, the Bugatti was gone and Adan was on his mobile. A Ricoh with an attached telephoto lens was on the seat next to him.

"...no, they're back...wait a sec, I'll check." Adan twisted in Ruben's direction to survey his passengers. "I don't see any blood. They look all right."

Ruben presumed the other party to the conversation was Dever. Sequent to being waved off when he asked for the phone, he turned on the camera and scrolled through the images of the man he and Rivka had talked to earlier.

"...yeah, okay...uh-huh...no, that's easy. I'll drop it off...no, he's chompin' at the bit. He needs to talk to you." Adan pulled the BlackBerry from his ear and shoved it toward Ruben. "It's Henry."

"We have a problem, my man."

For the next ten minutes Carver related their conversation with the creep who called himself Control, while relating what could have been a catastrophic event in the basement laboratory. Henry, in kind, related the details of Ryan Henderson's correspondence with the scientist.

"I've got no details, Henry, other than whatever

triggered the security lockdown appears to be contained. Like I said, the sleazeball we met was literally in a sweat, but I don't believe he was freakin' out because of the lab—at least, not directly."

"You think Bennet is a runner?" Spoken more as a declaration than a question.

"That's what I reckon. The guy doesn't believe our DARPA scientist was in the facility when the event occurred. He couldn't confirm it yet, but what he said was tantamount to exactly that. Bennet released something that caused the security sensors to alert and lock the space down.

Carver skipped a beat before continuing. "When you talk to Art about this, you should seriously consider getting the State Department involved and put a brief together for the President."

Dever reacted to the last comment with hesitation. "I don't know if we want to go that high yet."

"Hey, man, when Bennet split, he didn't just take an extra pair of socks. We have to assume he's got the bio-weapon with him."

"Art'll have to make that call. Adan is bringing me the photos he took of the person you talked to. Any idea what his nationality is?"

"He sounded French, but was a little too smarmy for polite society. You could squeegee the grease off his head. With the kinda bad juju this guy exudes, there should be a record of him somewhere. I'll bet Interpol has something. Did you run the plates on his car—a Bugatti Veyron?" Ruben gave Adan a sideways glance, with raised eyebrows. Adan responded with a short nod and a thumbs up.

Henry answered, "Yes, I should hear back in few minutes. Anything else?"

"A couple things. We need to get a fix on Bennet's target for release. Our best chance for that is to keep

Ryan talkin' to him.

"Also, the Frenchman wasn't too subtle about what'll happen to me and Rivka if we try to acquire the nutty professor. I don't wanna havta lose sleep over Sonny Xú's soldiers comin' after us—not while we're tryin' to sort things out. Can you get Art on that?"

"Yeah, Adan already mentioned it."

Rivka leaned forward and whispered in Ruben's empty ear. "I have a contact with the National Police in Marseille. I want to send him a picture as well."

Ruben held up his free hand. "Hey, Henry, I'm gonna put you on speaker." He searched the touch pad for an instant and punched a key. "Okay, Rivka's on...go ahead."

"Brilliant. I just mentioned to Ruben I have a contact at the Police Nationale in Marseille. If this fellow, who calls himself Control is French and has a criminal background, a discreet inquiry with my mate in Marseille would be faster and net us better intelligence. I'm going to send him a photo."

Carver noted his new partner didn't ask.

The reply took a few seconds too long. "Okay. Please keep me posted."

Moreau had a forum in thirty minutes and this time was diligent to secure a clear signal. "You've seen the video from the laboratory, have you not?"

"Yes, we've seen the images. Do you have Doctor Brody?"

"No, but he can't be far away. It's been less than two hours and he's on a bicycle."

The soft buzz came on, as Moreau's connection was muted. It lasted thirty seconds.

"Does he have the product?"

"The inference would be he does. Whether or not he left any behind can't be determined until the lab sensors release the door locks. I'm confident he didn't use it on his assistants, considering the speed in which they were dispatched."

The voice responded without hesitation. "We agree. Based on our analysis of the video, he probably used cyanide. We'll have a team on site later this evening to breach the facility and dispose of the bodies. If there is no evidence of a live culture remaining, the space will be cleaned and resealed.

"M. Moreau, the responsibility of reacquiring Brody is yours. Do you have a plan?"

A plan. Moreau was no stranger to tracking people. "I'll need you to apply your resources to monitoring his banking activity. Look at the accounts you've been seeding on his behalf. He'll be moving that money around. He's had plenty of time to open new accounts, transfer funds and obtain credit and ATM cards."

"If he's found a way to create a new identity, the documentation would have likely come to his address here. I trust your connections with the financial community will overcome the rigid personal information privacy restrictions.

"It's unlikely Brody's genius extends to the skills necessary to effectively disappear. I'm going to use a few of my old associates to help me track him on the ground. I'll forward their compensation packages for your review and handling."

Again the low hum, as his employers conferred.

"We approve the stratagem but insist you do not divulge anything regarding The Board, or the details of the project. This is, of course, in line with your pre-employment agreement. Failure to comply is grounds for...termination."

"*Naturellement.*" The veiled threat floating behind the innocuous comment made Moreau want to laugh. *I'm after the purveyor of doom and they're worried I'm going to tell someone.* Brody, his activities, and how they were financed, were no longer a secret. Moreau could only guess why the Americans and Israelis had elected to kept the affair to themselves.

That apparent fact had him pinging on the other reason for the call. "My search for the doctor will begin in a ten-kilometer radius of the university. Unless he plans on camping, he'll need a place to eat and sleep.

"He's smart enough to stay off the main roads, which will limit him to hiking trails, running and bike paths. I picked up a map of those on a campus message board—the same way he did, I'm sure.

"Before I sign off, there is one more issue in which you can be directly involved. I believe you've already assured me your solution is in the works."

The connection crackled. "We're listening."

"An hour ago, I had an interesting encounter with Ruben Carver and the Shabak woman. They came to the laboratory. Forgive me for asking, but can you tell me when you think the vendors you hired to *distract* them, are going to get to work?"

"We understand that is happening as we speak."

"Ah, some good news." Moreau couldn't mask the glib delivery, and pulled the pin on his next rejoinder. "So, Messieurs, before I bid you adieu, let me emphasize a single point: I'm frightened. I'm not talking about a phobia, like the fear of the dark or the monsters in the closet.

"When I was a little boy, I knew an old woman who lost her husband and two children to the Spanish flu. She said it killed more people worldwide, than all the bullets, bombs and gas of the First World War.

"I heard one of the lab assistants comment that what they were working on would likely surpass the Spanish flu for spread and mortality. I looked it up, Messieurs. It infected five hundred million people, and a fifth of those died."

"Calm yourself, Control. We don't believe Doctor Brody will go that far."

"*Bullshit!* Doctor Jerome Brody has every intension of using his creation. He's got an ax to grind."

"Now...I'll take care of this problem because you're paying me handsomely to do so. But know this: if you're not scared shitless, than you clearly do not understand the gravity of the situation.

"If he sets it off in a population center or transportation hub, nothing can protect you. You're wasted—like everybody else."

To no one in particular, Ruben said, "I want to get in that lab."

"How do you suppose we're gonna do that?" Adan was kneading the wheel with both hands as he steered the rental down Koç University road.

Ruben didn't answer. He was still thinking out loud. "The place was locked down without an alert to the university..."

"What makes you say that?"

Rivka answered with what was becoming signature pith. "Because the place wasn't going batshit barmy. It was nothing more than another school night for the learned."

Carver was definitely warming to the chick in the back. "Zactly. It's also an easy money bet the Frog has already contacted The Board. We know why he didn't stick around, his priority is to find Bennet, or Brody—whatever he's goin' by at this point.

"The Board isn't gonna leave the mess in the lab for someone else to clean up. They'll have a crew in there, but it'll have to be at a time when there aren't a lot of people around."

Adan came to a stop before merging onto Rumeli

Feneri Cd. "You want to go into a bio-hazard factory that's gone into shut-down mode because of an incident? Have you got a hazmat suit in that safari jacket?"

Rivka jumped in again. "They'd have a plan in place for this type of contingency and it'll happen fast. Let's go back and wait."

Adan didn't sound contentious when he said, "Dever's waiting for the memory card with the photos and should have information on the car registration." He looked at Rivka through the rearview mirror. "What about contacting your 'mate' in Marseilles?"

While it made sense to Carver to return, Rivka seemed to be mulling over the question.

As they made the right onto Rumeli Feneri, Adan continued gazing in the rearview. "We may have another problem."

Ruben turned and peered through the rear window. A white Mercedes panel van was bearing down. "What about it?"

"It was sitting on the shoulder with the engine running. As soon as we made the turn they punched it."

Before Carver turned to face front, he and Rivka had an electric eye moment. "Do you know who Sonny Xú is?"

"I never had the pleasure, luv. Is he a friend of yours?" Rivka didn't bother turning to look. She unholstered a compact Jericho 941 and flipped off the safety. At the same time, she pushed the power window switch.

"Not exactly. We've had issues."

Adan interrupted the interlude. "I can't outrun 'em. They're coming up on the left."

"I see 'em." Ruben hadn't skinned his H&K. He couldn't use it from that side of the vehicle. "See the dirt road up on the right?"

"Yeah."

"We're goin' in there. Rivka, can you discourage these

146

bums? I don't want 'em pitting us."

"I can kill the driver."

"That might be embarrassing if they're just folks in a hurry. Why don'tcha show 'em they're makin' a mistake."

Adan's voice went up a quarter tone. "The side door is opening. If you're gonna do something, now would be a good time."

Rivka spun left with her knee on the seat and her right leg braced against the driver's seat back. She gripped the padding around the door frame with her left hand and stuck the pistol, as well as her head, out the window enough get a sight picture. She then fired three rounds through the van's windshield.

Uh-oh. "That's not quite what I had in mind."

"You asked me not to kill him...and look, I believe we have his attention."

The driver of the van had slammed on the brakes, smoking the rear tires.

"You still want me to turn up that dirt road?" Adan took his foot off the gas, depressed the clutch, jamming the stick into second gear and moved his left hand to seven o'clock on the steering wheel.

"Yeah, let's see how motivated these dickwads are."

He yanked the handbrake, keeping his thumb on the release button, and jerked the wheel right. With the rear wheels locked, the Fiat fishtailed and Adan went into a controlled bootleg until he was pointed in the direction he wanted. He then dropped the handbrake, popped the clutch and stomped the accelerator. His hands were back at ten and two as the car lurched toward a brown spot between the trees.

There was a four- or five-inch difference in grade coming off the pavement to the dirt road. At speed, the car did a rocking-horse. The seatbelts caught Ruben and Adan but Rivka was catapulted forward. If Ruben hadn't been in the way, grabbing her as she went over the top, she would have smashed into the windshield.

With her torso in his lap, head against the dash and legs pinned between the two front seats, Ruben asked, "Hey, baby, how's it hangin'? You okay?"

Squinty-eyed and her mouth stretched across her teeth, she responded, "I love it when a man calls me baby." Waving her pistol, she added, "Help me up—I'm stuck."

Apparently unfettered by the flying body, Adan recovered control of the vehicle in less than a second. Grinding gears as he speed-shifted, he managed to keep traction on the grooved hard pack.

Ruben unfastened his seatbelt, leaned forward and wrapped both arms around her below the armpits. He then sat back, pulling her toward him. Aside from her slim, hard frame, he noticed she was wearing thin body armor. "I love a woman in a sports bra."

Adan glanced in the rearview. "I don't wanna break up the love fest but they've made the turn. We've got a 'T' coming up—which way?"

"Go left and stop. The woods will give us some cover."

"Why do you wanna stop?"

"Rivka and I are getting out. You drive another hundred yards and stop again. Did you bring a weapon?"

"There's a loaded shotgun in the trunk. You know this is a rental, right?" As Adan down shifted and feathered the handbrake again, said, "Okay, hold on," and spun the car left.

The slide on the dirt almost took them off the road but dropping the brake lever, lifting the clutch through the friction point and applying gas, corrected the motion. The dust gave them added concealment and twenty yards later he applied the brake.

The centripetal force from the turn helped Rivka free her legs, and when they came to a stop she was straddling Carver; their noses touching. "I'm ready, luv."

I'm glad I brushed my teeth this morning. He pulled the door handle and they spilled onto the road. His arms still around Rivka, Carver rolled them away from the undercarriage and yelled, "*Clear!*"

CHAPTER SEVENTEEN

The Distraction

Adan popped the clutch, and left another cloud of dust as Ruben and Rivka untangled. She checked the action on her pistol as she stood. Ruben's admiration for her firearm retention was only surpassed by his relief she hadn't shot him during the brouhaha.

He pulled his .45 and scanning the tree line, said, "Take cover on the other side of the road. They'll have to slow down to make the turn."

She nodded without the need for explanation and started moving. Ruben couldn't help getting a visual lock on her ass as she sprinted across. *Snap out of it, shithead. You've got work to do.*

"Hey..."

Rivka turned as she reached the trees. "*What?*"

"You can kill the driver now."

She rolled her eyeballs, not bothering to ask him what he was going to do.

Ruben jogged twenty feet up the road but didn't take cover. He wanted to be seen with the H&K. He waited about five seconds.

When he made eye contact with the driver, the van almost stopped. In that instant Ruben heard two pops and the dude disappeared from view.

The Mercedes continued to roll as Ruben back-stepped into the tree line. He could hear Rivka plinking rounds through the van's left-side panel. *You go, girl.*

As expected, the right-side door slid open and two men with auto shotguns came out shooting. It was cover fire, in controlled bursts. A tactical evacuation, but the vehicle's forward motion had them off-balance as they hit the ground.

Carver opened up, aiming at the belt line. Most body armor didn't protect anything below the navel. The copper grizzlies would blossom wide on the soft tissue, shredding their bowels. He also had a chance of hitting an artery or a kidney. They'd go into shock fast.

He double tapped on each man until they were both prone and the blood was flowing.

With one or two rounds left, he did a magazine exchange as the van crept by. A body was visible, lying face down. He peeped to his left when he heard another shot. Rivka was finishing up with one of the desperadoes who came out to play.

"Ya know, we may have wanted to question the fella."

"No worries, pet. He was in no condition for a chinwag."

Pistol at the ready, Ruben jumped into the van's cargo compartment. It had a bench along the bulkhead and light was coming through a half dozen bullet holes. He ignored the man on the floorboard when he spotted the crater in the back of his head. *Jesus, what kinda load does she carry in that shooter?*

The next order of business was clean-up. After pulling the wheel-man into the load bay, Ruben backed the van to where his friends fell. Rivka had already gone through their pockets, piled their weapons and was policing the shotgun shells and what brass she could find.

Adan was there thirty seconds later and began a search of the van, while Ruben examined the dead in the dirt. He started with the right forearms. *That fuckin' Sonny. I guess the truce really is over.*

The clothing labels revealed little; common wear throughout the Balkans and Near East. When Ruben pulled the trouser legs up, he yelled in the direction of the Mercedes. "Hey, Adan."

"Yeah?"

"Check the shoes. Are they black boots with lace guards?"

"Yep, for both."

He stood and walked three paces to the weapons Rivka gathered: two Saiga-12 shotguns, a pair of M84 machine pistols and an assortment of knives and pokers.

Adan stepped out of the van. "I found two cell phones—burners from the look of 'em. No IDs. A 9mm was in the glove compartment. One of the dudes in the back was armed like these two." Adan pointed at the two corpses stretched out on the road.

Ruben took a deep breath and eyed his compadre. "Let's get these two in the van. Rivka, do you want to hold on to anything we've found?"

"The cell phones."

The Special Agents nodded in agreement.

"Oh, one more thing." Adan said, throwing a thumb in the van's direction. "I found two seccade."

Raised eyebrows and a shrugged shoulder signaled Ruben's ignorance.

"Prayer rugs...at least two of these turkeys were practicing Muslims."

"Okay, let's finish up and get outta here. We'll talk it through in the car."

Moreau refused to think about what would happen if the quandary he faced wasn't handled with deft permanence. He was certain the doctor was still in the area and locating him under other circumstances would have been a relatively simple process of elimination.

Brody wasn't on vacation, though. The security briefings he sat through at DARPA would no doubt have left a checklist in his brain. An ordered set of practices he would use with the same methodical approach he did everything else.

Moreau also knew a disguise wouldn't fool the scientist. Getting next to Brody had to be done in a fashion that wouldn't alert him in time to release the agent.

The Corsican he'd called on for the assist was from a milieu that had ties to a Maghrebi organized crime family in Marseille. An association that spanned more than three generations.

The Algerian wanted to point him and his considerable resources at Carver and the Juif. The current state of affairs changed that. As he sat behind the wheel, nestled in Italian leather, he voiced Big Ugly's number to the console.

They'd met almost forty years before, not long after the Algerian boy was dragged to the address scrawled out by the woman. He'd been nabbed during one of his forays, lingering around a magazine rack.

In truth, he wanted to get caught. Tired, sick and alone, he used to say it was because his feet hurt. Stealing food was one thing, finding shoes that fit as he grew was another.

Musa severed the only short-lived affiliation he had with a street gang, when he cut the dick off the Arab leader. He didn't want it in his bum and could never understand why most of the Arab men he'd bump into shared that proclivity.

It came off as easy as slicing through a merguez sausage. The getaway wasn't difficult either. Most of the kids who witnessed his resignation from the club, got a kick out of the spectacle. That was one zebb no longer being stuffed in an unwilling culus. Word got around, though, and Musa found he was no longer welcome at any campfire.

The store owner cuffed him around a bit and called the Sûreté. Since the boy hadn't touched anything and was only in possession of a rusting knife and that weathered piece of paper, the police officer made a judicial decision on the spot. He gripped the youngster by the ear, and escorted him to a jeep parked at the curb.

The ride took him into a part of the city he'd never been: a European quarter called Bab El Oued. Most of the homes were deserted after the Pied-Noirs fled when French colonial rule ended.

The policeman found the house, and had Musa by the scruff of the neck to keep him from running. He banged on the door twice before it opened on a tall, lean figure with short cropped hair and a boxer's face. There were no introductions. Not much was spoken. The man at the door pulled the boy inside and that was the end of it.

He was Yves Moreau, an old army buddy of Musa's father, and the boy's new namesake. A good mass-once-a-year, confession-every-decade Catholic who elected to stay in Algeria despite the constant threat of reprisal. The new ruling party, the Front de Libération Nationale or FLN, had it in for those viewed as former French loyalists.

It was his contribution to an economy on the verge of complete collapse that saved him from the indignity of a noose. When his Pied-Noir gang repatriated to France and merged with a Maghrebi crime family in Marseille, he had ostensibly become a made man.

His efforts in reviving the casino business in Algiers were financed through that connection. He also provided an alternative shipping hub for North African cannabis and heroin produced in Turkey destined for ports in the

U.S. and Britain.

The initially slow but steady flow of foreign currency garnered him favor with a number of members of the fledgling People's National Assembly. He kept their pockets lined and they left him alone to conduct business unimpeded.

Through all this, he favored the boy as a potential protégé within his own growing family. However, it would take years of education and training before he'd become a valuable contributor in daily operations. The older Yves Moreau, with approval from Marseille, punted the kid in their direction.

One fine spring morning, the young Yves Moreau arrived in France aboard an Algerian freighter, laden with five hundred kilos of Moroccan hashish. It was bad form for a house guest to come empty handed—no matter how old.

His initiation fee accepted, he was moved into the home of an underboss, where his classic French education was augmented with street savate and edged weapons. As he got older, there was training in the short and long con, smuggling do's and don'ts, extortion techniques and methods of surveillance and counter-surveillance.

To take the bloom fully off the rose, he did a three-year hitch in the French Foreign Legion, slugging through muck in the Congo. It was either that or a two-year stint, on a robbery beef, in a rat-infested shithole called Baumettes. He discovered the Congo made Baumettes look like a summer villa.

All in all, it didn't matter. He remained engaged in the family business with the help of the raw-boned Corsican bruiser who'd been trained for assassination and vendetta campaigns. The big ugly who never learned how to duck, but always had Moreau's back—right up until the Algerian decided to carve out his own territory with his namesake in Algiers.

"So, whaddya want me to do...just drop you off?" Adan was clapping his hands clean after covering the blood pools with loose dirt from the side of the road.

Ruben was walking back from a spot inside the tree line where he'd parked the van with its dead occupants and their lethal paraphernalia. "Yeah, we'll be alright. How's the charge on your cell phone?"

Adan pulled his BlackBerry from its holder. "Ninety percent, it should be okay."

As they piled into the Fiat, Rivka spoke up. "Leaving the van in place might be fine for a day or two, but it's going to be found. I'd prefer a proper disposal."

Ruben pulled the seatbelt across his lap. "Whaddya got in mind?"

"I can have a couple of my associates out here in an hour. They specialize in hauling rubbish."

Adan double-clutched from second to third. "I could call our husbanding agent. His other business interests lend themselves to this type of enterprise but it would change the nature of my relationship——if you know what I mean."

Carver nodded. "It probably wouldn't be a good idea to go there." Another pause, then, "Art doesn't want us gettin' the Consulate involved in this kind of activity either, so we can't have Henry's help on this one. I guess it's on you, Rivka."

As she pulled a mobile from an inside pocket, Ruben glanced again at Adan. "You've got a lot to chat about with Henry. Do me a favor and make sure you're some place I can get in touch with you."

"Anything else?"

"Yeah, have Henry run the plates on the van." Carver twisted in his seat and focused on Adan's profile. "Besides being Muslim, is there anything else that stood out to you about those characters?"

"You mean besides the classic terrorist car stop and all the hardware?"

Carver's chuckle was brief. "Yeah."

"I don't know...what?"

"Well, they were wearing military issue combat boots for one thing—the kind with lace guards. They're not common anymore. The French are still wearin' 'em in their Ranger units and I'm pretty sure the Serbian Army is wigglin' its toes in a version.

"Along with the boots, the label on the body armor said Belgrade and the clothing was regional. The weapons were military grade. The shotguns were Russian but the machine pistols were manufactured in the former Yugoslavia.

"I read a report out of Headquarters a few months ago that the weapon of choice of the Serbian mafia was the Czech Škorpian and the Yugoslav knockoff of that gun is the M84.

"You put all that together, with the Muslim angle, you're lookin' at Serbian ex-military turned mafia hitmen, now moonlighting for Sonny."

Adan pursed his lips. "Uh-huh and maybe they were Bulgarian undergrads who bought their shit off eBay."

Holding up the cell phones they'd taken off the bodies Carver added, "See what Henry can get off these: last numbers dialed, text messages, shit like that. We need to know if they've got friends we havta concern ourselves about."

Ruben dropped the phones in the center console container. "Oh, and get Henry to contact Art about Sonny Xú. I wanna know what's goin' on with that fuckin' prick."

The final request, while it came out as an afterthought, was Carver's main concern. "Tap Ryan Henderson. See if he's made contact with the scientist again. He's our primary. We have to find that guy before the Frenchman does—before people start getting sick."

Within ten minutes, they were back in the university parking lot. Prior to stepping out of the car, Ruben screwed the suppressor on the H&K and slipped the laser sight on its accessory rail. Likewise, Rivka prepped her pistol with a six-inch baffled attachment and seated a fresh magazine.

Adan was ready to roll. He dropped his window and pointed at the Shin Bet officer, now standing on the pavement. "I'll stop at your consulate after I talk to Henry. Who's supposed to receive the pictures of the French dude?"

"Ask for Ari Levin. He'll download the images from the memory card. It shouldn't take more than a few minutes. He's expecting you."

Seconds later, Rivka locked arms with Carver as they strolled toward the engineering building.

Brody had taken his shoes off to lie down on the bed. He didn't bother undressing. He'd set the alarm on his wristwatch for ten pm. While sleep was impossible, he allowed himself to doze.

He figured he had no more than four hours before Control would find him. It was only logical he'd start his search within the beach communities. Brody, himself, had calculated rate of travel on his bicycle based on terrain, lighting, weather and his physical condition.

Based on those quantifiable factors he'd selected his first stop, the Golden Beach resort, as a place to lie low until dark. If he was out of the bungalow no later than ten-fifteen, he'd be gone almost an hour before Control showed up.

There was only one road into the resort. Fortunately, it was tree-lined. In the event Control made the Golden Beach an early choice for search, headlights could be seen for several hundred yards. Concealment was excellent three meters off the road.

Earlier in the week he'd made arrangements with the captain of a small fishing trawler docked at the marina in Rumeli Feneri. For five hundred Turkish lira he was more than happy to take the doctor out with his five-man crew.

They were leaving at midnight for three days in the Black Sea, hunting bonito. It was plenty of time for Brody to have the vessel to himself.

CHAPTER EIGHTEEN
Back at the Lab

Rivka's assessment of Carver continued as they found a spot on the quad with good visibility of the camouflaged doorway. She remained skeptical, knowing first impressions could be clouded given enough time. They weren't wrong, merely obfuscated through familiarity.

He was tough, she'd give him that. She didn't have to worry about him getting squeamish. The ambush she'd allowed him to direct clued her in to his tactical ability.

The other bloke, Adan, also proved to be more than administratively sound. He was an excellent wheelman. Cool under fire. She wondered if he didn't have military combat experience.

Neither man showed any signs of hesitation, and neither second-guessed the action. Other than the discussion of what was found on the bodies, they were dismissive. No high-fives, or celebration—no phony remorse endemic in what she viewed as comic American progressivism.

They were all business. It made her curious whether it was a matter of the NCIS selection process in its recruiting and training or if she just lucked out with these chaps. She fancied the answer was probably both.

"How long have you been with NCIS, Ruben?" She

tugged his arm while she kept her eyes on her field of fire.

"Why don't you ask what you really wanna know?"

"Oh, and what would that be?"

She heard a crack in his voice. "You want to know how old I am. When we met this morning you had the same look on your face I've seen on young hotshots since I was a boot agent. Of course...there is a difference..."

Rivka didn't need to be psychic to pick up on this Yank's tetchy tone. "Ahh, you're not about to get cheeky, are you luv?"

If there was a sardonic side to the geezer, she didn't hear it in his laugh or his following comment. "I've got a fiver in my pocket that says I'm not much older than you."

"Listen, pet, I know with you Americans getting on, it's not the age but the mileage that counts. I can also see when someone's on the edge. You move like everything hurts."

"I had a couple grand slams this year that went too many sets."

She caught him looking down at her as he said, "You can count on me to carry my own water. I just need you to hold up your end."

With that interchange she was convinced Carver had some reservations regarding his role. She also knew Arthur Sheppard couldn't afford to use a throwaway. He specifically picked the big Yank and trusted him to come through.

She decided to let it slide. The years she spent being judged on appearance hadn't made her any less susceptible to jumping to conclusions based on the image of a tattered cover.

When Rivka landed in Israel declaring her immigrant status, she had an uncle on her mother's side who welcomed her into his home. Also Haredi, he expected her to try to find work until he could arrange an acceptable suitor. He couldn't guarantee a mensch but a wife-beater was off the table—from his mouth to God's ears.

Her decision to take the Psychometric Entrance Test, a standard battery of university qualification exams, was some cause for concern. In hopes of quashing any ridiculous notion of escaping her familial and spiritual obligations, he told her there was no money for her tuition.

When she aced the Psychometric, she was accepted into Tel Aviv University under the Israeli Defense Force Atuda program. They paid her tuition in exchange for five years of her life after graduation. The family went *meshuga*. She, on the other hand, was in heaven.

Four years later, with a law degree in her pocket, she entered service, assigned to the Israeli Intelligence Corps. She quickly exhibited a talent for counterintelligence, with a particular gift for recruiting assets with high production value.

When she was recruited by Shin Bet in '81, the fact she had extensive training, was a decorated veteran, had a service jacket thick with commendations and recommendations for promotion, an expert rating in firearms and second-dan blackbelt in Krav Maga, meant very little to her immediate supervisor or male counterparts. She lacked the little stormtrooper below the belt.

It was assumed she'd be too weak, slow and emotionally ill-equipped for the type of work in the Israel Security Agency. Then there was the biological clock. They'd waste tens of thousands of shekels on training for someone who'd quit as soon as she found a soul-mate with whom she could start a brood.

These negatives, however, didn't in any way curb the

libidinous attention. She put three training partners in the hospital with broken wrists, a dislocated shoulder, a shredded knee and a few ruptured discs to convince the folks in the office that she wasn't gagging for it.

Rivka toiled for ten years under the gender bias, with stints in the Arab Affairs Department in support of Yamas operations in the West Bank and Gaza Strip, and in the Protective Security Department with two embassy tours.

Shin Bet was finally forced to acknowledge her contributions to the organization after moving her into the Non Arab Affairs Department. Two simultaneous and successful double agent operations against the French and the British, and the compromise of a blue-flaming CIA case officer, netted her first private office.

It was then that she started identifying assets for longterm double agent ops focused on science and technology. To keep them out of Mossad's sandbox, her efforts were tailored toward projects that represented an impending threat to State security.

Medleva Jankovic was one of a dozen youngsters Rivka had groomed from her post pubescent years. A brilliant young woman, but obstreperous to the point she would have been terminated from the program had it not been for the placement in Istanbul. She proved to be an agile asset.

The project she was embedded with constituted an imminent threat based on the data she'd provided. When the clandestine intrigue hadn't been briefed outside her department, Rivka began to worry the intelligence was not being taken seriously.

With the death of her asset. She began to piece together a scenario that meant only one thing: someone inside was working for the opposition. They had a fox in the hen house.

There were only a few people in her organization she

could trust with her theory. It was through their contacts with the CIA she was turned on to a report about a missing DARPA scientist. The very scientist Medleva had seduced.

Rivka liked to believe that fortune favored the prepared mind but in this situation having the compromised case officer leading the investigation was pure dumb luck. To a certain degree, she knew she still owned him. Although she wasn't sure how much more mileage she could get out of a handjob under a table at Delmonico's.

The information he'd provided on a couple of Russian assets, operating in Israel before the wall fell, she believed still carried some weight. In the end, however, Arthur saw a joint operation as beneficial. It spread the risk of failure.

They had no idea at the time how dire the situation had become.

Brody rode through the resort gate, leaving it behind not two minutes before a pair of headlights dotted the road. The plan was to use the trees and underbrush to hide from any traffic but he thought he'd have more time.

The practice runs over the last few weeks were proof of concept. It could be done. The problems were the lack of light and uneven terrain. On a moonless night, no matter how long he waited, his eyes couldn't adjust to more than a few inches of visibility.

The bike was designed to go off road, but after dark, riding it in a wooded area was impossible. It was an apparatus of little value. The energy needed to push the two-wheeler through and over obstacles, he could only feel, burned his muscles. They were spent in less than twenty minutes.

Out of desperation, the last item he acquired for his departure pack was a pair of night vision goggles. He found them during one of his insomnia-induced web-surfing marathons. A secondhand, head mounted, gen 2 monocular, that could be used passively, as well as with infrared illumination.

It worked. His ability to navigate in the bush increased but the green image and loss of depth perception gave him a headache. He could only wear it a few minutes at a time.

He crouched to avoid the high beams, yet looked up as it passed. It had a familiar sound. He didn't see the driver. He didn't have to. The shape of the car was unmistakable.

As he stepped out of the tree line, he looked once again toward the vehicle. For an instant, the headlights reflecting off the gate to the resort lit the sports car's interior. Brody thought he glimpsed the silhouette of two people.

Without taking the time to digest what that could mean, he was on his bike and rolling. With the goggles in passive mode, the blacktop was visible enough for him to pedal at a nearly normal pace. When he reached the outskirts of Rumeli Feneri, though, he lost the protection of the woods.

While central Istanbul was teeming twenty-four-seven, activity in the outlying villages was limited to a few restaurants and pubs. There were very few people out wandering the streets that late, which meant he would likely attract some unwanted attention, or be remembered if someone came asking about him.

It had only taken ten or fifteen minutes to get into the village. The houses and shops, however, had been built around paved-over cart trails. There wasn't a straight avenue anywhere in the small burg. It would take another quarter of an hour, veering along those disjointed streets, to make the marina.

He stood on his pedals, pumping up a steep grade

toward the lighthouse. When he topped the hill, he rested between two townhouses in a sprawling tract of old, custom *villalari*. He hadn't needed the goggles after entering town and had swiveled them to the top of his head. He now took the time to swap them for a pair of 6x binoculars out of his backpack, which he draped around his neck.

The lighthouse was fifty meters to his left. The marina stretched out below——visible from the deck lights of the fishing boats being readied to cast off. He had another two hundred meters to the water, but he could coast.

Jerome was congratulating himself until the first bullet whizzed an inch or two above his head. He wasn't sure what it was until it smashed into a wall to his right, dimpling a dime-sized hole.

The next two rounds were closer. One grazed the handlebar, spraying tiny shards of aluminum into his face that smacked against his glasses lens. The other was even more cause for concern as it nicked his backpack. His two cans of 'deodorant' weren't bulletproof.

Not having options was the only positive. He didn't need any time to think about what he should do. Ducking over the handlebar, he shoved off with his right foot, stomping the pedal with his left. A right turn down a thirty-degree grade allowed him to pick up speed with little effort. He stopped pedaling when he couldn't crank the chain fast enough to keep up with the tire rotation.

The shooter was now to his rear and continued to fire through the cascading first hundred meters. Jerome couldn't hear the reports but two bullets that came close sounded like a mosquito's buzz and a low whistle combined.

Near the bottom, to his left was a long, one-story building——a workshop primarily for net repair. At the end he yanked the brakes and skidded left, using the structure for cover as he headed into the marina.

He couldn't tell if anyone was chasing him. Once he got to the wharf and around people, he counted on whoever was shooting at him to stop. There was still another three hundred meters to go.

The marina was 'U' shaped, with a portion of it built on a natural jetty. The fishing boat he was going out on was docked on the Bosphorus side. To get there he had to make another left and ride the direction he'd come from. Then a right onto the jetty until he made the channel-side pier. From there it was another right.

He didn't know what time it was, but the crew would be waiting for him and he hoped they were ready to let go the lines. When he made that final turn, he looked to his right. Being the naturally curious type A, he couldn't help scanning the shore-side. He wanted to confirm it was Control trying to kill him——the logical deduction.

Brody spotted a car inching along the wharf. With his view obstructed by the boats, rafted three-deep along the dock, the 6x opticals helped. It wasn't Control's racer. When it stopped, a man with a pistol stepped out——someone Jerome had never seen before.

The gunman hadn't spotted the doctor yet, and Brody had the good sense to stay motionless. When the man turned to get back in the car Jerome dropped the binoculars to a dangle. He got off his bike, and in a half crouch, moved as quickly as his legs would allow the last hundred meters.

The boat's captain beamed when he saw Jerome at the end of his two-meter brow. At six feet tall and a lean one-ninety, the captain's worn leather face exhibited thirty years of weatherbeaten experience. The deep smile lines made the bristle around his mouth a parenthetical phrase, and the three parallel grooves across his forehead could act as rain gutters.

He covered his thick white hair with a ball cap, while his jeans were tucked into knee-high waders. His red gingham shirt was covered by a sleeveless down jacket.

In Jerome's mind the captain's appearance epitomized his profession. The aged seaman welcomed the lanky American aboard, shaking his hand with both of his. Brody smiled, comforted with the knowledge he would be the last person to see the captain alive.

CHAPTER NINETEEN

In Pursuit

The drive to the U.S. Consulate was a quick thirty minutes. With the shotgun in the trunk Adan knew he wouldn't be allowed to park his ride on the compound. He called ahead to have Henry meet him at the gate.

With Henry buckled up, Adan pulled back into traffic on Oçşehitler Sokağı. It was evident almost immediately, briefing the mission leader while driving was a bad idea. Congestion had him focused on the road, with his hands and feet in constant motion negotiating the moving obstacles in his path. Instead, he made a beeline for the Carrefour, a French big-box store, five minutes away.

The lot was about half full and he found a spot with some privacy in a section farthest from the store's entrance.

Before Adan could begin, Henry pointed at the rust-colored smudges on the country referent's shirt and trousers. "Are you all right?"

"It's not mine." Adan's inflection brushed it off as no big deal.

"Uh-huh. Let's hear it."

Adan acquiesced, detailing the attempted ambush. He made sure to include an explanation of the clean-up.

"Ruben believes they were Serbian in the employ of

Sonny Xú."

"What do you think?"

Adan didn't sense any skepticism in the question. It felt more like Henry probing his state of mind. "Ya might say the tattoos were a dead giveaway. I have to take Ruben's word the ink linked them to Sonny.

"As far as the Serbian angle goes...I don't know. Those guys could've been from anywhere in the Balkans. The end of the Yugoslav war produced a lot of groups that could fit their description.

"Have you talked to Art about the Chinese connection? Ruben wants to talk to this Sonny dude."

Henry nodded. "I'll text Ruben the number Art gave me. I don't know what good it'll do."

"I think Ruben just wants to get a feel for whether or not we're gonna have any more of these gangsters comin' our way. What kinda relationship does Carver have with this Chinese guy, anyway?"

"Well, first...I don't think the connection Carver has with anyone could be defined as a relationship. The exception would be the guy he opened the bar with in Tokyo, and I'm probably his best friend in NCIS.

"For sure, you're never gonna see Ruben get weepy and wring his feelings out to anybody. My wife Patty's been around him enough to believe he's never gonna be able to find a woman to stick with him for long.

"So, to answer your question, Carver and Xú have an understanding. As long as Sonny doesn't fuck with Ruben, Ruben doesn't go looking for Sonny. Sounds to me like our boy wants to put the Chinaman on notice."

Adan sat quiet for a few seconds. He was relaxed with his hands in his lap. "You brought a laptop?"

"Sure did. What've you got?"

"Gimme a sec. I wanna get the cable from the camera bag so I can download the photos I told you about. Once I drop you off I'm going to the Israeli Consulate to provide the photos to some dude named Ari Levin."

"What's that about?"

"Officer Levitan has a connection in France, who she believes can get information on the Frenchman faster than we can. Ruben and I don't have a problem with it—Art did put her on the team."

"How's Ruben doin' with her, by the way?"

Adan grunted a laugh. "I've got a feelin' before this is over, they're gonna take a break to go watch the submarine races." He then stepped out and went to the trunk.

Less than a minute later he dropped behind the wheel. Henry had his laptop out, and as soon as the camera was connected the download started. It took only a few seconds.

Unplugging the cable from the computer, Adan said, "The Frenchman called himself Control. According to Carver that's a term The Board uses for a project manager or handler."

"That's right. The big guy has had his share of run-ins this year with those folks. In both instances it nearly killed him. I'll see what I can find out. I'll run the car plates through Interpol, as well. If our NCIS rep isn't out of town, we should hear back fairly soon.

"Anything else?" Henry tucked his laptop into a soft-sided attache case.

"One more thing, and it's important. Ruben wants you to get in touch with Ryan Henderson and see if he's been in contact with the mad scientist. He may be able to get Bennet to disclose his plan. The nutjob apparently really has developed one of those flu bugs everybody's been worried about—an end-of-mankind sort of pandemic."

"*Holy crap!* You seem pretty calm about it."

"Yeah, well...I mean...how do you comprehend somethin' like that?"

"I'll tell you how I comprehend it. If Bennet is in the

wind, carrying a bioweapon that will unleash a super-pandemic, then Carver was right. Art needs to be briefing this up the chain.

"And let me tell you somethin', if you're havin' difficulty getting your head wrapped around it now, just wait 'til they throw politics in the mix.

"Carver and Levitan better find this guy quick, or we're in for the shitstorm of the century."

Moreau was searching Brody's Golden Beach bungalow when Big Ugly received the call.

"Hey, Musa...he's in Rumeli Feneri! They spotted him on a bicycle."

The Algerian came out of the cabin at a trot, straight to the Bugatti. "Let's go. He didn't leave anything behind. Where is he?"

"He was heading for the lighthouse. They're waiting for instructions."

"Call them back and tell them not to get too close. I don't want the boys catching what he's carrying."

Moreau could see Big Ugly had an inkling of what he meant. "Okay, but what then? You want him dead—right?"

"If they can put him down without the hassle of witnesses, then do it." Moreau wasn't sure what to do if they did kill the doctor. He had no idea how the agent was to be released, or if the doctor even had it on him. Although he felt that was a certainty.

The Board's disposal team was in the area but he didn't want the body left out in the open until they showed up. The fear of infection wasn't the only problem in that scenario. He had to keep the authorities from getting involved. *Why not get them involved? I could drop the whole thing in their laps. Maybe get a message to someone in the police about a level four biohazard...*

The thought actually appealed to him. The

gendarmerie would be all over it like stink on a pig. It'd force The Board, *ces fouteurs*, to pull a rabbit out of their hat. A situation he clearly considered within their bailiwick.

The Bugatti's needle hit a hundred and thirty kph as they went through the gate. They were in the village in less than a minute, pulling the speed off the tires just short of threshold braking.

Big Ugly had his right hand on the dash to brace himself—the cell phone was at his ear in his left. "They missed him. He's going into the marina."

"Merde. Can they still see him?"

There was a break as Big Ugly spoke Corsu into his hand, then, "They lost the visual. He's hiding."

"Tell your men to sit tight. If he shows himself they can take him down. Otherwise, have them wait for us. I'll decide our next move when we get there."

Carver was jonesing for a cup of coffee. The elixir of life on a stakeout. Adan had checked in with an update on his conversation with Henry. No surprise there. He wondered how long he'd have before Art was forced to escalate.

He checked his watch—eleven-fifteen pm—and did a rough calculation in his head. He hadn't been on the ground forty-eight hours yet and everything was already turning to shit.

The news he and Rivka both found interesting was from Ari Levin, her man at the consulate. He didn't need to contact anyone to identify the man in the photos. A window source at Turkey's National Intelligence Agency—Millî İstihbarat Teşkilatı or MIT—came calling about the guy several months before.

Rivka had taken the call from Ari, while she and Ruben sat secluded on the quad. When she finished, she filled Ruben in. The Sussex accent, sprinkled with

Yiddish slang, had him engrossed as she related everything from the briefing.

A copy of a French passport, in the name of Yves Moreau, had been provided to Ari. The Turk who presented it wasn't at liberty to divulge too much regarding the information request. It was a two-parter.

First, the MIT wanted to confirm the business interests Moreau had in Tel Aviv. Then whether or not he had a criminal record, or considered a person of interest in any ongoing investigations.

Since the MIT wasn't forthcoming about the reason for the background inquiry, Ari wasn't fully on the up and up with the intelligence he'd acquired. The man in the photos taken by Adan did, in fact, go by the name of Yves Moreau, along with a number of aliases.

His early criminal history was sketchy but connected closely to a crime syndicate in Marseille with Algerian roots. Mostly involved in small-time extortion and protection rackets, he disappeared for a half-dozen years in the late 70's and early 80's.

In the mid 80's he emerged around allegations of a rash of homicides linked to turf warfare and Corsican-style vendetta killings. There was also talk of arms dealing, drug trafficking and racketeering. Nothing ever stuck.

About the time the Wall fell and the freedom-loving west was celebrating the end of the Cold War, Moreau popped up in North Africa—Algiers and Casablanca. He'd apparently changed allegiances, going into the construction business with a man with whom he shared a name.

Rivka explained the Israeli connection began there. Moreau had become adroit in building casinos and gambling houses, that could fly under regulatory radar.

Maghrebi Jews who'd repatriated to Israel after the Algerian war had formed a number of crime families.

Aside from battling each other over control of the cookie-cutter criminal activity of drug distribution, prostitution and racketeering, they went knocking on Moreau's door to seek his assistance in establishing their underground gaming.

They liked him because he had no interest in sticking around after the job was done. He worked on a fee basis and while he was pricey, he never demanded a percentage.

Rivka finished by advising Moreau fell off the grid about three or four years ago. While the casino business had been lucrative, it was rumored he'd also gotten involved in mobile production of munitions and chemicals used in weapon manufacture.

That last bit of intel closed the loop for Carver. The Board found in Moreau the skill set necessary to build out and manage a laboratory environment. Unfortunately for everyone, the scientist they'd scooped up from DARPA turned out to be the wildcard in the deck.

The doctor was shown into the galley and presented with a cup of muddy Turkish coffee and a plate of fresh baklava. The captain, who spoke decent English, invited him to get comfortable while the crew got underway.

The diesels were already fired up. With the galley lights low, Brody could see through the windows the cleat on portside aft being unwrapped. Since he had the space to himself, he pulled the cans from the side pocket of the backpack. He'd found the spot where the bullet grazed the fabric and was amazed neither container was damaged.

He'd begun the process of peeling the tape from a lid, when motion from the starboard side caught his eye. It was the Bugatti pulling onto the wharf. The deck lights from the boats, along with the wharf lamps on that side of the marina, made it quite visible.

Notwithstanding the dim galley lighting, the small porthole and a distance of over a hundred meters, Brody didn't take a chance. He slid down in the booth low enough to mask his silhouette, while still able to peer over the sill.

The binoculars came up and Jerome studied Control exiting his driving machine. He was right when he thought he saw another person in the car. A giant unfolded himself from the passenger side. Both he and Control were then engaged in a back and forth with the gunman from the car that chased Jerome into the marina.

That conversation lasted no more than fifteen seconds. Control leaned down, pulling a pair of binoculars from his speedster, and began scanning the boats along the jetty and Bosphorus side moorings.

Jerome could tell Control's attention lingered on the vessel he'd boarded, and he slid sideways to disappear completely from view. The engines revved as the crew pushed the fishing trawler away from the dock but it wasn't like opening the throttle on a speedboat.

The anticipation of forward motion was agonizing. As he lay in that awkward position, picturing, any second, the thug with the pistol bursting into the space, Jerome stripped the rest of the tape from the can, freeing the lid. If he was going down, so was everybody else.

Big Ugly moved up next to the Algerian, the toes of his shoes extending a half-inch over the pier. "What do you think?"

Moreau was motionless, binoculars up, examining the trawler leaving the marina. "I want the hull number on that boat and its transponder frequency." He handed the binoculars to the Corsican. "Can you do that for me?"

The man looked through the glasses at the name

painted on the stern. "I can do that."

With his clenched fists resting on his hips, feet shoulder width apart, Moreau said, "Have the men check each vessel. If the crews are on board, find out if they know anything about the doctor. Make sure they have money to spread around.

"If they find him, they have to keep their distance the best they can, but I want him dead."

"What about my men, if that happens?"

Moreau took a long, hard look at his friend with the Fellini-esque features. "I'll try to get your men out of the country as fast as possible—as long as they're not infected."

Only half his face could express displeasure in what he'd heard but he nodded his agreement. He handed the eyepiece back to the Algerian and walked to the two with their instructions.

As Moreau watched the fishing boat move into the shipping lane, headed for the Black Sea, he had no worries for the men's safety. He was simply reminding his Corsican comrade what the stakes were.

CHAPTER TWENTY

Tearing Down the Lab

Campus security showed little interest in the couple on the bench—a pair of faculty lovebirds. Ruben's ass had been aching for a while and he wondered how Rivka was making out. There wasn't much padding in the seat of her pants.

As if reading his mind, she stood, placed her palms at her waist, and leaned backward. She then raised her arms above her head, stretching as she balanced on the balls of her feet. The motion lifted the bottom seams on her cotton blouse and silk jacket.

It gave Ruben a peek at lean abs and the tip of the suppressor she spun onto her pistol earlier in the evening. The total image sparked a physical reaction. His next shift on the hard seat had nothing to do with sore gluteus maximus.

She caught him gawking. "Relax, Bronco Billy. The show's going to be over there." She pointed at the door to the lab.

He tried on a deer-in-the-headlights look as his eyes sidled up her frame. When they rested on her face, he said, "Stop doin' that."

Even in that tenebrous setting Carver could tell the difference between a smug mouth and a smile. "Hey, I'm just sayin'..." He then redirected his focus to the lab door.

Rivka glanced at her watch. "If a crew is coming in to mop up they better do it soon. It's going to take more than a few minutes to sanitize that space."

Carver nodded toward the engineering building. "Speak of the devil, or maybe it should be *devils*."

A squad of eight, dressed in dark coveralls, walked in from the direction of the parking lot. They were each pulling a Pelican transport case attached to a two-wheel trolley. From what Carver could make out, the lead man inserted a silver, 'T' shaped, hex key into a slot near the door seam.

He had to use both hands on the device to turn it. When the latch released, the door popped open like a hatch cover. In less than ten seconds, and without a sound, they were through the opening. The door closed behind them with a solid thud.

Still staring at the once occupied spot, Rivka quipped, "Shall we knock?"

Carver took a second to think. "Ya, know...they had to come in something big enough to carry all that gear."

"And it'll have to be equipped to manage hazmat," she agreed.

With his hands on his knees, Ruben pushed himself to his feet. "Should be pretty easy to spot. Whaddya think?"

"I think we'll probably find what we need to open that door. Those goyim don't look the sort to leave home without a spare."

They didn't run, but this time Rivka didn't take Ruben's arm. Both hands free were necessary and he grooved with it.

Although the quad was empty, there were people in the surrounding buildings. They didn't want to do anything that would attract attention.

The parking lot was well lit, with pole-mounted circular LEDs, on a twenty-five meter spacing. The twenty-two foot white Freightliner, which filled the front of the lot, would have been visible in ambient light.

Using the shadow from the engineering building to mask them, they stopped to check the area around the truck, looking for security. They didn't see anyone in the cab.

Ruben spoke first. "I don't know...I'm guessin' two, maybe three in the cargo bay monitoring what's goin' on in the lab. Although, I don't see any antennas or cabling. They must have some kind of wireless comms. Do you see any camera mounts on the truck for exterior surveillance?"

Rivka scratched her chin with the nail of her right index finger. Then, using that same finger, pointed at the truck. "No, but let's go see who's in there."

"Let's agree on somethin' first. If I'm right, that'd be the best place to watch them strip the lab. They probably have somethin' to drink and eat in there."

"You want to make yourself at home?"

"Well...yeah. I didn't see any of those guys goin' into the building sportin' guns. Did you?"

"No."

"They're in there to collect the research and destroy anything they can't safely carry out. I don't want to be around for that. Then they have to scrape up what I'm assuming will be the bodies of the lab assistants."

Rivka shook her head. "You can't assume that."

"Whaddya mean? That lab was ostensibly their home. If they're not with Bennet, then what's left of them is in there. Anyway, when that crew is finished, we'll look for any clues of where Bennet may have gone."

Carver could see what he was saying wasn't sitting well with the Shin Bet officer. She didn't shrug him off altogether, but he perceived there was going to be some compromising.

Rivka squinted her eyes and set her jaw. "I want to

know what they found. I want to look at it. If we wait until they come out, they'll seal the entrance and we'll be in the same fix we're in now. We need to persuade them it would be in their best interest to help us."

"There are eight of them."

"You said you didn't see any guns."

The fishing boat was a fifty-foot stern trawler with the galley situated below the wheelhouse. Brody waited until they'd cleared the marina entrance and motored into the shipping lane leading to the Black Sea, before climbing the ladder to the bridge.

As he stepped through the wheelhouse door, he was greeted by the captain and his first mate. They were both resting against an instrument console, behind a third man who was at the helm.

"Ah, Doctor Brody, is there a problem?"

"No, no. I was hoping it'd be all right for me to come up here for a while. I've never been on a boat this size. I think it's fascinating how you're able to navigate at night."

The cabin interior was illuminated by red lanterns located along the deck line. It saved the helmsman his night vision to the extent he'd be able to see other ships' running lights but it didn't do much for vision-fixing navigation.

The captain said something to his first mate, who moved away to study a screen flashing data on one of the electronic instruments next to the helm.

"Well, it's fairly obvious we can't see much at night outside the marina. We navigate entirely off of an integrated system of electronic chart displays, radar and global satellite positioning. We also have sonar here," he touched the console he was leaning against, "and depth sounders over there."

Brody nodded with enthusiasm. "This is really

interesting stuff. I hope you don't mind me spending time in here over the next few days. I'd like to learn how all of it works."

"Not at all. If you get proficient, I'll put you to work." The captain belched a laugh and nudged his first mate with his fist. "Would you care for a cuppa? We've got a kettle on."

"Yes, great, I'd love one."

As the captain turned toward a hotplate, attached to a bulkhead cabinet, Brody pulled an aerosol can from his coat pocket. He removed the lid, and depressed the actuator at eye level for two seconds.

Afterward he wanted to kick himself. He didn't need to use that much. As he put the can back in his pocket, he chocked it up as a learning moment. The unanticipated nerves and sudden adrenaline rush wouldn't be a factor the next time.

A moment later, the captain approached with a steaming metal mug, which Jerome accepted with gratitude.

There was no 'sneaking up' on the Freightliner. The best they could do was a casual sangfroid.

Ruben let the tips of his fingers slide along the side as they walked the length of the van. "Is it big enough for ya?"

"Men—you've got such a size fixation."

"What? No...that's not..."

"Always worried if it's big enough. Your nightmare scenario: 'Is it in yet?'" she cackled.

"Oh, yeah? Well, I've got two words for you: *boob job*."

"Have you ever heard it described as a boob measuring contest?"

When they reached the end, they stood in front of two six-foot cargo bay doors on vertical hinges.

Rivka pulled her Jericho and moved laterally and back

two steps. "Look, if you're experiencing any performance anxiety, please let me know now."

He held up a fist and glanced her way, with a cocked eyebrow and half-cocked mouth. "After talkin' to you, I'm beginnin' to understand that whole gay pride thing."

"Oh, sure. Get mad and take the football home, why don't you?"

Fuckin' typical. Always with the last word. Ruben hit the door twice. Then twice again after a few seconds. When it came open, he was peering up at a man in his late thirties or early forties. Clean-shaven, with a blond crew cut, he wore the same coveralls Ruben saw on the group going in the lab.

"Hey, pal, where's your parking permit?"

With that he landed a right cross to the guy's groin, then grabbed his ankles and twisting at the hips, yanked the chump's feet straight out. Ruben tried to get enough leverage on the throw to pull the man clear of the door.

He missed by a few inches. The fella's head smashed on the deck, at the edge of the door frame. It was accompanied by a loud, unmistakable snap, as his neck separated from the occipital at the atlas.

Two fingers on the dude's carotid confirmed Ruben's immediate suspicion. Rivka then juked past him, apparently not feeling the need to stick around for the diagnosis. With pistol up she climbed into the cargo bay, covering down on two more similarly uniformed gentlemen.

"Keep you mouths shut and remove the headsets."

Another blondie opened his mouth. "What the hell do you think you're doing? Do you know who we work for? Lady, you are in so much..."

The bullet went through his left eye and spattered chunks of his brain and bone on the front bulkhead. Before the wiseass crumpled, Rivka had the pistol trained on his partner.

"Do you have anything to say?"

The man's hands flew up, as if invisible strings had jerked them. With his lips in a tight grimace, he shook his head until Rivka instructed him, once again, to remove the headset.

Carver watched the drama while he lifted his dead man into a fireman's carry in order to roll him into the cargo bay. Pushing the feet out of the way, he climbed in and closed the door.

As he slipped past Rivka, he asked, "Wanna get a beer later?"

"Ruben, you are such a mashugana."

Carver poked a finger at the guy. "Where's your hazmat gear?"

Without dropping his hands, he pointed with his nose at one of three Pelican cases laying on shelving fastened to the opposite bulkhead. Before Ruben turned, he gazed at three seventeen-inch monitors that showed activity taking place in the lab.

One of the video feeds was coming from a stationary CCTV, and two were helmet cams.

"You recording this?"

"O-of course."

Carver turned and opened a container and pulled out a roll of duct tape. He then stepped behind the man in the chair and pulled his arms behind his back. The duct tape was used liberally to secure the arms at the wrists and elbows.

"Why am I a mashugana?"

"If you want a Jewish woman to go out with you, don't mention beer."

Seated in front of the monitors, Rivka slipped on a headset and Ruben turned his focus again to the man with the duct-taped arms. "What's your name?"

"What? Why do you want to know my name?"

"I know that accent. You're an American?"

184

"No...no, Canadian."

"You *are* an American——U.S. Citizen to be more precise."

"No, why do you say that?"

"'Cause when Americans overseas find themselves in a tight spot they always claim to be Canadian. An interesting non sequitur, since Americans on the U.S. side often find Canadians quite offensive——and vice versa, of course.

"The reason I want to know your name is I feel my friend here and I have, sort of, started off on the wrong foot. We're really the good guys..."

He stared at Ruben unbelieving. "I've got nothing to say to you. You are completely out of your depth."

"Yeah, I've heard that before, but you're the one tied up. And without being too poignant about it, you're the one with dead comrades layin' around.

"So, anyway, I'm gonna call you Mr. Roberts, since that's the name stenciled on *your* Pelican case."

Ruben spun his chair, turning his attention once more to the monitors. "See anything of note?"

Rivka tapped a screen. "They've loaded the bodies into what looks like an incinerator. The radio chatter suggests Bennet left nothing behind but the equipment. The servers are fried."

"Any indication how his lab assistants bought it?"

"Hydrogen cyanide. They found the trays in the air ducts."

"I want to have a chat with Mr. Roberts without being disturbed by his runnin' buddies. How much time do you think we have before they finish up?"

"They're packing up now, waiting for the bodies to burn. Thirty minutes——maybe."

Ruben got up and shuffled to the driver's compartment. "We're in luck. They left the keys in the ignition."

* * *

The big six-cylinder diesel cranked over with a quick twist. He released the brake, pushed the lever into drive and gave it some fuel. There was a slight delay before the rear differential began spinning the wheels. Once they were rolling it was a smooth ride.

Jet lag had been nagging him throughout the day, but sitting at the wheel, fatigue was setting in. He looked at his watch—after midnight. *Cinderella and the dainty glass slipper.* He had to find a way to take a break without losing too much time.

When he reached Rumeli Feneri Cd, he decided not to go right, toward Istanbul. Rather he turned north and headed for the village where the road ended.

They had to locate Bennet and so far they had nothing to go on. Mr. Roberts might be able to provide some of The Board's insight into the matter; however, Ruben was asking himself some basic questions.

When Rivka stuck her head through the hatch to check on him, it presented the perfect opportunity to see if she came to the same conclusion.

"If you were in a foreign country, on the run, and you couldn't speak the language; had no idea where you could hide safely; knew the train stations, airports, bus terminals and other public transportation were being watched; and couldn't reach out to anyone for help, what would you do?"

Ruben could almost feel her ruminating.

"I'd do the same as you."

"What's that?"

"I'd have a plan. I wouldn't just run off. Neither would he. He left when he had his exit already arranged. He prepped the lab for shut down, to include what I'm sure he believed was a humane termination of employment for the people who worked for him.

"He destroyed any vestige of his research, or at least

what he had to leave behind." She paused for a few seconds, staring out the windshield. "You're going north. This road ends at the Black Sea. You think he went out by water."

Oh, yeah...it doesn't take a genius to figure that one out.

CHAPTER TWENTY-ONE
Executive Order

They didn't have to canvass the marina for long. Big Ugly's men leveraged the information Moreau needed using wads of Turkish lira. Brody had indeed hitched a ride with the trawler Moreau watched motor out to the channel.

The captain hadn't made a secret of the weird American. The entire marina was aware of the excursion. It was a sea-based community, tight in more ways than one. To have a university professor agree to pay enough to cover the expenses for a few days at sea was a cause célèbre.

The Algerian had been assured by the Corsican bruiser they'd be able to locate the boat. What they'd do after that was the mare's nest.

His first inclination was to sink it from the air with everyone aboard. The problem with that solution had to do with verification. Brody may have had the crew drop him off across the channel. The doctor's duplicitous nature would make that a very real possibility.

Moreau was alone when he left the village. A progress report was expected and while it was unlikely The Board's entire complement would join the call, there would be a few individuals waiting up for him.

He'd initiated the sequence for the conference after leaving the village on Rumeli Feneri Cd. It would be a short conversation, with a few very specific requests. Before he uttered the final code to make the connection, he was blinded by a pair of high-beams drifting into his lane.

The reflex was to stomp the brakes and hit the horn, but the size and speed of the machine coming his way caused a change in reaction. Instead of braking, he punched it.

There had never been an occasion for him to floor the beast and the engine response was radical. If he could make it to old age, he'd probably enjoy an anecdotal bon mot about g-force. He might even read up on horizontal and vertical inertial trajectory and weight calculations based on Pythagorean theorem.

In that instant, however, his colon was ready to eliminate. The car's forward lunge crushed him against the seat back. His arms, fully extended with elbows locked, formed a ridged posture. The fortunate paradox was that while he felt as if he was careening out of control, he was physically unable to over-steer. A jerk on the wheel left, then right amounted to no more than a few centimeters in adjustment.

The Bugatti did the rest. Its tight suspension, hydraulic assisted rack and pinion steering and all-wheel self-adjusting drive distribution, made it appear he'd slipped laterally into the left lane. From the instant he saw the headlights, to the flash of a large, white delivery van blasting past on his right, was a blink of the eye—literally.

Ordinarily, he'd brush such an insult off with a wave of a few fingers. Not this time. He thought he'd seen the van from earlier in the evening. As his foot came of the accelerator, he considered turning and following the *enculé grossier*. A fleeting self-indulgence to be sure, and

189

until the call went through, he brooded about what he'd do if he saw that truck again.

Rivka was hovering over Carver's shoulder from the hatch between the cab and load bay. If it was anyone else he would have been annoyed. It was the way she smelled. Her natural body odor made his skin tingle. He would have loved to lay his nose on that patch of dermis where her neck met the shoulder. *Breathe her in.*

When she touched his deltoid, his body jerked. A natural polysynaptic response to a tactile stimulus served up by the woman whose bones he wanted to jump.

Her hand came off and then rested again on the same spot. "Are you okay?"

"Oh, yeah. I was just thinkin' about something."

"Look at that car."

Ruben could see the headlights, as the automobile came out of the village, but had obviously missed what had attracted her.

"It's the Bugatti Veyron."

"Are you sure?"

"Absolutely, luv. I'd never mistake that piece of art."

"Do ya think there could be more than one in this neighborhood?"

"Not a chance."

"Well, then...let's say hello. Find a way to brace yourself."

Ruben pulled the seatbelt with its shoulder harness across his body and snapped it in place. Rivka pulled Mr. Roberts to the floor face down. She then sat down with her back against the bulkhead, feet braced against a seat at the monitoring station. She wrapped her arms around her thighs and dropped her head between her knees.

When Ruben heard her yell, "Ready", he pulled the turn signal lever, switching to high-beams. *Oh, man. I hope this is going to be fun.* He pressed the accelerator a half-inch and eased left, pinching off the Bugatti's lane.

It was rare Carver felt the itch to fuck with someone, but he wanted to see how the Frog would react. He had to believe even this snail-snapper would be disinclined to play chicken with a million dollar toy. At the instant he thought he'd overestimated the competition and braced for impact, the Bugatti vanished.

Relieved, he steered back to his lane and shouted to Rivka. "You okay back there?"

She appeared at the hatch and asked, "What happened?"

"I don't know. Whatever he did...it was pretty fuckin' amazing. I need to make some phone calls."

"It's late, Control. What's your status? Have you located Doctor Brody?"

A new voice, but the telltale intonation made Moreau wonder if someone didn't just try to run this *connard* off a road. Since The Board dispensed with the pleasantries, the Algerian replied in kind.

"He's gone fishing."

The dead air lasted long enough for rigor to set in. He'd gotten a stiff neck waiting. "Are you still there?"

"Yes, Control. We don't understand the metaphor."

"That's because it's not a metaphor. Your scientist boarded a fishing trawler at midnight and is now somewhere in the Black Sea. I won't have the vessel's hull number and tracking code until later this morning."

"Then what?"

"I'll need a fast boat with long range fuel tanks. Something innocuous but with good communications, radar, infrared sensors, and GPS with AIS and VTS tracking capability. Are you getting this?"

"Yes, please continue."

The curt brevity allowed him to remain on the same tack. "I also need an FGM-148 Javelin. It's a U.S. antitank, shoulder-fired missile. Three re-loads will be sufficient."

Again there was a delay in reply. "The boat we can have ready for use by this afternoon. It may take a day or two to acquire the Javelin, another day for delivery. Will that be a problem?"

"I don't know. It depends on how long the trawler plans to stay out. I need to be in the water in two days."

A soft buzz came on, as the joining members cut Moreau out of their discussion. A minute later: "We want the data Brody is carrying. Sinking the fishing boat with him on it, is obviously counter-productive."

Moreau shook his head in disbelief. "You still don't get it. There is no way to take Brody without exposure to his creation. Give me the missiles. I'll sink the trawler and then come back in a few weeks with a salvage team to search the wreckage."

"I'll have to get back to you. We need a consensus from the entire membership."

"Okay, but don't take too long. The window is still two days."

"I understand."

I don't think so. "That's it for me. Do you have anything?"

"The CIA has raised an alert regarding Doctor Brody. The President of the United States has been briefed and the entirety of the country's intelligence community is aware of the situation. It appears, however, that Carver and his Shin Bet counterpart will be allowed to continue their investigation. At least for the time being.

"On another note, there is something else we want you to be aware of. As we discussed yesterday, a team was sent into the lab to search and sanitize. Brody's three assistants were killed with hydrogen cyanide, not the bio-weapon.

"Disposal was relatively simple. They used the lab's

incinerator for everything. They had nothing to haul away."

Then what's the issue? "I'm hearing a 'but'."

"Yes, well, after sealing the lab on exit, they discovered their vehicle, along with its three member monitoring team, were gone. We do not believe they went fishing."

Moreau didn't wait for them to finish before he had the Bugatti in gear and was executing a U turn.

The STE rang at eighteen-seventeen. Art sat with a half-empty white porcelain mug in hand, emblazoned with the emblem of the eagle, globe and anchor. The only items on his desk were the secure phone and the twenty-four-hour clock next to it. Before picking up, he took a sip. The cold, acrid liquid fit his mood.

The caller ID showed it was Henry Dever. A ripple of ambivalence caused him to let it ring a few more times. After Dever's call earlier in the day, the incident management domino effect was in full force.

Art briefed his boss, the Director of the CIA, who in turn provided a synopsis to the newly appointed Director of National Intelligence. He went to the President, through the Chief of Staff, and in less than an hour the National Security Council, the Homeland Security Council, and the remaining seventeen members of the Intelligence Community had received emails.

On top of that the President demanded the Director of the Centers for Disease Control and Prevention be brought into the loop, along with the Joint Chiefs of Staff, since DARPA belonged to them.

Art had no doubt The Board was fully aware of the national security circle jerk taking place and wondered when Katie Couric and Matt Lauer would be brought up to speed. He figured the only reason it hadn't been leaked to *Good Morning America*, or the *New York Times* for that matter, was because nobody wanted to alert the

Turks.

Then came the data calls. Each of the heads of the agencies placed on distribution had their own sycophantic minions, with armies of analysts below them. In typical fashion, the avalanche of demand for sitreps, point papers, briefing modules, solution schedules and other mindless, but top priority data requests, filled email inboxes to capacity.

When the answers to those queries weren't instantly forthcoming, a negative wave began that also reached the oval office. The question of whether or not the operation should be managed by someone with a better understanding of the *big picture* had begun to be bandied about.

When the scrimmage ensued over which individual or agency had a better big picture perspective, the President was informed the Israelis were already up to their nuts in Art's op. As the leader of the free world, he expressed no desire to give America's only true ally in the Middle East the idea the Executive Branch, once again, had its head up its own ass.

In putting the quietus on any suggestion Art Sheppard, and the people he already had on the ground, were not up to the task, Art received a call directly from the man himself. In a voice that had not yet been fully rid of its Texas drawl, the President's only directive was something Art had heard more times than he wanted to remember: "You've got the ball. Don't fuck this up."

Rather than setting his mug down, Art accepted Henry's call through the speaker.

"Gimme some good news, Hank."

"Is there anyone else in the room?"

"No. If you want to go secure push the button." Art's crypto card was perpetually in place.

After Henry went secure on his end, it took almost a minute for Art's unit to register SECRET.

Henry's voice came back on, tinny but clear. "Can you hear me?"

"Yes. It's a good connection. Are we still operational?"

"We are. I just got off the phone with Carver. He and Levitan are in a village called Rumeli Feneri, about twenty-kilometers north of here. I've prepared a report I'm sending you now."

"Okay, thanks, I'll need that in the shark tank."

"I figured. Anyway, let me give you a dump on their activity. Then I'll tell you what support Carver's requested from Ryan Henderson."

During the ensuing fifteen minutes Henry discussed the situation at the lab, to include the current body count, the eight stranded members of the crew sent in by The Board to clear the facility, and the man Carver had taken with them for additional Q&A.

He also laid out Carver's reasoning regarding his belief that Bennet had likely found a way to leave the country by sea. While that was in Carver's mind the most feasible option, Henry wanted to cover a few other bases. He had Adan use one of his well-connected sources to check if a taxi or limo service picked up a fare at or near the university the previous day.

The background check on Bennet revealed he didn't own an automobile in the States. His mode of transportation was bicycle or public. It was unlikely that would change in a foreign country—an assumption confirmed by Carver's Shin Bet partner.

Art broke in on Henry's monologue with: "What did Carver want Ryan Henderson to do?"

"Well...besides his continued attempt to make contact with the scientist, Carver wanted him to access the Turkey Straits Vessel Tracking System, and get a fix on every boat leaving the Rumeli Feneri marina yesterday evening."

"Why there?"

"It's the only marina in the area and an easy bike ride from the university. Apparently there are also a shitload of back roads and trails he could have taken to avoid the main arteries.

"The place is a nice sized facility, with not only mooring services, but dry dock and boat repair as well. One of the few Turkish fishing fleets ties up there and it plays host to dozens of yachts and cruisers."

Art leaned back in his chair and dropped a heel on the corner of his desk. He worried the cup handle with a thumbnail as he asked, "How does Ruben know any of this? He just got there."

"Adan, our country referent. Carver called him before me."

Art responded with a grunt, wanting Henry to continue.

"According to Rivka, Bennet didn't get out much, but the marina at Rumeli Feneri would definitely fit in his exit plan. He would've had plenty of time over the last several weeks to scout the area and make arrangements. Essentially, she agrees with Carver."

"Okay, anything else?"

"Maybe a heads-up."

The tone in the delivery affected Art in the same way a creaking stair at home had him reaching for a pistol. He sat forward with his forearms on his desk. "I'm listening."

"Carver also asked Ryan to get the last known location for any of The Board members within a six-hour drive of Istanbul. I got the impression he hopes he doesn't have to go that far."

"No, no, no. We're not ready to move on them. Carver needs to stay focused on Bennet. You need to call him back. Tell him I'm not authorizing action against known members of The Board. Did he tell you what he planned to do?"

"All he said is he needs a phone number."

"I gave him Sonny's number."

"Yeah, and he says thanks, but he needs another one you can't give him."

CHAPTER TWENTY-TWO
Rumeli Feneri

They sat facing Mr. Roberts, now propped against a bulkhead, his legs straight out, ankles taped. After the near miss, Carver settled on a spot east of the village in a new tract housing and condominium complex. While his decision to follow the road north to its end may have been impulsive—a noodling instinct—the appearance of the Bugatti added confidence to his hunch.

He was rarely in a situation where his cognitive faculty couldn't fill in factual gaps. His ability to enter a state of clarity, where more than forty years of chunked information he'd organized in his *memoria loci*, allowed him to devise solutions on the fly. It relied, however, on placing his circumstance in a context that triggered the mental process.

When that wasn't happening, he improvised. He found directed activity got the percipient juices flowing. Even though he didn't visualize an answer right away, he did what everybody else did—he followed his nose.

Adan was on his way and Ryan had his orders. The BlackBerry battery was at twenty percent and while Carver wanted to dial Sonny's number, he saved the cell for Ryan's call back.

Carver had leaned forward, forearms on knees, staring

down at the man they'd brought along for the ride. "Let's make this simple, shall we? My name is Special Agent Ruben Carver. I'm with the U.S. Naval Criminal Investigative Service. Perhaps you've seen the TV show. Anyway, I've taken you into custody as a suspected member of an international terrorist group. I want to ask you a few questions."

The downturned mouth and defiant eyes were mitigated by Roberts' fidgety attempt to adjust his position. Ruben figured the man's arms must be aching.

"Bullshit! You can't do this. I'm not talking to you."

"Come on. Why do you wanna be that way? You answer a few questions and we let you go. Shit, we'll even leave the truck so you can go pick up your friends."

"Or what? You gonna torture me—a fellow American? You're a Federal Agent and I have rights."

"Well, you're right about that. Fortunately, I have my friend here." Ruben tapped his forehead. "Oh, sorry. Where are my manners? I haven't introduced her yet."

Roberts shifted his focus to the woman. Her lips pursed as her brow went tight and her ears seemed to flatten against her skull.

"She happens to be a citizen of the second greatest country in the world." Carver stressed this by gesticulating with the back of his fist—two fingers elevated.

Confusion etched across Roberts' face. "What? No...England's not..."

Carver turned the hand with palm out and swiveled his head Rivka's direction. "It must be the accent." Returning his gaze to the idiot who was beginning to remind him of a mid-level government employee, he declared, "*No, stupid*...Israel."

"But Israel isn't..."

"Don't say it." Ruben shook his head and waved both hands in warning. "While I wouldn't feel good about doing anything that would violate your rights as a citizen of the United States of America, she would *love* to."

Carver maintained eye contact but let his last few words sink in before continuing. "Now don't get me wrong, it would really bother me to watch her go to work on you. So, I'm gonna step outside for a while. I need to take a leak anyway."

As Ruben stood, Rivka bent down and lifted her right pant leg exposing a knife sheath strapped above her ankle. With a silky smooth *swoosh*, a seven-inch black Dustar appeared.

"Wow, is that the Model-1 I've heard so much about?"

Her eyebrows dropped a fraction as they seemed to come together at the bridge of her nose. It was the accompanying smile, though, that made the skin on Ruben's neck prickle.

Roberts couldn't take his eyes of the cutter, as the Special Agent interjected: "I hope it doesn't seem too aggressive, but ya know, we're in kind've a hurry." He redirected his next comment to his lady friend. "I'll just be outside. I don't think you have to worry about noise."

He took exactly one step.

"Okay, wait...*wait.*"

Ruben shrugged a shoulder. "Too late, my man. She took the big dog off the leash and you know what that means."

"No, I, uh...I don't know what that means."

"Ya gotta let the big dog eat." He copped a peek at Rivka, who had no idea what the expression meant. "No, really. It's an old American axiom. Mr. Roberts, here, knows that. He's just foolin' around."

The whimper from the man on the deck kept Ruben from taking that second step. "Kinda gives you the willies—don't it." He rotated his eyes toward his partner, keeping his head stationary. "I don't know. You think you can hold off for now? Our boy here sounds like he's had a change of heart."

After all the haggling, Mr. Roberts was not the wealth of information they expected. It turned out the contentious whiner, like his compatriots, was a PhD with specialty training in biosafety.

He and his team worked for a multi-national pharmaceutical in Paris. A subsidiary of a global conglomerate with interests in everything from banking and real estate services to arms manufacturing.

The members of Roberts' team were from different departments and except for this collateral duty as an on-call fly away team, they had no contact with each other. In most cases they didn't even know each other's names. They were experts in biodefense and biohazard removal and their assignments were doled out by a designated team leader when they were in the air.

They had no idea what to expect when they arrived in Istanbul, other than being told there was a lab accident involving a highly virulent, genetically engineered, biological agent. Their job was to first quarantine survivors, isolate the agent and any contamination and then sterilize the environment. The second phase of the operation was to collect all research data, the lab servers and if possible a viable sample.

Ruben and Rivka were witness to most of what Roberts detailed. He had no idea who called the team out, who the research fellows in the lab were and what they had been working on.

Carver leaned back in his chair, incredulous. "You mean to tell us, you came here from Paris on a company jet, big enough to haul this truck, along with all your gear. You then passed through Customs and Immigration without raising any flags and drove straight to the university.

"Then you knew where the lab was and even had a

key to manually open the outer door. You can understand why I find your story hard to believe—right?"

"But it's true. There were a couple guys at the airport waiting for us who expedited everything."

"What guys?"

"I don't know...two guys. Both of them French, I guess. We laughed about it. They looked like they came off a set of the *Addams Family*. The guy who did all the talking looked like Gomez and his friend could have been Lurch—the guy was huge. There was also something seriously wrong with his face.

"Anyway, they apparently had all the necessary documentation. We went into a VIP lounge where they had our passports stamped and we waited for our truck. When it was ready, we followed them to Koç University."

"We saw your team enter the engineering building. The Frenchman wasn't with them. How'd they know where to go?"

Roberts blinked at the question. "He told us, how do you think? I mean, he pointed straight at the building and handed the team leader a hex key. We're not stupid, you know. We've handled things like this before."

"Yeah, sure. What happened then?"

"Whaddya mean, what happened? You happened."

"No, no...what happened to Gomez Addams?"

"He said he couldn't stay. He had other business in the area and left."

"Did he have a fancy sports car?"

A nod, then, "French, I guess." Roberts bobbed his head toward Rivka's contribution to the body count. "He kept calling it a Bugari or Bulgatti. I don't know, something like that."

"He didn't by chance leave a contact number?"

"Of course. It's taped to the table next to that last keyboard. We were supposed to call him when we finished. He'd contact the airport and let them know we were on our way. We didn't expect to see him again."

With a pang of regret, Carver sliced the tape away and handed Roberts the truck key. "Go back to the university and see if your crew is still there. As far as these two are concerned," Carver pointed at the dead, "if Customs and Immigration didn't hassle you on entry, you should be okay at departure.

"Stuff the bodies in Pelican cases and have your team leader collect and manage the stamping of the passports for everyone.

"Oh, and if for some reason you feel the need to report us," Carver now waved the index finger between himself and Rivka, "either here or in France, just remember you'll have to divulge why you were in Turkey. Your employers won't like that much and you'll probably wind up in the same condition as your friends here."

His final comment—in the form of advice—was the man should ask a few more salient questions before jumping on an airplane for parts unknown.

When he arrived back at the marina the Corsican, along with his men, were gone. Moreau would hear from him in the afternoon with the particulars about the fishing boat. As he pondered the American and Israeli, the notion of backup, however, hovered for an instant.

He wanted to take care of those interlopers before he went after Brody. His problem was time. He needed sleep and food, in that order. When the fast boat was delivered he had to be available to put it in the water and prep the systems. He could depend on his big ugly friend to help with that but the Javelin wasn't something he wanted dropped at the pier without supervision.

A quick scan confirmed the Freightliner was also absent. As he drove away from the marina, Moreau had more than a vague suspicion that finding the pair wouldn't be an issue. If they indeed where the ones who absconded with the truck, then the direction they headed indicated they'd already pieced together a likely narrative.

At that point, the doctor's escape route was an inevitable deduction. Whether or not they concluded he actually made it out to sea was another matter. Moreau was fading and he had to presume the nemetic pair were in the same condition. They needed to sleep, eat, use a toilet—normal human functions—and they'd be at their most vulnerable.

He wondered if the vendor The Board hired to act as a diversion was still in the game. The Board's enlistment of the Serbian gangsters had initially pissed him off—mainly because of the way it had been presented. Moreau now wanted them back on the field. It would be the first subject on his shit-to-discuss list after he got some shuteye.

As he merged on the quiet road leading out of town, still cogitating on the variables in his plan he couldn't control, he spotted the Freightliner. His pulse jumped, and while he wanted to chase the truck down, his affection for the twelve-hundred horses he was sitting on curbed his zeal.

He was content picking up the tail, lying back to avoid immediate detection but close enough to spot any deviation. When the Freightliner made the right toward the university, Moreau accepted what he knew would come next. As he followed the truck up the road, he shot the cuffs on his jacket, one hand at a time, anticipating the confrontation.

What he hadn't anticipated was the disappointment he felt when the truck came to a stop. The driver's door slid open and out stepped a mech in dark gray coveralls moving toward the lab. The Algerian remained seated and pulled the Bugatti forward to cut the man off.

When the window slid down, he propped his elbow on the sill, and asked, "Where have you been?"

The response bordered on hysterical. *"Where have I been? Where the fuck have you been?"* The dude took a breath and calmed a fraction. "I was kidnapped by a maniac claiming to be a Federal Agent and some crazy-ass bitch I think was Israeli."

"Where are the two other men who were with you?"

"Dead!"

"I understand, but where are the bodies?"

"In the back. You know what that fucking psycho told me to do?" Roberts took another breath.

Moreau had no sympathy or patience for this joker's frustration. "Do you want me to guess?"

"What? No...he told me to stuff the bodies in Pelican cases to get them through Customs."

"That's an excellent suggestion. One I also recommend. I believe your team is back in the lab. Can your reestablish communications?"

"Probably."

"Then do it. You have to get out of here."

The pilots were on standby and Moreau had paid extra to have an immigration official waiting for their return.

"Wait! Aren't you staying?"

"No, I have to go. Good luck, Monsieur."

"Where are we going from here?" Rivka asked.

Ruben hesitated for a few seconds as he looked his partner over. She stood with her weight on one foot, the knuckles of one hand planted above her hip. The longish hair was a limp tangle, and with makeup absent, her face looked drawn; her eyes tired. "I don't know about you, but I need somethin' to eat. And things are definitely gonna go sideways if we don't get some sleep ."

Rivka looked toward the village. "Oh, like that hasn't

happened already. Maybe we can find something there."

"It's three o'clock in the morning."

"I saw a sign for a beach resort. The parties go all night in those places." She pulled a soft pack of Camels from a pocket and shook one up, offering it to Ruben. He eased it out with a thumb and forefinger. She freed one with her lips. From a small pocket on his vest he pulled his Marine Corps Zippo and fired them up.

"We could, I guess, but I have to recharge my cell phone and I don't have a charger on me. Adan'll be here soon. We can decide then. Besides, do you want to schlep one of these through town?" Ruben tapped the lid on one of two Pelican cases he'd dragged off the truck.

Rivka had her left arm across her waist. With her right elbow resting against the knuckles, she was lazy-handing the smoke to her mouth with her right index and middle fingers.

"Did it occur to you, if Moreau was coming out of the village, he might have already found your DARPA scientist? He might even have had him in his car."

Ruben sucked the red ember bright. "Yeah, I thought about it but I didn't see a second person. It would've been tough to hide him.

"Anyway, that's why I've got Ryan searching archived intel on The Board. Until a couple of months ago, the NSA was capturing most of their comms traffic. If there were calls traced to Istanbul, chances are we'd be able track the Frenchman that way."

"Maybe."

"Don't you think a guy with a set of wheels like that, would have it loaded with more than extra cup holders and great audio? He'll have traceable comms gear. Even if it's connected to a secure network, it's got to emit a signal. We just needed to know his number, which by the way we now have—Ryan can do the rest.

"Ya know...I'm a little disappointed in the Frog. I

hoped I pissed him off enough to come looking for us. I realize I stashed the truck in a place he'd have to make an effort to find but jeez...nothin'."

Rivka's gaze slid right. "Here's your man.

"Listen, luv. I don't think it's a good idea for you to go back to your hotel. There's a safe house about thirty minutes from here with plenty of room—well stocked, too. I can probably find a charger that'll work for your phone. There'll be a fresh shirt and maybe some clean underwear as well.

"You're gettin' kind of funky, mate."

CHAPTER TWENTY-THREE
September 17, 2005

The clattering chains on metal railings, revving diesel engines and clanking net drums, dragged him from the sleep of the dead. There was no disorientation. With the smell of fuel oil mixed with sea brine and the bobbing motion, he remembered where he was.

What Jerome couldn't remember was the last time he didn't have to will himself to sleep or woke up fully rested. He was alone in the six-man crew quarters, which was no surprise, considering the noise, but another sensation had him dropping his feet to deck. He was hungry.

Dressed in five and on his way to the galley, he detoured at the head. After draining a liter and examining the john for some number two action later on, he continued in his quest. He hoped there'd be someone in the kitchen that would be willing to throw something together.

He checked his watch and calculated his remaining training hours. He felt great. No sea sickness. His only concern was how long he slept. He had to get the basics down of boat driving, night navigation, fuel consumption and how to turn systems on and off.

He'd spent time googling ship tracking and had to

learn what instruments installed on the trawler could wreak havoc with his plan. Deductive reasoning didn't seem to be outside Control's skill set and Jerome assumed by this time, the astute Algerian had identified the vessel he was on.

If Control knew that, then he could acquire the equipment necessary to track the boat. The entire crew would be debilitated in thirty-five hours, dead in forty-eight. Depending on fuel reserves and consumption, he'd try to push the vessel beyond the effective operating range of a helicopter.

Control would have to chase him in a boat. If he caught him, it was unlikely he'd want to board. Jerome had made a point of illustrating, to the man who brought him to Istanbul, the potent nature of the weaponized agent he'd developed. The only other option, and well within Control's ability, would be to scuttle the trawler.

After the doctor satisfied his first priority, he'd start climbing the learning curve.

The safe house was a three-story Ottoman style, wood and brick structure that reminded Carver of a cross between a San Francisco row house and Brooklyn brownstone. A vertical living space, with two bedrooms on the first floor; a kitchen and dining area on the second floor; and a bedroom and a full bath on the third.

They'd reached the place before sunrise. Carver didn't wait for a room assignment. He climbed the stairs, checked each room and, satisfied there was a back way out, stripped and crashed on the bed on the third floor. He decided to worry about his personal hygiene when he got up.

The sun was at apex when his eyes popped open. He could hear the other two shuffling around and could smell something being fixed on the four burner, a floor below.

He had a mild headache centered behind his forehead and would've sworn he'd been gargling gravel. He figured his breath would gag the lady of the house and decided to do something about that as soon as he drained the lizard.

The bathroom was across the tiny hall. The door sat open enough to make him think it was unoccupied. He didn't bother pulling on his trousers to traverse twenty-four inches. As he slid through the door, Rivka was sitting on the toilet. An extra-large white T-shirt drooped over her frame and her hair was wet, exploding in ringlets on her shoulders.

His face felt hot and he tried to avert any further embarrassment by stepping out. "Sorry. I thought it was free."

"Oh, don't be an idiot. You can come in. I'm finished."

He stared at the floor as she stood and pulled up her panties. He didn't want to be too weird about the situation, but when he looked up he could see her hard nipples tenting the thin fabric and her breasts swayed as she moved. Her bare legs were smooth, olive, and muscled; the toenails painted blood red.

She pulled on the mirror above the sink, revealing a medicine cabinet.

"Here's a toothbrush you can use. The paste is with it. If you want to shave you can find what you need in this drawer." She pulled a knob on the cabinet below the sink. "There's body wash and shampoo in the shower. I'll throw some underwear and a clean shirt, I think will fit you, on your bed."

"Is Adan here?"

"He's been up for a few hours. He had a chinwag with Henry he'll tell you about, and he's been chatting online with that bloke in DC...Ryan. How are you doing?"

"I'm hungry, I have a slight headache and my shoulder's sore." Ruben rolled his delt forward and back, touching his trapezoid where a pink scar from a bullet wound was on display. "I could use some aspirin."

She pulled the mirror again, took a bottle of Bayer off the shelf and handed it over. "Did you get that in Iraq?"

He shook his head. "China—a few months ago."

"Whoever fixed you up did a good job." She reached up and poked the pink with an index finger. "By the way, you have sleep apnea and you snore loud enough to wake the neighbors. You ever try to do something about that?"

Ruben peeped her way and considered a less than snide retort. "I live alone—for a lot of different reasons."

"Uh-huh. You know, pet...I'll bet you're not half bad looking, on a good day. You even seem reasonably fit. There's the shower," she pointed behind him, "let's see how well you clean up."

She spun on the ball of a bare foot and headed to the door. The way she moved reminded him of another woman—a hairless six-foot-something, in Shanghai. A stunner who wanted his balls for hors d'oeuvres.

That woman had some serious issues. He couldn't help but wonder, however, what it would have been like to spend some quality time with the broad—aside from getting the crap kicked out him and nearly barbecued. After meeting Rivka he decided he needed to be more careful what he wished for.

The water pressure was better than the hotel's and with the fogless mirror suctioned to the tiled wall, he took advantage of the razor. A shit, shower and shave: the daily jumpstart. After a cup of coffee and whatever was still in the pan, he'd definitely be ready to slay the dragon.

Rivka had tossed some tighty-whities on the bed along

with a brown canvas work shirt. There was also a pair of boot socks in his size.

The wooden stairs announced his arrival in the kitchen. Adan was sitting at a round, four-chair maple table, pounding on a small laptop. An empty plate with crusting egg yolk was next to him, as was a ceramic mug. He acknowledged Ruben with a head bob.

Rivka was on her feet, leaning against a kitchen counter. Her hair was in the tight, short ponytail, and she'd dressed down for the day. She wore an olive drab T-shirt under an unbuttoned and untucked canvas work shirt, similar to the one she'd loaned to Carver. He could see the outline of the body armor she'd worn the day before.

Her trousers were beige tactical pants, cinched with a thick leather belt, that had a Sam Brown buckle. A pair of canvas Scout Commandos hid her feet.

The Jericho was field-stripped, on an open newspaper and Ruben caught a whiff of cleaning solvent. He'd slipped into his own shoulder holster before he came down for breakfast and noticed an unopened box of ammo at the end of the counter.

"That's IMI .45 acp, jacketed hollowpoint. It's a little hot—about like a +P," Rivka offered.

"Sweet. This is definitely better than a tie for Christmas." Ruben tugged at a velcroed pocket flap on the vest he had slung over his shoulder. He jammed his hand in the pleated pocket and retrieved an empty magazine he set next to the box of ammo.

"There are eggs in the refrigerator, and some turkey bacon and pancakes in the oven, thanks to Adan. There's also coffee in the pot."

"Excellent." He pointed at the paper. "Is that today's?"

"Yes, but it's not the English language version."

"I was wondering if The Board's biohazard crew

made it out last night. If they got busted, it may not have made the news yet."

"Don't know. It would be easy enough to find out."

Adan piped up. "I agree. It'd take a two minute phone call."

"I felt bad about leavin' poor ol' Mr. Roberts in that fix last night. He didn't know he was playin' for the wrong team. Shit happens, though, and we can't have the Turkish authorities nosin' around, yet."

As he pulled a carton of eggs out of the fridge, he asked, "Hey, Adan, what did Henry have to say?"

"He said Art doesn't want us ruining some Board member's day, with an unscheduled visit."

"I'm not surprised. I wonder why Henry decided to bring that up?"

"Who knows...I guess because we work for the guy? Anyway, we have what we need to keep tabs on Yves Moreau.

"Turns out the Bugatti has a factory installed locator. Kinda like a LoJack, but with a GPS transceiver."

Carver poured a couple of tablespoons of olive oil in a hot pan and broke three eggs into it. "Wouldn't Moreau know about that?"

"Probably, but from what Ryan could tell he never used it. With the photos I took, the NSA identified the specific Veyron Moreau drove off the factory floor.

"When Ryan switched the unit on, he initially got a signal. Apparently, however, the Frog installed some type of RF jammer that went active as soon as he started the car. The Veyron disappeared."

"So what's the answer? We can't track him?"

"No, Ryan figured it musta been a fairly narrow directional, otherwise he wouldn't be able to use his cell phone. He changed the GPS transmitter frequency. We've a got signal—it's weak but it's there. He sent me a dandy little tracking app I loaded on this laptop. He also provided the software I needed to turn my BlackBerry into a 3G modem. I can run everything off the car battery."

Carver scraped the scrambled onto a plate. "Cool. I guess we didn't need the phone number after all."

"No, it's good we have it. The Bugatti doesn't have a phone. It has a Bluetooth setup. He uses the car's satellite antenna and audio system to make calls from his cellphone. We can also track him when he's not in the car as long as he's in range of a cell tower."

Ruben looked at his watch. It was almost one pm. "Any idea where he is now?"

"As a matter of fact...he's on his cellphone at a restaurant called Van Kahvaltı Evi—about a five minute walk from here, if the Google map is accurate."

A tablespoon of strawberry jam went on a pancake Carver laid next to the eggs. "It's one o'clock in the afternoon on Saturday. He's sippin' a demitasse, gabbing on his mobile. Anything wrong with that picture?"

Rivka joined the conversation, as she slipped the barrel into the slide assembly, along with the recoil rod and spring. "The bloke got a late start to the day, just like us. Let's find out who he's talking to. Even if Brody did make a getaway, Moreau could be our best bet in locating your itinerant scientist."

Adan began tapping on his laptop. "I'll have Ryan create a call log from the phone the guy is using. By the way, I contacted the husbanding agent the U.S. Navy's been using for its ship visits in Turkey. He and I are… kinda related, and I think I already mentioned the guy's well connected."

Carver nodded but said nothing.

"I told him we were looking for an American that went missing: a professor at Koç University. I also said I believed he may have hitched a ride on a boat leaving Rumeli Feneri last night. He told me if the guy did leave from the marina, he'd have the information for me this afternoon."

The Van Kahvaltı Evi was an open-front cafe on Defterdar Ykş in Istanbul's Chihangri. One of a half-dozen Kahvalti Evi in the area, it had a reputation with locals for its better lunch menu.

Its appearance was unremarkable, even questionable, with a dingy whitewashed interior and oak plank floor. Bolted to a wall facing the street was its only distinguishing feature: a five-foot by three-foot Greek orthodox icon carved out of cedar.

Eight or nine thin butcher block tables lined the inside. Another half dozen pedestal tables were parked on the cobblestone sidewalk. Moreau, overdressed as usual, lounged in a wood-slatted chair next to the curb, enjoying a surprisingly exceptional coffee.

He'd been on the phone with the Corsican bruiser, who'd delivered as promised. They had the trawler's Turkey Straits VTS profile, and as a bonus the boat's AIS transceiver was active. As a final touch, the trawler was contacted by radio. The Corsican, spoofing Koç University administration, confirmed the professor had made it aboard without issue.

A sensation began to creep over Moreau that he'd been missing since the doctor's love troll had been butchered. He was at ease. In his mind it was over. The next thirty hours were nothing more than a technicality. While he'd also been assured by The Board that morning Carver and Levitan would not be an obstacle, he couldn't ignore the irony.

The instant he'd laid eyes on the two the evening before, their intention was manifest. It was essentially what his had become: ending the doctor along with his project. Despite The Board's continued desire to acquire the research, Moreau's plan had been green-lighted. He couldn't feature wasting anymore time, money or resources on Carver.

As he drained the cup to the mud, he allowed the thought to drop away. In a few minutes Carver would no longer be anyone's problem.

CHAPTER TWENTY-FOUR

Another Day at the Office

The buzzing of Carver's BlackBerry, still connected to a charger next to the bed he'd slept in, could be heard in the bathroom. He and Rivka were sharing the sink, brushing their teeth. Adan had packed his gear and was standing in the bay window, working on his third cup of coffee and checking out the brick-paved road below.

The street had a steep, thirty degree gradient without any signs of terracing. The bright orange exterior of the safe house would have been conspicuous, if it wasn't for the electric blue house on one side and emerald green on the other.

From his position in the window, Adan could glimpse the surrounding tenements. They were all ablaze in the same kindergarten palette.

Rivka eyeballed Ruben, and with her mouth full of foam and brush, asked, "'Ou 'onna 'et 'at?"

He spit in the sink, bent down and with his hand cupped under the spigot, rinsed his mouth.

"Don' 'ink ih'," she mommied.

He wiped his mouth on a towel, as he took another look at the charmer beside him, then strode out to fetch his phone. The number had been withheld. The call hadn't gone to voice mail yet and waving it another second between thumb and index finger, he pushed the green button. "Carver."

"Ruben Carver, I was told by a mutual acquaintance you wanted to talk to me."

"Sonny Xú, you always did like to take the initiative. So, tell me, how long have you been operatin' in the Near East? The competition's got to be tough—what with the Corsicans and Italians and Albanians. Those characters have been in your line of work for a couple millennia."

Ruben expected the Chinaman's stoic reaction. "You understand, the *arrangement* we've had is exclusive to the Far East. When the contract came available, I couldn't resist. As usual, however, you've—how do you Americans say it—upset the apple bin?"

"Yeah, no...that's cart, but..."

"Anyway, it hasn't been easy trying to run a business in a region with so many divergent interests and agendas. You know what I mean?"

Aside from the Chinese accent, the cadence in Sonny's voice as he got his rant on made Ruben wonder if he'd acquired his command of the English language in the Bronx.

"You think the Chinese are bad about paying their bills? I always have to get the money upfront with those Eastern European *huàidàn*. And don't get me started about those fucking *fēngzi* ragheads...they're the worst!"

"Sonny..."

"Okay, so you're not interested in the P and L. Just be aware, after some discussion with Art Sheppard—he can be pretty pushy as you know—I've backed out of the contract for your head. At least for the time being."

"I'm pleased to hear it. It'll save me the trouble of knockin' on your door."

"Yes, well, don't start popping any champagne corks. Apparently, what you did to the team I sent your way, has gotten back to some of their relatives.

"I have to tell you, Carver, I thought the extended families in China were enormous. My ethnic group, as proud and an ancient as it may be, has nothing on those Serbs. And can they hold a grudge—*gàn!*" Sonny chuckled. "With me it's always been about business, and you are invariably bad for business. No offense intended."

"Uh-huh."

"With them, though, it's vendetta time. They want you and that Israeli woman, bad."

"How'd they find out? All that shit went down yesterday. Even you couldn't know that fast."

"What can I tell you, *lǎowài*? It's not about ideology anymore, and The Board can satisfy just about anybody's sweet tooth. Government agencies always talk shit about tossing the green around. I've heard that *shuǎzuǐpí* first hand. In the end, though there's always some quibbling, pencil neck *wángbādàn*, clutching the purse strings."

"What are you saying?"

"Aren't you listening? You've been *sold out*. You've got Serb gangsters coming your way."

"When?"

"They're not there yet?"

"Did somebody order a pizza?"

After the first two steps, Carver leaped the rest of the staircase to the second floor. He ran to the bay window next to Adan, whose finger was already extended toward the street.

"That look familiar?"

A black Mercedes Sprinter had stopped in the middle of the road. "Whaddya think they do in those vans, in their off time?" Ruben turned to yell for Rivka and found her already at his shoulder.

She carried a pair of CTAR-21 assault rifles with

quick-detach suppressors mounted. "You two ever use a bullpup?"

"The Chinese version gave me the hole you were playin' with this morning."

"Then you know what it can do." She handed them to the men, while gazing down at the van. "The doors on this house are steel, with inch-and-a-quarter bolt locking systems; the windows are three-quarter-inch ballistic glass, and the walls have been insulted with eight inches of ballistic foam. Unless those tossers are coming super heavy, you can keep your peckers up. We've got some time until they figure out what they want to do."

She pointed at the bullpups and continued. "The sight is an M21 red-dot reflex." She moved closer to Ruben and pulled the boxy shooter from him. "Here's the magazine release. You'll note it fires the NATO round and the thirty-round magazine looks suspiciously similar to that of the M16. That's because it is, essentially. They're interchangeable.

"Here's the charging handle. The bolt locks back after the last round. To chamber a round, put in a fresh magazine, and punch the bolt release switch—here. This is the fire selector nob. Only two modes: semi and full."

She pulled the suppressor off and then reattached it. "No threads. It locks tight and after that first round pop, it's as quiet as the grave." She handed it back to Carver. "And Bob's your uncle. Any questions?"

"Where's yours?" Ruben asked.

"I'll stay with my pistol until we're in the car. Then I'll use the one Adan has."

Adan held the rifle out. "Take it now. I prefer the shotgun and I've got a couple boxes of double-ought in my pockets."

She accepted the weapon, absently thumbing the safety. A habit ingrained after hundreds of hours on the range. "They're not getting in here with the kind of weapons their friends were carrying yesterday."

As she spoke, Carver and Adan looked up from the window at each other. Ruben then glanced at the Hebrew hammer and asked, "Would a shaped charge do the trick?"

Her eyebrows raised. "Well, chaps...I believe it's time to go. I'll check the back to see if it's covered."

Carver's smile was grim. "I guess that's a yes." He then asked Adan, "Where's your shotgun?"

"On the floor under the table, ready to go." In four steps he had it on his hip. "I saw six, plus the driver. You?"

"That's my count, too.

"*Rivka*——how does the back look?" Carver could hear her voice coming up from the first floor.

"It seems clear to the car. We can go now but I'd rather not have them get their hands on some of the stuff we have in here." She then appeared at the landing, a thirty round magazine packed with 5.56mm in hand. "Here's an extra," and lobbed it at Ruben.

She ran the steps to the third floor two at a time. "I need a few minutes."

Adan asked the obvious. "Do we have a few minutes?"

"You two go to the hatch on the second floor."

Adan zeroed on Carver. "Oh, man...you don't think she's puttin' on her face, do ya?"

"I heard that! Get going!"

The hatch was exactly that. It was two feet square, hinged on the left. The release lever was similar to those found on a naval vessel. A rope ladder was bolted to the floor.

"*Rivka! We're waiting!*"

Thirty seconds later, Carver felt her tap on his shoulder. He pushed the lever and pulled the hatch; Adan threw the ladder. The explosion they heard didn't come from the front door. The assault team was smart. They left the door alone and blew the window next to it.

"Come on, let's go. I've got the incendiaries on a fifteen-second delay once the lasers are tripped."

Ruben moved aside, shouting, "You first...then Adan."

The shaped charge must have tripped a laser. Carver had a leg, arm and his head out of the hatch when the blast from the incendiary lit the gas lines. The big guy may have been the last one out, but he was the first one on the ground.

If it wasn't for the branches of a *quercus frainetto*, aka Hungarian oak, he would have needed a stretcher. He was flat on his back, struggling to catch a breath when Rivka's upside down face appeared.

"Are you hurt?" Her voice was muffled but he could make out the words.

"Incendiaries? *Mrs. O' Leary's fucking cow, Rivka!*" The shouting helped him get some air in his lungs.

"I don't know who that is, mate. Can you move?"

"I think so, gimme a hand."

"Where's the rifle?"

Ruben moved his head left and peered up. He saw it swinging from its sling on a branch. "There it is."

"For Christ's sake, Carver. Would you quit messing around."

"Oh, yeah, that's easy for you to say, I was raised Baptist." He forgot about her help, as he rolled onto his stomach and pushed himself up on his hands and knees. "Where's Adan?"

"He's in the car. Let's go."

On his feet, the rifle was just out of his reach. "Come 'ere, doll." He intertwined his fingers to make a stirrup. With an exasperated expression only a woman in a hurry could make, she stomped back to him. She set her foot in his hands and lifting with his legs, hips and back, he executed a close-hold power clean.

She assisted with a leg press that gave her additional lift. She'd gripped the weapon with both hand, her feet swinging three-feet off the ground. Ruben hugged her at the waist and pulled. The branch bent and they were showered in leaves and twigs the sling peeled away.

When the branch snapped, Ruben was flat on his back again, with Rivka straddling him. She shoved the rifle in his chest, using the motion to stand. "Would you *please* stop fucking around."

Ruben rolled to a sprint, trying to keep up with the no-shit femme royale. She yanked open the door behind Adan and dove in. A cool move in Carver's book, if it wasn't for the CTAR-21 slung on her back. The butt of the rifle smacked the top of the door frame and she spasmed to a stop in midair.

When she came down, her knees smashed on the hardpack, her ass waved in the breeze and her face bounced on the firm seat cushion. Carver wouldn't have been surprised if she'd lost a few front teeth. All in all, though, he thought it might be a good position to try later, if she was game.

As Ruben reached for the handle on the front passenger side, she was already pumping her legs to get in next to a Pelican case. At that instant the black Mercedes skidded into view, with dust flying from locked brakes.

Almost forty years of muscle memory kicked in. The rifle came up, he flicked the fire selector two notches, and he stitched ten rounds through the van wall and sliding door. He was careful not to shoot the driver, who did what any decent wheelman would do—he punched it.

Adan didn't wait for an invitation. Before Carver's door closed, the clutch came up—the accelerator floored. Carver sunk his fingers into the seat back, his right hand pressed against the roof. The door slammed on its own, with a power shift into second.

They skidded through a left hand turn. When Adan yanked the wheels straight, jamming into third, Rivka was on her knees shooting through the rear window. Four three-round bursts aimed at the back panel of the van as they pulled away.

"*This is a rental!*" Screamed Adan.

He down shifted hard to make a right turn on the first street with pavement. Amidst the sound of screeching tires, horns blaring and the smack of metal on metal, Adan gunned away from approaching sirens.

Ten minutes later, when they were sure they hadn't been followed, Adan turned down a side street and parked under the shade of an oak.

Both hands twisting on the steering wheel, Adan spoke first. "Okay...what are we doin'?"

"We lost your laptop?"

"Yep, and my BlackBerry."

Carver's lips disappeared as they went tight under a stubble mustache. "Before we figure out how we're gonna track the Frog, we need to talk about what just happened. Rivka...according to Sonny, you've got someone in your dugout telegraphing our signals to the other team."

"My side? Didn't Arthur bring you into this operation because he couldn't trust his own agency?"

"Yes, he did, but Art didn't know about the safe house."

Rivka scrunched down as if to physically avoid the direction the conversation had gone. "After Medleva was killed, I have, in point of fact, been trying to identify the leak."

"Who'd you contact about where we were staying?"

"A Shin Bet officer who's in charge of consulate security. He functions much like your Regional Security Officer. I'm sure he pushed it up to the Institute."

"Where?"

"The Institute for Intelligence and Special Operations—you know it as Mossad. If they were notified then there's no telling who else was aware of us using the place. The Mossad isn't happy with me anyway."

Carver could relate. "I bet they don't like you steppin' on their toes, with a cross border operation."

"That's right, but after years with Yamas, I've been given a certain amount of leeway. As long as I can show a direct link to state security, or a threat to Israeli personnel, assets and facilities, I can go after whoever I want, wherever I want. That is, of course, within certain parameters."

"You be sure to let me know when we're about to color outside those lines. What are your reporting requirements? NCIS has to be fed regularly and on time or it gets hypoglycemic—fuckin' anxiety attacks."

"Tachycardia." Adan piped in.

Ruben grunted, "Headquarters folks get downright hostile over late paper."

Rivka sighed. "I have people I'm required to report to and after what just happened, they're going to want an immediate after action report and my status. They'll likely order me in for a debrief and you can lay money on a major dressing down.

"Turkey authorities are certainly going to be brassed off. The Ambassador will get stitched up and there'll be a call for some official apology from Sharon."

Ruben looked at Adan for some kind of reaction, then said, "Ordinarily I'm the one havin' to weather this kinda shitstorm. It's definitely fubar. Do you want us to drop you at the consulate?"

The reaction was trenchant. "Don't be daft. The only way I'm—we're—getting out of this fix is to find your scientist. I have to leg it, and you're going to help me.

Now...as far as I can tell, at this point, your Henry is the only one we can trust."

Carver saw Adan's nod and they were all in agreement. He pulled his BlackBerry from an inside pocket. "I'm callin' him now. We have to get another laptop."

Adan added, "And another BlackBerry, charging cables, and maybe a sidearm. I like the street howitzer but it's kinda conspicuous. Oh, and one more thing..." Adan caught Rivka's eye in the rearview mirror. "We need a new rear window. I can't return this thing, with the window like that."

CHAPTER TWENTY-FIVE

Gestation

Jerome had spent the day in the wheelhouse. To his relief there was very little conversation. The captain was busy on the stern, with occasional visits to the bridge. Jerome learned almost everything he needed to know by watching. Anything he couldn't discern intuitively, he jotted down in a small notebook, to ask the captain when he made his rounds.

There was another aspect to this adventure he hadn't considered. He found he enjoyed deepwater navigation. He hadn't learned how to swim. It was an activity which never entered his consciousness. When a person's work demands an ethical approach to killing people, there's time for little else.

He understood the concept of buoyancy. While hydrodynamics weren't his specialty, the mechanics behind closed-conduit and open-channel flow systems, and the calculation of forces on submerged bodies was never a mystery. *It's water—what's the big deal.*

There was, however, something he found thrilling about being out of sight of land. Although foul weather would lend itself to his decision, Jerome discovered where he wanted to spend his remaining years.

As he pondered this catharsis, he had in no way lost

his original resolve. If anything he was more intent on culling the world of troublemakers and evildoers. To that end, Islamists made the hit list, with a bullet.

He didn't have a shift in his thinking. The destruction of the Zionist gangsters hadn't been abandoned. His ambiguous rage over the loss and revelation of the only woman he'd ever have a chance to embrace, set off a series of introspective forays. The result of which was an epiphany.

When he left his life in the U.S., he didn't see it as a betrayal. For him, it was a reckoning. He'd begun an exhaustive study of the Qu'ran to better understand the struggle he was down for. Medleva's death, however, forced him to come to grips with the truth: he wasn't a Muslim, and never would be.

No matter how sympathetic he'd become to the plight of a downtrodden people, it meant nothing to those he'd committed himself to. He was a non-believer, unwilling to submit to Sharia and therefore unworthy to continue breathing. Simple.

As a scientist, he hadn't resolved internally the God issue. He was convinced, however, the solution to the riddle could be managed in a manner most acceptable to both the Jews and Muslims. To make it ultimately fair, it involved all of humanity. Jerome was going to let God sort it out.

When the captain came into the messdeck at eight pm, his sweaty pallor signaled an early onset. Jerome had considered the possibility that outside the lab, the gestation period for a toxin release would be different.

In a controlled environment he could almost set his watch by the process. With a one-percent margin of error, it entailed fifty-six hours from infection, to symptoms being exhibited, to full incapacitation leading to death. The captain was ahead of schedule by more than twenty-four hours.

"Captain, you don't look well. How do you feel?"

"I feel like shit. Almost like I got hold of a bad oyster. I've been in the head for the last thirty minutes." The explanation caused an eruption of coughing.

"Anybody else sick?" Jerome had been writing in his journal for almost an hour and now noticed only two other crew members seated. He couldn't smell anything coming from the galley.

"It hit most of us at about the same time. We damn near didn't get the nets in before a couple men were dropping trou over the side.

"You're a doctor. Maybe you could look at the crew and tell me what hit us."

"I'm not that kind of doctor, but I'll see what I can do. Who isn't sick?"

"Those two over there, I think." It took some effort for the captain to raise his voice, as he said something in Turkish to the two men. After their reply he turned back to Jerome. "The man on the left is Furkan. The other one is Yusuf. You spent the afternoon with Furkan at the helm."

"Yes, that's right. I enjoyed his company."

The comment would have produced a quizzical smile, had the captain felt better. "That's only because he can't speak a word of English."

"Exactly." Jerome was aware the captain was being droll, but the lack of verbal communication with the man called Furkan made the hours spent on the bridge pleasantly productive. "So what did they say?"

The captain's mouth came down at the ends, as he shrugged his shoulders. "It seems they're okay."

Jerome checked his watch and studied them for any signs of the toxin at work. Assumptions began to emerge, centered on environment and physical activity. He stood and said, "Sit down, Captain. I want to go get a few things I brought with me. I'll use them to check you out.

229

It'll just take a second."

He could barely contain his excitement. The possibilities of its effectiveness on a grand scale had him humming *Just a Spoonful of Sugar*. A little ditty that always made him tap a toe.

As he grabbed his blood pressure cuff, stethoscope, ophthalmoscope, otoscope and a reflex hammer, he considered for the first time what he was going to do with the bodies, as they began to drop. It made him giggle when he decided to put them on ice. The fish hold contained a few tons of the stuff.

The doctor couldn't stop cracking himself up, as a number other pithy metaphors began to bubble up. It was days like this that made Doctor James Bennet, under his nom de guerre, Jerome Brody, happy to be alive.

By ten pm the yacht was delivered to the marina at Rumeli Feneri. A forty-seven-foot Rio cruiser, with twin 500 horsepower Cummins diesel engines, it had been modified to carry twenty-five hundred liters of fuel, giving it a range of about seven hundred nautical miles at a steady thirty knots. It wasn't a cigarette boat, neither would it raise any eyebrows.

The delivery issues surrounding the shoulder-fired missile continued to crop up during the day. It couldn't be acquired locally. The dealer with whom The Board had placed the order, happened to be someone Moreau had had previous business dealings.

The last time the Algerian met the man, a misunderstanding occurred over product quantity and price. After the discussion ended, the dealer had to have a few feet of intestine removed. Apparently, the perforations and the accompanying sepsis didn't agree with him.

It was wishful thinking the man wouldn't remember Moreau. The Board had wire-transferred the money request, without negotiation. While that should have assuaged any hard feelings, the Algerian didn't believe the dealer would be that forgiving. A missile detonating in the tube would be the type of elegant tit-for-tat Moreau could expect. A close examination of the hardware would be in order before it went aboard.

The solution to getting the Javelin in country eventually came down to which skid to grease. Intel from The Board indicated the manager of the Airport Authority, at a domestic airstrip twenty-kilometers northwest of Istanbul, had a gambling problem.

Moreau made arrangements for Big Ugly to acquire the deadbeat's markers. The Corsican didn't waste much time explaining the new arrangement. He was cheerfully kissing the manager's cheeks over their mutual understanding, several minutes before the hemorrhaging from the man's nose finally abated.

Even with light traffic, the missiles and launcher wouldn't arrive at the marina until four or five o'clock in the morning. A big positive to his current situation was the non-appearance of Ruben Carver. The sound of the explosions coming from the Israeli safe house that afternoon, could be heard at the cafe.

The subsequent sirens from the fire engines and police wagons suggested the American and his Juif, if not dead, were up to their eyeballs in crocodiles. Moreau added to the fix with a few of his own phone calls to the General Directorate of Security and the Gendarmerie General Command. BOLO alerts were soon issued all over the country.

With the local media broadcasting their images, they'd have difficulty staying on the street, or for that matter, finding a place to go to ground. The consulates and embassies were out of the question. Since he hadn't heard of their capture, he mused on the odds that their bodies were among those found in the burned-out shell.

231

Moreau remained in the Bugatti, while the crew who delivered the motor yacht took their time putting it in the water. He had enough experience from his smuggling days to operate the vessel at sea; however, the tracking equipment that came installed would require instruction.

There was plenty of time. He was ahead of schedule, despite another six to eight hours before the missile delivery. Once again dropping Carver from serious consideration, his thoughts wandered to Doctor Brody.

Moreau had given The Board a twenty-four-hour window. The amount of time he'd spent with the evil genius clued him into a few things about how his head worked. Brody wasn't on a joyride. He had no plans of returning to the marina—of that Moreau was certain.

On the other hand, if he viewed the boat as his transport into destiny, as the Algerian suspected, the crew was irrelevant. They were an opportunity to test his weapon outside the lab.

The doctor may have been a social misfit, but he wasn't autistic. While it may have been a painful exercise, he was capable of masking normalcy long enough to ensure the crew's complacency.

Moreau's confidence in Brody's ability to learn what he needed to operate the trawler, set the window he'd dictated to The Board. The agent in the bioweapon needed forty-eight hours to gestate in its host—eight hours for the toxin to kill.

Moreau had to catch the trawler before the doctor had control of the vessel and disappeared at sea.

Henry Dever wasn't happy. He couldn't believe how fast things had gone sideways. Art's encouragement to "keep the pressure on", and "we've got the President's confidence our people have things in hand", didn't square up with the facts on the ground.

Rivka was wanted by her own people over the cockup

at the safe house, and Carver's and Adan's names and images had made the news as persons of interest. They were on the defensive and on the run.

Then there was the matter of where he could meet the trio. Hotels were out of the question. They couldn't talk business in a restaurant. Henry agreed with Ruben the diplomatic establishments were being watched. Since the mission was still on, they couldn't beat it out of town.

But that wasn't the worst of it. To Henry's consternation, Adan drove the two folks he was on the lam with to the Istanbul office of the U.S. Navy's husbanding agent in Turkey. The only fella Adan said he could trust, with enough juice to help them out of their jam.

It was well known within NCIS that Henry's assignment to the CIA in Mexico City was the result of a Carver operation in Malaysia, nine months prior. That undertaking involved the investigation of a corrupt husbanding agent—a redundant expression in the minds of most—who met an untimely end.

Husbanding services tended to be universally viewed as an indispensable enterprise. The agent's support was critical to ship readiness when navigating government regulations on pilotage, towage, and customs entry and clearance. They handled berthing, medical support, ship's stores, and use of repair facilities, along with assisting in crew changes.

A decent husbanding agent had the ability to make a ship visit a seamless and trouble-free lark for command and crew. To ensure the experience, the Navy had shown for years its willingness to shell out the big bucks, without complaint. Like a masochist begging for another one.

Graft, bribery and other forms of corruption were normal in the course of conducting business. As far as Henry was concerned, trust and husbanding agent were mutually exclusive terms. A sentiment shared by NCIS headquarters and an issue plaguing Adan for the last several months.

When the facts in Carver's Malaysia investigation came to light, anyone with a close relationship to those providing ship support and husbanding services became suspect. What made Adan's circumstance even more tenuous had to do with a familial connection. The owner and CEO of the maritime corporation providing husbanding services was his wife's cousin.

One of the richest men in Turkey, he was an industrialist on a first name basis with the Prime Minister and the military's Chief of the General Staff. Henry might have featured some help from the guy, if wasn't for the added reputation of having godfather status with organized crime groups in Turkey and throughout the Balkans.

The taxi dropped him in front of a four hundred and fifty-foot glass and polished steel work of art, that housed forty-two stories of office space. It was after hours, and the guard who let him in handed over a visitor badge that allowed him through the security gates. Henry had a briefcase the guard only glanced at, as he waved him on. A second swipe of the card in an elevator transported him straight to the penthouse.

The doors swept open to a twenty-meter square bay room. In the center was a conference table, laden with a buffet of what he'd soon find out was lamb shish kebab, a dish called mantı that reminded him of ravioli, cheesy börek, dolma, a range of meze and baklava. There was a tub of bottled beer on ice and two unopened bottles of wine.

Henry's first instinct was to crack wise, but seeing a scuffed-up Ruben engaged in a conversation with a pretty boy, who was obviously the host, caused him to hold his tongue. If nothing else, Dever was imbued with a keen sense of decorum.

He'd caught Adan's eye three feet into the room. As the country referent walked over to greet him and prepare for introductions, Henry scanned the space. Besides the food, there was a white board on a tripod. A poster-sized photo, attached to it, displayed an aerial view of a docking facility or marina.

Next to the wall on his left were two opened Pelican cases, Rivka seemed to be inventorying. On the floor propped against one of the cases, muzzles up, were a pair of bullpups. Several boxes of ammunition, magazines and what he assumed were flash bangs, sat on a two-shelf trolley a few feet from the assault rifles.

As Adan stuck his hand out to greet the boss, Henry glimpsed the remnants of a pastry lining his lips. He accepted the hand, grateful it was still connected to the Special Agent's arm, and asked, "What's all this going to cost us?"

Quid pro quo could be a bitch with a guy who liked to dance with the devil.

CHAPTER TWENTY-SIX

Husbanding

While the introduction between Henry and Ishmael Demir had a cordial air, Ruben sensed a chilly composure in his good friend. From the vocal restraint, stiff posture and refusal to make eye contact, Carver could tell Dever had a major case of the ass.

He had to pull Henry into the discussion post-haste. Whatever the man had crawling up his butt would make its way into the conversation, and they could all deal with it together.

Ruben nodded at him, doing the best imitation of casual he could muster. "Hey, Hank, you made it."

"Did I have a choice?"

"Well, actually...no. You need to have your hand in what we're planning."

Henry's expression was slack as he grab the back of a chair and pulled it from under the conference table. When he guided his backside into the cushion, it signaled an ease in his acerbic comportment. "This is a nice spread."

Demir's laugh didn't suggest mirth. "Help yourself. I was careful not to order anything that would offend a culinary restriction."

Henry leaned forward, with his feet under his chair;

the tips of his shoes touching the floor. He braced himself with his elbows and forearms on the tabletop, one hand over the other at the edge. Ruben watched him survey the dishes, as Adan named each.

Finished, Henry's irises rotated up, followed by his head. The rest of him stayed motionless. "It all looks good, but I'm not really hungry. What are we doing here?"

Rivka, now at the table next to Adan, pointed a finger at Ruben from a hand resting on the chair back next to her. He bobbed his head, but before he began raised his hand palm up, and using the swivel on the ergonomic mesh where he was planted, directed Henry's attention to the proprietor.

At five-nine and weighing in at a pinch over a buck-fifty, the forty-seven-year-old CEO could have made it to the top on his looks alone. A deep olive complexion, his skin was tight along a jawline that ended at a square, dimpled chin.

He had the shadow of a beard. The proud expression of his manhood; however, Ruben got the distinct impression this dude wouldn't sprout anything more. He wouldn't want to mar the countenance.

The ultra-white capped teeth dressed up a pair of ordinary lips. The nose also had some work done to it—designed to avoid any distraction from Demir's eyes: pale Persians with long, thick lashes shaded by heavy, but shaped eyebrows.

His black hair, with flecks of gray, was combed straight back and long enough to touch the white collar of a starched, blue cotton Brioni. The top two buttons were open at the neck and its tail tucked into a pair of lightweight, tan gabardine slacks—the cuffs buckled with perfection over handmade, blue velvet loafers.

"Mr. Demir, here, is aware of our current dilemma and has been gracious enough to let us in anyway."

Dever cleared his throat. "How aware?"

"We've told him everything, Hank. Seems only fitting since we're asking for his help."

The face Dever made, when the words out of Carver's mouth registered, would have fit someone who discovered he'd had his pocket picked. Before he had a chance to howl, Demir spoke up.

"From what I understand of the situation, Mr. Dever, and please correct me if I'm wrong, the United States has known about the location of your so-called missing scientist for several months. The fact that you've kept this information from Turkey's Prime Minister would, under any circumstances, be viewed as remiss." Demir's pregnant pause was met with silence. He continued after a few seconds.

"My cousin's husband," he bowed his head in Adan's direction, "was smart to come here. I've already contacted my friends in the Ministry of National Defence. They've decided to give your Special Agent Carver, and team," Demir waved a hand at Rivka and Adan, "one chance to take the scientist into custody.

"After that it becomes an international incident the government of Turkey will assume control over. Be assured, should your team fail, Turkey will make political hay out of this in way that would be most embarrassing to your country." There was another hitch in the monologue.

"What we indicated, which may or may not be true, but is nonetheless important, is the trawler he's riding is currently outside our territorial limit. We've also elected not to disclose the weapon payload he may be carrying. It would create a panic and all bets—as they say—would be off. A military option would most likely come into play."

Henry's reaction was muted. Carver had hamstrung his friend and he was under no delusion their relationship would not suffer. In the interest of time and logistics, Ruben went a direction contrary to what he believed would be NCIS dictum. The saving grace being this was a CIA-financed operation, using NCIS assets.

Ruben had no idea what the protocol would be for engaging the husbanding agent. It hadn't been discussed. The time-worn adage that the correct solution is not necessarily the acceptable one, was followed almost immediately with the equally aged cliché: better to beg for forgiveness than ask for permission.

His home-boy would deal with it; he always did. Whether or not Ruben would have a job to return to was another matter.

"What's the plan?" Henry asked in a measured tone.

Confident the worst of the awkward moment had passed, Carver stood and went to the white-board. "Mr. Demir was able to quickly locate the last known position of the trawler." He rolled a map down over the aerial photo, which showed the Turkey coastline along the Black Sea. He then touched a circled spot about hundred and fifty nautical miles northeast of the mouth of the Bosphorus.

"One of his guys had a brief ship-to-shore call a few hours ago. It seems the crew has come down with some kind of food poisoning. They're laid up and according to a description of their condition, they're in bad shape. Apparently, Bennet is fine and looking after them. You can imagine what that means."

Dever fingered a piece of baklava and popped it in his mouth. "If he's made them sick, the boat will have to be quarantined. We should also assume the crew is on its way to being dead. How do you propose taking him down without scuttling the boat?"

"If we miss our chance, that's something you'll have to seriously consider. I can't say we anticipated Bennet using the weapon on the crew, but we did anticipate having to board a boat to get to him. We helped ourselves to some equipment brought in by The Board's clean-up squad. It's in those Pelican cases."

"Okay, but how do you plan on doing that?"

"Thanks again to Mr. Demir, we're aware of an Italian made motor yacht that was delivered to Rumeli Feneri marina, this evening. Yves Moreau took delivery. It seems the Frog is also preparing to go after Bennet."

"How does that answer my question?"

"Our host, here, has been commissioned to deliver a specialty item to Monsieur Moreau. The dealer is having it flown in from Romania as we speak and the Airport Authority is being surprisingly cooperative. I'm thinkin' it's time for one of those magic Hallmark moments."

The doctor was beat. He couldn't remember when he'd ever gotten a blister from anything but a new pair of shoes. Even after using gloves, his hands felt raw. His shoulders, arms and lower back ached. The fittest part of his body were his legs and they were spent to the point he had difficulty negotiating the ladders.

Most of the crew were dead by three in the morning. Furkan and Yusuf had to be helped along. They hadn't begun to exhibit symptoms until midnight. When the captain and the rest of the crew retired to their bunks, unable to move, the two decided to turn the boat towards home.

Jerome used a gaff hook to remedy that situation. It turned out to be a dandy tool in managing the other bodies as well. He'd discovered that lifting limp deadweight couldn't be accomplished by hand.

Back at the lab, he had his assistants handle disposal. When he did help, there was a gurney, and an autopsy table that could be rolled to the incinerator. They never had to move the remains more than a few feet and they didn't have to deal with ladders.

He'd taken the time to rig a rope and pulley system to hoist the bodies to the deck. With gaffs set in the armpits and the rope threaded through the hooks' eyes, he cleared the crew's quarters in a few hours. It was exhausting work nonetheless.

The other issue that grossed him out was the fecal release. The smell gagged him. He expected a fluid purge but this was different. It mystified him that as much as these guys defecated while they could still move, they had anything left. The boys in the lab managed the odor with fans, filters and quick disposal. Clinically induced mortis hadn't prepared him for a real world death scene—it was the mess.

After stripping the bedding and tossing it in with the bodies, he went to the wheelhouse, cranked the engines and turned the navigation systems on. He confirmed his position, and set a course for a spot in the middle of the Black Sea that showed an absence of AIS or VTS activity. He then turned on the autopilot, went below for a shower, cheese scrambled and sleep.

They had all thrown in to load the van. With the two Pelican cases were sixteen thirty-round magazines for the bullpups. Ruben elected not to dwell on why Demir would have them and gave Henry the high sign to let it slide. The same went for the half-dozen flashbangs.

Adan sat behind the wheel, and Demir claimed shotgun. Not to be left out, Henry jumped in the back with Ruben and Rivka on a bulkhead bench.

It was forty-five minutes, or thereabouts, to Hezarfen Airfield. A privately run airstrip on the northern shore of picturesque Lake Büyükçekmece. Ruben had a good ear, and broke the pronunciation down in syllables—*bee-yu-chek-may-say*. The attempt to pronounce the name of the popular vacation spot evinced an approving nod from Demir.

Ruben and Rivka stuffed their pockets with ammo and grabbed a pair of flashbangs a piece. The big Okie went through his routine of patting himself down, tapping his tactical knife, and the ASP baton. The suppressor for the H&K, along with the green dot laser sight, were in place on his weapon.

Rivka had her ritual, which included checking the Dustar and tightening the sheath strap on her ankle, eyeballing the magazine in her pistol, and confirming a seated round. By the time she adjusted her body armor, Carver was mesmerized. It was like being back in high school, treated to an up-skirt.

He snapped out of it with Henry's elbow in his ribs.

"Jesus, Carver, would you get a grip."

Unfazed, Ruben averted his gaze only when Rivka turned her attention to Henry.

"What's the matter? Did something happen?"

Henry shook it off. "Nah, I'm just bustin' my man's balls, here."

She twisted her head Carver's direction, cheeks sucked in.

Ruben's ears burned, and he hoped the dusky interior camouflaged a flushed face. "Don't look at me. I'm fine...good to go."

When they arrived, Adan was allowed to drive directly onto the apron. Along with a three-story control tower, Hezarfen had a flight school with a dozen turbo-prop trainers sitting outside a hangar they'd been invited to enter.

With boots on the tarmac, the team assembled at the rear of the van. Demir stepped forward to greet the airport manager, who was approaching in an obvious snit. His round belly shook, and sweat dripped over quivering jowls, as he wrenched pudgy fingers. Ruben could hear him grinding his molars.

Demir draped an arm over the man's shoulder. In a

consoling voice he comforted the blubbering recreant—assuring him the bad man who hurt his feelings would soon be dealt with. Then he calmly asked where the package was that needed to be delivered.

The Javelin was in a military standard carrying case, inside a twin engine Cessna Citation resting on the apron near the hangar. The pilot was still aboard and made no effort to help, other than to drop the luggage compartment hatch.

It took the three Americans to wrestle it out of the aircraft onto a heavy duty trolley and then hoist it into the van. The extra missiles were easier to transfer. They were in launch tubes that had shoulder straps and carrying handles.

Ruben assumed the reusable command launch unit, which fired the missiles, was in the case and connected to a launch tube—ready to go. He had only watched a Javelin launch demonstration, but couldn't help wonder how a ground-pounder was expected to hump this stuff in the field.

Loaded up, Dever and Demir shook hands all-round and stood back. Adan was again behind the wheel, while Rivka and Ruben snugged in next to him. They waited until they reached the outskirts of Rumeli Feneri to get in the back.

Nothing was said until they drove onto the quay at the marina. The pair in the back heard the exchange between Adan and the guard. When Adan craned his head in the cargo space to let them know what was coming, Ruben gazed at Rivka with moony eyes. "Would you like to do the honors?"

She smacked her lips and battled a lid. "Oh, you...you're such a romantic."

The foamy wake, from a number of fishing trawlers headed for the channel, rocked the Rio against its fenders. The lines were tight on the cleats and bollards but Moreau had both hands on the console for balance. The Algerian had been trying to shake off a groggy head, when a shrill whistle from a kettle in the galley signaled help was on the way.

As soon as the yacht went in the water, Moreau had gone aboard to test the engines, and familiarize himself with the navigation and tracking equipment. When he finished, satisfied everything was shipshape, he dropped onto a bulkhead couch.

Rotating sentries had been posted twenty-meters out, draped in open front jalabiya to hide their Barreta CX4 carbines. Big Ugly had brought along five guys for the ride and Moreau felt safe to rest his eyes.

Five hours later he opened his orbs to a thin blue line forming on the horizon. A new day had begun the push against the night sky. Moreau rubbed his eyes, and then the crystal on his Yema. He jiggled the linked stainless steel band around his wrist before taking a peek—five forty-five am.

A filtered dark roast in a mug with Disney characters appeared in the console cup holder. Half of Big Ugly's scarred face seemed pleased with the presentation.

"I can have one of the boys fix us something to eat if you're hungry."

"Maybe later. Does the man delivering the launcher have a contact number? He should have been here by now."

The Corsican pulled his cell phone to check the call register. "The only call that came in was from Airport Authority. You already know it was loaded on the truck."

Moreau shifted to face the pier and pointed an index finger. "This might be it." A silver-gray Ford cargo van descended the steep inlet to the marina.

When the van made the left past the repair shop, it drove straight onto the quay and stopped. Moreau saw an arm extended from the driver's window, with a hand waving at a man in a fluttering jalabiya. Five-seconds later the Corsican sentry pointed at the Rio.

"Your man has a radio?"

"Of course."

"Tell him to check the cargo."

Big Ugly barked the instruction into a handheld he'd wrested from a holder on his belt. The van had already started moving, but stopped as soon as the guard started yelling. The driver's willingness to comply was a positive indicator they were about to get what they ordered.

Not long after the guard disappeared behind the van, it became apparent they were about to get what they deserved.

CHAPTER TWENTY-SEVEN

September 28, 2005

She nudged the switch one notch off safety, as the bullpup came up. When the rear doors came open, the chump had his own weapon in a ready position, but his finger wasn't on the trigger. If it had been, things might have proved more interesting.

When the round punched through his sternum, a few centimeters above the xiphoid process, the copper jacket fragmented and the soft lead core flattened. It crushed a dime-sized hole through the right aorta, with enough temporary cavitation to shred a large chunk of his heart.

If he wasn't dead before he hit the ground, he wouldn't have felt it. The bullet exited at the T2, severing his spinal cord.

"*Do you have a count?*"

Adan yelled back. "*Four on the pier. I don't know how many on the boat!*"

Ruben jumped down to the search the body. The rifle sling had a quick disconnect and he tossed the gun on the truck bed. When he found the radio, he was back in the van.

"*Okay, find us some cover.*"

Adan yanked the gear lever into reverse and floored it. "*Hang on to something.*"

Carver braced himself. After thirty yards, Adan let his foot off the gas and jerked the wheel port, with his left hand. The van spun starboard a hundred and eighty degrees. He then jammed the shifter into drive and crammed the pedal to the metal again, heading for the repair shop.

Ruben glanced at Rivka who'd pulled herself to a knee. Like Ruben, she was doing her best to avoid the Pelican cases that were bouncing around, while at the same time trying to cover down on the open rear doors.

She muttered something Ruben didn't catch. The next string of words were more clear. "Why aren't they shooting at us?"

The answer came from the walkie-talkie pulled off Rivka's first kill. "*Ne tirez pas! Ne tirez pas! Tirer Sergio et venez au bateau. Rapidement!*"

She glanced Ruben's direction. "Did you understand that?"

"My French is a little rusty, but it seems the bad guys aren't ready to light the place up yet. They're gonna scrape what's left of Sergio off the concrete and fall back to the boat."

Instead of driving to the rear of the repair shop, Adan made a sweeping left toward the mouth of the marina leading to the channel. Ruben moved to the passenger seat to scan the area.

"This place is a junkyard."

Most of the fishing boats in the water had motored out to go to work. The section of the pier they'd driven into was dotted with piles of old netting and fenders, along with conex boxes, storage shacks and boats—lots of boats.

From a sixty-foot trawler on a timber stand, to dozens of smaller crafts scattered around, lying cantered on their hulls, there was no lack of cover and places to hide. Ruben's worry had to do with locals.

The situation wasn't going to end in harsh language and vulgar hand signs. The last thing they needed was having civilians in the crossfire. It dawned on him that was probably why the Frog's reaction to Sergio's demise was a tactical retreat.

Nobody wanted to do anything that would get the police involved.

"Pull up over there—behind that green container. We need to figure this out."

Moreau watched the van roll into the boneyard. *Quel connard...*

The body of the henchman, formerly known as Sergio, snagged on the undercarriage when the vehicle backed over it. The remains—a flopping tatter—were flung with enough force during the "J" turn, to skip it fifteen or twenty feet.

The Corsican was in a rage and it was all the Algerian could do to talk him down to a controlled boil. Big Ugly lost men before but this was different. They were caught with their pants down.

The first inclination was to unload on the van with all the bullets at their disposal. Moreau's brutish compatriot, ever the professional, listened and waved that off. An ostentatious display of firepower would have the gendarmerie dropping in—a major game changer.

The other concern had to do with the missiles and launcher. He couldn't afford to have any of the hardware damaged. Bullets wouldn't set the munitions off, but they could harm the launch unit, or infrared seeker mechanisms. That would be as big a plan killer as having the cops show up. *I really hate that American.*

The Yank and Yid were daring him to go get his cargo. Fine. Once in the boneyard, the playing field would be leveled. The years he'd spent in the Congo made search and destroy his bailiwick. He was already feeling at home.

The CX4s were chambered in 9mm. With the suppressors attached, the only sound would be the clicking of the bolts, as the casings were ejected. Any citizenry they came across were to be put down, and piled with the trouble makers. The Algerian didn't want witnesses and it eliminated any confusion from a shoot-don't-shoot scenario.

After the tenderized Sergio was weighted and dumped over the side, Big Ugly formed three two-man teams. Moreau said nothing. He sipped his coffee, taking in the tactical scheme. The two best shooters were paired. The other two were split up, one assigned to Moreau, the other with the Corsican.

Big Ugly used the coffee table in front of the bulkhead couch to draw the lines of attack and the use of cover and movement. He also emphasized confirming a target before pulling the trigger. He didn't want to worry about being shot by one of his own.

The sun was an inch over the horizon and would be at their backs when they left the boat. Big Ugly tapped the chest of each man to confirm body armor, another issue resonating from the late Sergio. Fresh batteries for the radios were doled out, and cables from the earpieces were taped to their shoulders.

Bolts released and rounds chambered, they were ready. Moreau didn't need to check his pistol—a Baretta Compact L. However, in the spirit of the psych job his substantial friend was laying on his men, he dropped the magazine into his hand and verified a full load.

Before he gave the final signal to move out, he inserted an earbud and keyed the radio.

"Special Agent Carver...this is Control. We noticed our man was missing his handset when we checked his body. I'm assuming you are now in possession of the item." He didn't have to wait long for the reply.

"Hey, Yves. We thought you'd forgot about us. So what's the deal? We're gettin' bored." There was an instant of squelch when his thumb came off the key.

"You Yanks, with the pseudo bravado. You're so predictably jejune."

"You know, I'd love to get into a discussion about American exceptionalism, but I'm guessin' this isn't a social call. You want to tell me what's on your mind?"

"I want my missiles. If you give them to me, we'll let you live."

"Oh, please! You didn't just say that. Do you have a bad-guy script you read from, or what?"

"Anyway, just so you'll know, these Javelins aren't that hard to figure out. I'm guessin' you already know that. If you and the rest of the dipshits on that dinghy don't want to get smoked, I suggest you toss your guns and get the fuck out."

"Now who's reading from a script? You have the Javelin...I have the boat. It's obvious you came here to take it.

"Prepare to defend yourselves."

The trio found a high spot near the base of a sixty-foot cliff face, that marked a boundary of the marina. There was a corrugated steel conex behind them. To their front and flanks were stacked concrete blocks and piles of fish netting, truck tires and stand timber. The van, with the hazmat gear, was ten feet below and thirty yards to their left, behind a green cargo container.

Carver was squatting on his haunches, as was Rivka, examining the Javelin launcher. Adan was in a sniper kneel, cradling the CX4.

"Don'tcha just hate a smartypants bad guy?" Ruben groused to no one in particular. "Who do you suppose the Frog brought with him to this party?"

"Mr. Roberts and the airport manager talked about a

big, scar-faced gentleman," offered Rivka.

An image of Lurch floated across Ruben's memory. "Yeah, right. If they're gonna stay with radio comms, then they've already changed their channel. You can dick around with this thing if you want," he waved the handheld, "but you gotta figure they'll go radio silent until they pinpoint our location."

Rivka countered. "That's assuming they've got enough men to split into teams."

Adan shifted on his heel. "I counted four on the pier and the dock lights were bright enough for me to know Moreau wasn't one of them—neither was Scarface."

Carver nodded. "With that sized boat, I'm thinkin' squad strength—no more than eight guys. That would include the Frog."

The shrug from Rivka was noncommittal. "That count would also include the one already down. So...three two-man teams or two three-man teams. They'll want to leave someone back to guard the yacht."

The two men dipped their heads and Ruben added, "If they're in a hurry, it'll be three teams. They cover more area that way.

"We need to decide now where we go from here. We've got the high ground but they've got plenty of cover. Once they've spotted us it wouldn't take 'em long to pin us down. Then they could get somebody up there." He pointed at the clifftop.

Adan tapped his rifle. "I'd like to think we could pick 'em off, but we haven't zeroed these rifles. We'll have to make sight adjustments once we see where the first rounds land. At this distance, if they're wearin' body armor, all we're gonna do is hurt their feelings. We can't depend on head shots. We'll have to get closer."

Another nod from Carver. "We've got plenty of ammo for the bullpups, but you've only got the one magazine for that." Carver pointed at the CX4. "And two extra for your sidearm."

Ruben stared at Rivka. "Are you sure you know how to use this thing?" He touched the launch tube.

She sucked in her cheeks and smacked her lips. A patented expression Ruben now understood as the Jewish princess sign of incredulity. "America's generosity with its own arms proliferation is without peer. We used the Javelin to develop our own version, called the Spike. I've been fully trained on the system."

The woman went into rapid fire. "The operations are almost identical. Turn it on here." She touched a switch on the lower left of the command launch unit. "First notch is for daytime use. The main fire control display you'll see by looking through here." She touched a lens shrouded with a padded absorber.

"Once you find the target with the launcher, you switch on the IR tracker on the missile. You do that with the seeker trigger on the left hand grip. It also locks the missile seeker on target. The range finder is on the left grip as well. That'll be important because of minimum distance issues.

"The right hand grip has the attack mode selector..."

Ruben tried to interrupt the flow. "So, I guess you've got this."

"...switch to adjust the track gates to acquire a seeker lock-on, and the fire trigger."

"Uh-huh, that's great." Ruben started checking avenues of escape.

"There's more to it when you talk about the battery coolant unit, or minimum engagement time...but that's basically it. Get target lock, pull the trigger and *voilà*...the missile does the rest. Shoot and forget."

Carver understood the term *basically*. "Fabulous. What's the blast radius?"

"Look, Mr. Cheeky...you asked."

"Yeah, that was my mistake. How far do we have to be

away from a target?"

"It's a shaped heat charge used to defeat armor. It'll ignite a high explosive on impact and kill everyone in close proximity. For direct attack mode, we'll need at least sixty-five meters to target."

The woman is into it. "Okay, so it fires a heat round."

"Hey." Adan spoke as he raised his weapon.

Ruben turned and spotted two at about a hundred yards, when he heard the bolt on Adan's rifle click three times. One man went down and was quickly dragged behind a boat lying on its hull.

"Nice shot."

"Yeah, but I don't know where I hit him. Even if he's not dead, they're gonna sit for a second. They don't know where the shots came from."

"A two man team. So, where are the others?"

Ruben and Adan raised up enough to scan the area. "Have you seen any civilians this morning?" Ruben asked

"No, and I've been looking, but it's Sunday and early...people sleep in. The sardine fishers must have gone out before sunrise. The marina's nearly empty."

"Officer Levitan, you wanna give that bad boy a ride?" Carver's head bobbed toward the Javelin.

Using the right-hand grip she raised the nose of the missile launch tube and set it on a cinderblock next to her. She slipped three fingers under a wire rope connected to a retaining pin on the front tube cover. It took a few tugs to pull the pin free. She then turned the cap latch and the cover slipped off with ease.

A quick check of the seeker and the launcher was on her shoulder. "Where are they?"

"A hundred yards straight out." Ruben handed Adan Rivka's bullpup. "Look for the bullet strikes on a white hull. It's next to the path we came in on."

The Special Agents were plinking when they started

taking fire from their right flank. At least that's what they thought. They couldn't hear the report of the weapons, but the sounds of the rounds hitting the concrete blocks, timber and buzzing by their heads, caused them to redirect their fire.

"It looks like the scar-faced dude, with a second man." Adan shouted.

"I see 'em. Rivka, do you have the first target?"

With icy calm she said, "Yes, luv. Sighted. The two you spotted are there. I've got a lock on the hull. On the way..."

They were clear of the backblast but still felt the heat and pressure from the launch tube. Ruben turned his eyes to avoid the impact flash, but the detonation was jarring, even at a hundred yards. The hull came apart with burning splinters, raining over the boneyard.

"Fuck! Ya think anybody heard that?" Ruben wiggled a little finger in an ear.

"*They're still shooting at us.*" Adan ejected an empty. "I'm out."

Ruben tapped him on the shoulder with a fresh magazine and looked back at Rivka. "We can't stay here all day. The neighbors are gonna complain about the noise."

She'd disconnected the command launch unit from the spent tube and was busy snapping it onto another missile. "You and the bloody neighbors."

Rivka glanced up at him and then beyond to where Adan was returning fire. "They're too close for a missile. Can you move around them from over there?" She peered right, at three or four boats in a pile.

"Yeah, maybe we can flank 'em. Are you stayin' here?"

"I'm taking this back to the van." She hoisted the Javelin. "Then I'm going for the boat. Do you think you can take care of those blokes before the bobbies get here?"

Ruben locked eyes with his new heart throb. "Take the radio and gimme your rifle ammo."

CHAPTER TWENTY-EIGHT

The Marina

Carver and Adan, hunched over in a near duckwalk, headed toward a stack of weather-worn boats on their right flank. Their contorted movement didn't allow Ruben to check on Rivka's progress. She may have been comfortable on her own, but the Okie had grown accustomed to her being around. He'd begun to worry about her and it bugged him a little. He couldn't afford the distraction.

Adan's breathing suggested the initial adrenalin rush was wearing off. They didn't talk, using only hand signs, and Ruben wondered how his man's legs were holding up. A thirty-meter jog in a squat had Carver's quads in a quiver and they burned like hell.

He knew Lurch's last position, but without the benefit of whining rounds and bits of debris from bullet strikes, there was no telling if he and his partner were in the same spot. Carver had lost the visual in their effort to move to Scarface's flank.

Twenty feet from their objective, Adan raised a fist to stop. With the same hand, he patted his chest, then brought two fingers to his eyes and finally jabbed the air with straight fingers toward the starboard side of the derelict boats. He wanted to take a peek.

It'd been a long time since Carver found himself in the back seat. The thought bubbled up that his fatigue might be showing. *No time to get indignant.* He took a knee and nodded. Adan rose to a crouch and proceeded. Ruben watched him scan over the bullpup's sights, in a sixty-degree sweep. *There's no such thing as an ex-Marine.*

When he was ready to move behind the stack he gave Carver the high sign, waving him forward. In his own crouch, Ruben followed suit with weapon up. A second later Adan had disappeared. Then the shooting started.

The immediate response was to enter the fray. As he stepped behind the flaking hulls, he was body-slammed by Adan. Almost six inches shorter than Carver, and already going down, the man's momentum caught him low.

Ruben's instinct was to try to catch the guy, but his combat sense had him shuffle step backward, search for a target, and let Adan fall. He wasn't dead—he was still shooting. Carver could also hear him gasping for air and cussing.

The other party to the gunfight appeared to be in the same condition. He was going down, plugging away in their direction. It registered with Carver the dickhead's partner was absent, but he had to put an end to this nonsense before the prick got lucky.

He left Adan to find cover on his own, taking long strides toward the gunman. The schmuck was on his back, pushing with his heels and pulling with his shoulder blades in a panicked attempt to escape Ruben's approach. Two three-round bursts, directed at a spot two inches above the dude's shoulders, did the trick. *It'll be a closed casket.*

As Carver looked to engage another quarry, he back-stepped and pivoted right. Unless Lurch caught a round, which was a distinct possibility, Carver couldn't afford to be blindsided.

He whisper-shouted, "Adan."

The response came equally restrained. "I'm here—over here."

Leaving the cover of the boats, he went into a crouch. "Where?"

"Here." The disembodied voice came from the direction of a four-foot high pile of netting.

Carver found the Special Agent propped in a half-recline, legs outstretched. He was bleeding from his right delt and left quad. There were also signs he'd take a few rounds in his vest.

"You got him?"

"Yeah, but where's the other one?"

"Beats me." Adan coughed and winced. "Fuck, that hurts. I think I've got a few broken ribs."

"We've got to get you back to the van. There's no arterial spray, but you're bleedin' pretty good. Do you think you can walk on that leg? I can't tell if it's broken."

"It doesn't feel like it. I should be able to put some weight on it."

"I'm worried about those ribs, too. I don't want you to puncture a lung. What side are we talkin' about?"

"Right side."

"Okay, leave the rifle and your ammo. If I have to drag you, I don't want the extra weight."

"What...are you kiddin'? I'm not leavin' here without a weapon. Besides, that shit's got my prints and blood all over it. Just help me up. I'll be all right."

Carver leaned his bullpup against the netting and squatting on Adan's left side, positioned the crook of his right elbow under Adan's armpit. Straightening his back and pushing with his legs, he was able to lift Adan enough for the man to get his feet under him and help in the process.

Ruben was fully focused on the task, when Adan's "Oh, shit!" alert came seconds too late. The body's natural proximity sensor is an amazing physical attribute for folks with good reflexes. Like ducking under a low hanging branch, milliseconds before it poked an eye out, or slipping a punch, thrown outside of peripheral vision.

Lurch had managed to move around the two NCIS agents without being heard. He charged them at that vulnerable moment. If Carver hadn't bobbed his head left, at the instant of impact, Lurch's shoulder would have done to him what Jack Tatum's did to fools who tried to run a crossing route.

As it was, the hit still connected on his right pectoral and deltoid, spinning him right and knocking him over, face down. Adan wasn't so lucky. He took it square on the chin, and was out cold before the netting broke his fall.

Carver rolled left onto his back in time to jam the sole of his right shoe a centimeter above an attacking Lurch's left kneecap. It didn't hurt him, but stopped him long enough for Carver to gain his feet. With fists ups, they were now doing the dance.

Lurch had about an inch and maybe twenty pounds on him. In Ruben's mind, the size difference was manageable. He'd kicked bigger ass; however, by the look of the cheesedick, it was apparent he didn't mind mixing it up.

He couldn't chance a glance at Adan. If he let himself fret about the former devil dog, they'd both wind up dead. The guy moved with confidence and Carver didn't kid himself. No matter how much he kicked, punched, and trapped, this fight would end in a grapple on the ground. The next few seconds confirmed it.

With shoulders hunched, chin tucked and fists cocked close to his cheeks, Carver bounced slightly on the balls of his feet. He stepped-dragged, right foot forward, and landed a right jab on the nasal spine, followed by a left cross on the chin and right hook to the mandible. He grunted an exhale as the knuckles connected, with a satisfying vibration that rippled to his elbow. A beautiful three-punch combo with legs and hips twisting into each blow.

He might as well have been beating on a heavy bag. When Ruben rotated right to deliver an uppercut, the big man with half a grimace did a lapel grab on Ruben's photographer's vest. As he began to twist inside for a shoulder throw, Ruben blocked it with a palm strike on the right bicep. Lurch countered with a head butt, using his forehead boss, against the bridge of Carver's nose.

Stunned and partially blinded, Carver staggered backward, smashing his forearms down on Lurch's wrists. When the grip relaxed, Carver's instinct was to lean in, bob right and weave left, for a right uppercut.

He was either too slow, or had telegraphed the move. Lurch grabbed the right shirtsleeve at the top hem with his left hand and pulled. With his right, he hit Carver with a knife hand on the left shoulder, spinning him left. Lurch was now behind him, working on a choke hold.

Carver never considered himself full of warrior spirit, but fear pissed him off. The Frog's droog got the better of him and he was about to go down. He was scared and the resulting anger fueled adrenalin reserves.

Lurch was trying to apply pressure to Ruben's carotids with his right forearm and bicep. He stepped back and pulled down to get leverage, but Ruben tucked his chin in the crook of the guy's elbow. He trapped the arm with his hands and bit into the soft flesh, going after the medial cubital vein.

At the same time, Ruben shoved his glutes into Lurch's hips, an inch above his groin and stepped right to get his left leg between Scarface's legs. With his right foot planted outside, Ruben jerked forward and twisted clockwise in a single motion that brought Lurch over his right shoulder—heels over head.

Ordinarily, dropping someone onto pavement with that much force took the fight out of them. At least long enough for Carver to draw down. Not with this asshole. Carver was about to find out he was exactly where he wanted to be.

As Ruben reached across his chest inside his vest, to yank his pistol, Lurch rolled onto his side and spun on a hip. The shin of his right leg caught Ruben on both Achilles tendons and swept his feet straight out. He landed hard on his upper back and neck, between the C7 and T1.

There was a flash of white light as pain radiated down his spine. He'd slapped the ground with his left forearm and palm on impact, which helped transfer some of the energy of the fall. He wasn't dead yet. He rolled onto his stomach to push himself up.

Before he could get the soles of his shoes on the ground, however, Lurch was on him again. He straddled his back, with his left hand over the top of Ruben's head, fingers in his eye sockets. He pulled Ruben's head back, while trying to snake his arm below Ruben's neck for another chokehold.

When he had the appendage in the position he wanted, Lurch rolled onto his back with Ruben on top of him. He wrapped his legs around the waist, crossed his ankles and squeezed. Ruben was locked up and as the pressure increased top and bottom, black spots appeared in his vision.

He couldn't get a breath, and blood from his broken nose began flowing down his throat. With circulation to his brain being cut off, he knew he would pass out in less than a minute. He'd aspirate on his own ichor.

The pistol was gone. Lurch's left leg should have been crushing it into Ruben's side. Struggling to stay awake, his fists and forearms smashes did nothing to break Lurch's body scissor. He scratched and clawed at the killer's face and arms, trying to gain purchase on the back of a hand. It might as well have been a vault door.

In a panic, Ruben could feel himself slipping away. His arms and legs flailing, he wrenched some of his vest free from the flesh vice crushing his lower ribcage. That's when he felt it and with a frantic hand, snatched at the velcroed flap until the Recon 1 spilled into his hand.

With a single, hard flick of his wrist, the tanto blade snapped open. He had it in a reverse grip, blade edge out, when he began stabbing and ripping into Lurch's right quad. The shriek was exquisite.

He felt the leg spasm, as the pressure on his neck subsided. Carver continued to stab and rip as he twisted on top of Lurch, opening gaping wounds in his side. Lurch tried to hold on, but each jab robbed him of power.

The blade went in to the hilt at the armpit and Carver knew he'd punctured the prick's lung. When he finally straddled the big man, he looked down into his eyes. The dude knew what was coming.

Devoid of any emotion, other than a joyless sense of relief, Carver switched the knife into a hammer grip, the edge down.

"What's your name?"

In a gurgled whisper, the grotesque face uttered, "Fuck you...asshole."

Ruben rammed the tanto into the side of Lurch's neck and twisted the blade. He removed it by tugging straight up, tearing out the throat.

Ignoring the now inanimate object, Carver staggered to his feet. He wiped the man's residue off the knife with a pant leg, and then folded and tucked it in a slot in his vest. Before turning his attention to Adan, he kicked around the area of the scuffle, looking for his pistol and anything that may have fallen out of his pockets. The .45 had skidded a yard or two from where the body lay.

He holstered the H&K, testing the snap on the retaining strap as he walked toward Adan. His partner was still out, but breathing, and his pulse was strong. Carver looped the bullpup's sling over Adan's head and laid the weapon on his chest.

With one hand, Carver grabbed the canvas handle at the nape of the Adan's body armor and pulled him off the fish netting. He then grabbed his own bullpup, and getting his bearings, began to drag the Special Agent in the direction of the van.

The jostling must have brought the fallen man around. "What hit me?"

"Remember the big scar-faced guy everybody was talkin' about?"

"Yeah..."

"Him. What's left of him is over there."

Adan's head swiveled right. "How long have I been out?"

"Three, maybe four minutes. The guy really rang your bell."

"You okay?"

Carver's chortle was more of a hiccup. "Well, I'll tell ya...I'm glad I'll never have to run into that motherfucker again."

"Did you get his radio?"

"Oh, shit. Why didn't I think of that?" Carver eased Adan down.

"Wait a sec. Let's see if I can get to my feet. Help me up."

Carver pushed Adan into a sitting position, and using the same process they had going before the ugly son-of-a-bitch showed, lifted him to his feet. Ruben held onto to his buddy until he was confident he'd stay that way.

"Oh, man...I'm still bleedin', but I think my face and ribs hurt worse than the bullet holes." Adan's griping stopped when he got a load of Carver's condition.

From the expression, Carver checked himself over. The knees on his cargo pants were torn, with the ragged edges stained with dirt and blood. His photographer's vest was smeared with the same grime, but intact.

The knuckles on both hands were bruised and scuffed and his right hand was caked in blood up to his elbow. As he spit snot mixed with blood, he imagined what his face must have looked like.

"I guess I could do with a shower."

"All those fuckin' stories I heard about you are true then?"

Carver touched the bridge of his nose with the tip of a little finger. "That depends entirely on who's tellin' the story. Do you think you can drive?"

"Yeah, probably. I'm a little woozy, and have the mother of all fucking headaches. I'm not nauseous, yet. I got that goin' for me." Adan pointed at the body. "Do you know who that guy was?"

"He said his name was Fuck-you Asshole."

"Oh, yeah? I think I know some of his relatives."

"We need to get back to the van and find Rivka. Once we get the gear on the boat, I want you to beat it back to your cousin's. You can brief Henry and get patched up."

"What are you gonna do if she's dead?"

"Have a little faith, brother-man...she's one of God's chosen."

CHAPTER TWENTY-NINE

The Frenchman's Foreplay

She didn't wait to follow their progress. While Art Sheppard's confidence in those blokes began to make sense, she was glad to be shot of them for a few minutes. The Javelin was a tick over twenty-two kilograms and Rivka didn't want Carver seeing her struggle with the weight.

It had been the first time she'd actually fired one. The price tag on those babies prohibited a knock about on the range. The relief of not going cack-handed in front of the Yanks, after showing off her knowledge of the system, was punctuated by the pleasure of toasting the first pair of baddies. *Bloody fucking brilliant! I'm keeping this toy.*

Rivka could neither crouch nor run, with the Javelin slung across her back. The steep slope down to the van had to be traversed sliding on her bum. She managed to keep her head up, and with pistol out, she did repeated visual sweeps for Moreau's goons.

The panel truck Ishmael Demir anted for their crap shoot was the size of a small lorry. The container Adan parked it behind provided only partial concealment. A motivated party with an interest in its cargo would have no difficulty locating the vehicle. She hoped, however, she'd be the first on site.

The tube dug into her trapezius and the external obliques at her waist were stiffening. She couldn't fight effectively, encumbered to that extent, and wondered if she didn't make a mistake sending the NCIS muscle a different direction.

The thought was stuffed. Rivka may have been a proud estrogen producer, prone to second-guessing as much any smart, willful woman, but she'd learned early in her career to stick with initial instincts. What good was feminine intuition if a person didn't follow it?

Unless there was another punter in Moreau's crew as imposing as the scar-faced gentleman, she could manage on her own. While she didn't cock a snook at who might be coming her way—they could put a hurt on her—she and the boys had to clear the field before the coppers showed. That wouldn't happen, if they hadn't split up.

The concealment she'd been using ended ten meters from her destination. A dash to the lorry was possible, but not with the launch tube. Rivka positioned the dangling end of the casing cover over a two-foot-high stack of concrete blocks and took a knee. The pressure from the sling released, and as she balanced the missile with one hand, pulled the strap over her head.

Careful not to drop it, she used both arms to lay the tube on the ground next to a six-foot pile of stand timber covered by a blue tarp. With more effort than she wanted to apply, she managed to tug enough of the cover down to lay over the tube. She then pulled her pistol and made her move toward the lorry.

She stretched her legs out in a sprint. The balls of her feet pulled her along the pavement, as her arms pumped in time. She'd covered the distance in less than three seconds, sliding to a stop next to the right front tire. A pirouette right one-eighty, revealed nothing—she was still alone.

Backing up to the passenger side door, she peeked through the window and saw the key in the ignition. Decision time. If Carver and Adan had found themselves in a face-off with more than Scarface and his companion, she likely had a free run to the boat.

She could pull the lorry up to the edge of the stand timber, where she'd left the Javelin, retrieve it and drive pier side. If Moreau stayed with the vessel, she'd deal with him there. The assumption in all of this being Carver's ability to overcome any opposition.

If he went down, the Americans would bite the bullet, inform Turkey of the situation, and a military option would go into effect. She might even be witness to it, in the event she secured Moreau's yacht and made it into the channel.

As she opened the door and climbed in, she tucked the pistol away and crawled across the passenger seat to drop behind the wheel. She wondered if a military option, in the end, might be the best solution. That outcome obviously mirrored Moreau's panacea. Otherwise, he wouldn't have ordered a million dollar can opener.

The engine coughed to life on the first turn, but before she could put the lorry in gear, she felt the cold business end of a suppressor poking her in the right temple.

Except for the painful ringing, Moreau had gone completely deaf in his left ear. The hearing in his right was only muffled—saved because of the earbud.

When they left the boat twenty minutes before, the plan was simple. He saw the direction the van went and fanned the teams out to pinch off any routes of escape. He sent Big Ugly left, the two best shooters up the middle, and he took his man to the right.

The idea was to have the shooters situated along the only avenue large enough to navigate the vehicle, which happened to be the road they used to enter the boneyard. Their backup would be Moreau. The Corsican's job was to move in behind the van and kill anyone trying to exit from the rear.

If the American's decision was to make a stand, or charge the boat on foot, they'd want to stick together. In that case, Moreau and his crew had the tactical advantage of numbers and position. No matter what Carver and his friends elected to do, they would eventually have to go through them. What happened was exactly what he didn't expect.

After one of the shooters had been hit, Moreau shifted to a spot behind a metal storage shed, fifty meters to the right front of the two men. His movement had been covered by the Corsican, who radioed he had three people pinned down with flanking fire.

The man who'd been shot took the round on his vest and although winded, was ready to engage. However, everyone had employed suppressors and the shooters couldn't get a fix on where the enemy sat.

In a squat, the Algerian shuffled from behind the shed to a pile of netting where he had a clear view of Carver's position. What he couldn't believe was what that *salope Juive* appeared to be doing. When he started yelling into his handheld it was too late.

Moreau experienced mortar fire in the Congo, but this was different. It was the shockwave from the sound, heat and concussive force of the blast that rattled him to his core. He couldn't get close enough to the ground.

It felt like his organs moved and his heart skipped a beat. For an instant he'd passed out. The metal shed and the four feet of piled fish netting between him and the carnage, were what saved his life. He lay for almost minute before sitting up to look around.

The stripped boat hull the shooters were perched behind was gone, as were the shooters. He peered in Carver's direction and saw him and another man, in a low crouch, moving left from cover. Moreau used his radio, the earbud still in place, to warn Big Ugly. The response, while difficult to hear, was reassuring.

The bitch didn't go with them. He watched her sling his Javelin over her shoulder and start slowly to the right. When she disappeared from view, Moreau surveyed the area below her position and spotted her end point—the Ford van. He knew what he had to do.

The Italian hitman Moreau partnered with, had also survived. The Algerian found him on the ground behind the shed, addlebrained, with his fingers in his ears. He'd straddled the man's legs, and shook him until his eyes focused. When he was certain his instructions were understood, he grabbed him by his body armor and hoisted him to his feet.

Moreau had jogged back to the boat, and was now standing in the cockpit on the stern. The ringing in his left ear unabated, he pulled on the lobe and flexed his mandible for relief. He'd taken the radio off his belt and unplugged the headphone. He left it powered, and slipped it in a charging unit on the bridge. If Big Ugly reported in, Moreau believed he would hear him.

No matter how anything else played out, he was confident the Jewess was coming alone, with his property.

The youngish man spoke French. "Where's the rocket?"

Rivka was beside herself. Cheesed-off she'd stepped into a trap she half-expected, she took a few deep breaths through her nose to clear her head and slow her heart rate. "I'm not going to tell you where the rocket is. What's the matter with you?"

"You tell me, or I'll put a bullet in your brain."

"Well, that's smart isn't it? How're you going to find it then? I mean, I've hidden it...right? What are you going to tell your boss? 'I shot her because she wouldn't tell me?' Oh, yeah, he'll be pleased. What's he going to do to you then?"

"*Shut up!*"

"Oh, now you want to me shut up. How did you get this job?"

He pressed the suppressor hard against the side of her head. "*If you don't shut up and tell me where the rocket...*"

Rivka slapped the barrel away with her right hand, grabbed it with her left and pulled it for leverage to spin right in her seat. The knife on her ankle was an easy reach and freeing the blade from its scabbard, she jabbed it in his left tricep, with enough force to get it stuck in the humerus.

Screaming, the henchman dropped the rifle. He howled in horror at not only the pain, but the sight of the woman, gripping his wrist with her left hand, her foot braced on his hip, wriggling the hilt back and forth trying to yank the blade loose. The tip of her tongue sticking out of the side of her mouth as she worked.

As it dislodged in a cascade of dark red gore and bits of bone, he stumbled backward into the cargo bay, weeping.

"Hey! Where do you think you're going? I'm not done with you yet." Rivka hadn't gotten past being snookered and she reckoned a little more conversation was in order.

It was slow going with Adan, but they were back in their initial firing position in two or three minutes. Carver didn't want to sit him down, primarily because of the hassle of getting him up. The possibility of more bad guys, however, necessitated the use of cover.

Carver could see their ride and thought his eyes were playing tricks on him.

"Hey, man, does the van look like it's movin'?"

Adan's grimace suggested even the slightest motion racked him with pain. "No. It's sittin' right there."

"That's not what I mean. It's rockin' like a Saturday

night at the drive-in."

"Huh?"

"Never mind." *Anachronisms and tired metaphors—fossilized cool. Fuck me. My throat's sore and my back hurts. I wonder if she's married...*

Ruben keyed the radio. "Rivka, are you on?" He waited a five seconds and tried again. "Rivka...Ruben."

"Hello, luv. It's nice to hear your voice. Do you think you could pop over and help me with something?"

"Where are you?"

"I'm in the lorry."

"I'm sorry, where?"

"Oh, for the love of...the lorry, the truck...the *van.*"

Carver checked Adan's leg, tugging gently on a strip of cotton fabric he'd tied over the wound. Fuck-you Asshole's pants had been the source of several bandage strips. "Whaddaya think blew up her skirt?"

"Don't ask me. You better go. I'll be fine here."

Ruben thumbed the mic. "On my way."

In thirty seconds he was standing at the rear of the Ford. "Rivka, it's me."

The door swung open to Rivka kneeling over one of Moreau's men, bound with duct tape.

"Help me with this wanker."

"Is he alive?"

The look she gave him reminded Ruben of his grandmother, just before she slapped him for asking something stupid. "Do you think I'd go to this trouble if he was dead?"

She squinted past him. "Where's Adan?" Concern was creeping into her voice.

"He's banged up, but he'll make it. So what's with this guy?"

"Help me pull him out of the lorry. We'll dump him where I left the Javelin."

Ruben figured it was better to say nothing and do as

he was told. He leaned over the bumper, burying his hands in the armpits and pulled the body straight out. The unconscious man's heels smacked the bumper, before dropping hard on the ground.

"Are you gonna get his feet?"

"You're doing fine, pet. Let me show you where to put him."

Two minutes later, Ruben had the man under the blue tarp and the Javelin slung on a shoulder heading back to their wheels.

"I'll stow this and go get Adan. He's up there." Ruben pointed at the location. "You wanna me tell what's goin' on? You don't seem to be too worried about Moreau. Is he dead?"

"He's on the boat, waiting for me and this thing." She tapped the missile launcher.

Ruben shrugged, trying to find a better spot on his shoulder for the weight. "Oh, and I'm fine by the way."

"I'm sorry, luv. Do you need a hug?"

Ruben and Adan sat on the bulkhead bench, their boots resting in goo. Rivka insisted on driving and Carver wasn't interested in arguing. If Moreau's invitation was extended to her only, she was the one he needed to see behind the steering wheel.

Ruben took no more than a dozen breaths from the time she put the van in gear, hit the gas and put it in park at the pier.

Adan stared at the back of her head and then at Ruben. "Are you really gonna let her do this?"

"What makes you think I can stop her? Besides, aren't you even a little curious..."

She dropped her head to speak into her lap. "I can hear you talking about me."

The driver side door opened and she stepped out, pistol in hand. Ruben did a magazine exchange and confirmed he had round in the chamber but didn't move. He saw a shadow drift across a cabin window and three heartbeats later, Moreau appeared in the cockpit.

He and Rivka had begun a dialog, but Ruben couldn't make out what was being said.

"That's not Arabic. What is that?"

Adan coughed and winced. "It's Hebrew."

If the two Americans thought things had gone to the surreal, what happened next was downright medieval. The door came open and Rivka dropped her pistol on the seat. Without looking at Carver she said, "I don't want you to interfere."

She pulled off her jacket and looped it around her left hand and up the forearm to the elbow. She let the tail dangle about ten inches. Propping her right foot on the door jamb she reached down and skinned her Dustar and spun it in her palm. She left the door open as she stepped away.

Moreau, with a flourish, came over the brow to face her. Ruben watched in fascination, as the knives appeared and the two combatants began to circle. At that point he'd seen enough and glancing at Adan said, "I'll be right back."

Carver pulled and turned the handle on the rear door to keep the latch from making any noise. On exit he turned left to use the van as concealment as he walked its length. When he cleared the front, the two were at each other. He heard knife blades clanging and detected a few places on both where they'd nicked each other.

We haven't got time for this. Carver raised the bullpup, and put a round through Moreau's sphenoid. His left eye plopped onto his cheek as he rag-dolled.

Rivka turned and glared at Carver, her chest heaving with each breath.

He dropped the rifle to his side. "We don't need to be dickin' around with this guy."

"Well then, what took you so *bloody* long!"

CHAPTER THIRTY

On The Water

Adan had settled behind the wheel and was on his
BlackBerry, while Carver moved the gear to the boat.
The idling twin diesels sent a soft vibration up Ruben's
legs as he stacked the Pelican cases in the cockpit. Rivka
was in the salon, below deck, rummaging for a first aid
kit.

"Hey!" Adan yelled after he finished the call and
cranked the engine.

"Yeah?" Ruben came across the brow and took three
steps to the driver side window.

"Ishmael said the cops are waiting for me to leave so
they can come down here and find someone to arrest.
They've had the road blocked to keep the locals away. I
guess they're getting antsy. Are you ready to go?"

"In a minute. I'm a little worried about our girl. She's
got a couple of cuts on her arms that look pretty deep.
They didn't go to the bone but they'll need stitches."

"Are you thinkin' about tryin' to do this thing on your
own?"

"It crossed my mind."

The answer to Ruben's immediate quandary emerged
from the salon with a white plastic container under her
arm. "What are we waiting for? Let's go!"

Narrowed eyes and pressed lips precluded Carver's calm demeanor. "You're a good man, Adan——a genuine snake eater. I'm honored to know you. You take care of yourself. You're gonna be swimmin' in shit for a while, but you should come out of it okay."

As they shook hands, a hint of skepticism crept into what would have been an optimistic response. "Yeah, sure. I'll see you when you get back."

Ruben let go the lines, and after pulling in the brow, used a pike pole to push away from the pier. Rivka sat in the pilot seat, operating a bow thruster to help move away from the mooring. When Ruben yelled "clear", she shoved the twin shifters to engage the screws. With a hand on the helm, she pressed the throttle controls to ease the bow toward the marina's mouth.

As they passed through the marina gate, she opened the throttle to begin a long sweeping turn into the channel. At more than thirty knots the yacht's planing cut through the chop, but it wasn't a smooth ride. If it wasn't for the padding in the leather helm seating, it would have been downright uncomfortable.

Rivka had stripped the sleeves off her shirt and applied gauze patches and ace wraps to the cuts on her arms. Ruben figured she found a way to close the wounds since they weren't bleeding through the dressings. He wondered how long that would last and decided he wanted to examine the cuts.

At that speed they'd be in the Black Sea in a few minutes. Once they made the deep water, he'd have her throttle back. The sun was fully up and he could see for several miles in every direction. There were other boats visible but none along the line they were traveling. The GPS and VTS also indicated a clear path. The autopilot would maintain their course.

A check of the first aid kit, as they bounded through the open water, was difficult; however, to his satisfaction it revealed packets of braided suture, curved surgical needles, a needle holder, forceps and two pair of scissors—one labeled iris and the other suture removal. All of which were in sterile packs. *Good stuff.*

Along with those, he found a bottle of povidone-iodine, tubes of other antiseptic ointments, boxes of surgical tape and several gauze rolls.

Before he could say anything, Rivka spoke up. "Did you find what you were looking for?"

"Yep."

"Do you know how to use any of that stuff?"

Carver spread his lips in what he believed to be his most ingratiating smile, and said, "Nah, but how hard could it be...really? Do you know where we're goin'?"

Rivka tapped a handwritten note inside a plastic sleeve, that had been taped to the AIS tracking system console. "Moreau synced the fishing trawler's AIS transponder frequency with this boat's GPS tracker and auto-navigation system. We're on a heading to intercept."

"Any idea how long it'll take?"

"At this speed, maybe six and a half hours. It'll be on our radar in about five. If the weather holds, it'll be visible about four miles out."

"Throttle back a bit. I can't see the monitor for all the bouncing."

"What's the problem? You getting sea sick?"

"Excuse me, lady, but I am with the *Naval* Criminal Investigative Service. Just slow down, I want to check his heading."

With an exaggerated reach for the throttle controls, Rivka pulled the speed off the screws. As the bow nosed down, the planing ceased and the yacht gravitated into a comfortable twenty-knots cruise.

Carver pointed at the screen. "Is this him?"

"Aye, that's him."

"This shows him heading due north at about ten or twelve knots. Where's he goin'?"

Rivka peered down at the monitor and answered, "He's not stupid. Your scientist knows someone will be coming after him. And honestly, I'm surprised he still has the AIS transponder active. He must have the trawler on autopilot."

"If he wants to rid the world of Israel, he's goin' the wrong direction. He's going north and you believe he's on autopilot."

"Uh-huh."

"I bet he's resting. He's been up all night with a dying crew. He can't feel much different than we do. That boy got something to eat and went to sleep. Which is what we need." Ruben laid his hand on hers. "Let's go below. If Moreau had this," he waved the first aid kit, "then there's a stocked galley."

"I don't know..."

"Come on. If that trawler changes direction, this scow will tack to a new heading on its own. I want to check your wounds. From what I saw earlier, you need some stitches."

To Ruben's surprise, she didn't object.

It took Ruben almost an hour to suture Rivka's arms. The cuts were longer and deeper than he thought. He was amazed she hadn't lost more blood than she did. For the discomfort, he found a box of morphine sulfate tablets at the bottom of the first aid kit. A couple of those with a shot of brandy and she conked right out.

They lay together on a queen-sized bed, but Ruben couldn't sleep more than four hours. The boat's noise and motion wouldn't allow him to get past a doze for most of the period.

While concerned about Rivka's chances for infection and the job he did on her cuts, he had his own problems.

His right shoulder ached from what he hoped was only bursitis and his throat was on fire. He had difficulty swallowing.

He didn't have to speak to know his voice was a croaker; no better than a whisper. The mirror in the head showed the bruising—dark purple marks on the sides of his neck.

They'd heal, but he saw something else during the examination even more annoying. His nose, clearly broken, reminded him an inflated condom. On top of that, the scapha and antihelix on both ears were red and swollen; a formation of large puffy blisters where the skin had been pulled away from the cartilage. *Cauliflower fucking ears...I hate this job.*

When he finished cussing at his reflection, he busied himself prepping the hazmat suit. He laid it out to make it easier to climb into when the boat was back to planing through swells at thirty-five knots.

Earlier, he found level IIIA body armor he figured was meant for Fuck-you Asshole. It was too big for a proper fit, but it would be fine under the hazmat suit. He had to forget about the shoulder holster, but he could probably get away with slinging a bullpup.

As he examined the suit, and tried putting it on solo, a number of issues presented themselves. The gear was designed to give maximum protection in a bio-hazardous environment—airtight head to foot. Its sheer bulk, with the double-lined gloves and the Mickey Mouse boots, made it unconducive for gripping, climbing, pulling triggers, grappling, or movement in tight confines.

Another issue was the oxygen tank. It was rated for only thirty minutes. Each man who went into the lab had a spare in his Pelican case and the suit had a coupler that could be connected to the lab's clean air filtration system. Fine for them, bad for Ruben.

If he was in the suit when the air ran out, he wasn't

sure he could free himself before he lost consciousness. He therefore made a decision on the spot how to proceed. Rivka wouldn't like it, but he couldn't divine a better solution.

He'd go onboard with the tank and respirator, a long-sleeved shirt, nitrile gloves and the photographer's vest for ballistic protection. If the doctor exposed him to the concoction, he'd go in the drink, strip and hope the salt water would rinse him clean. That's, of course, after he killed the demented fuck.

Once he got back on the yacht he'd shut himself in the forward berth and wait it out. If Rivka was right, it wouldn't take long to confirm his status.

Nodding to himself, the suppressor came off the pistol. He left the green-dot laser sight in place. He didn't want to hassle with finding a sight picture through the respirator mask.

He was making coffee when the radar proximity alert sounded. Rivka met him in the salon, and the two climbed to the helm together.

She stared at the radar screen through puffy lids, still groggy from sleep. "It looks like he's about ten miles out. Dead in the water."

"What's wrong with the guy? You think he's sick?"

"He's supposed to be immune. I just think he hasn't seen us yet. Get ready. Once you're suited, I'll give it the gas and we can be there in thirty minutes."

Jerome couldn't remember ever being so sore. When he opened his eyes, everything seemed fine. As soon as he tried to move, he found himself immobilized with excruciating muscle pain and stiffness. It seemed at that point the only things that didn't hurt were his eyelids.

This was a first for a man who'd spent his life avoiding the kind of physical exertion he threw himself into the night before. He read about delayed onset muscle soreness from eccentric activity and understood what his body was going through. He was a man of science after all.

Brody was well versed in all the theories from microscopic damage of muscle fibers, lactic acid buildup and muscle spasms, to connective tissue damage, inflammation and enzyme efflux. Knowing why he couldn't move didn't help. *Whoever said knowledge is strength needs a dose of my medicine.*

Through arrant willfulness, he raised one arm, then the other, to grip a frame rail on the underside of the bunk above him. A groan gurgled through clenched teeth as he pulled himself a quarter-inch off the mattress. It was enough to allow him to pivot his legs.

When they dropped over the edge, he used the momentum to slide out of the bunk. The cold deck against his bare legs was a mild comfort, but the torment twisting to his knees, made him wonder how he'd negotiate the obstacles around the trawler.

He grabbed the bunk to climb to his feet. After the painful discovery of what muscles were necessary to maintain balance, he concluded he needed a plan to pull his pants on. The laces on his shoes became a superfluous detail.

If he could negotiate the ladder to the wheelhouse, he'd pack in what provisions he needed for an extended stay. He'd use the head when his bladder and colon could no longer stand the pressure. He wasn't looking forward to the task of getting on and off a toilet seat.

It was apparent from the sound of the engines idling he'd slept the entire trip. The trawler had traveled to the designated point he'd entered on the GPS chartplotter. On arrival it throttled back to idle, tacking only enough to adjust for drift and relative position.

Brody checked his watch and determined he'd been out for almost eight hours. It was after two pm, and a certain apprehension began to form. The GPS and AIS transponder had been active the entire time. Control would have a fix on his location.

Fear induced adrenaline, powered his legs, but they ached with every step. To move over the hatch coamings, as he went from berthing to the head, meant pulling a pant leg to help. Careful not let his trousers fall as he stood in front of a metal trough, he was irritated by how long it took to piss. It was like a never-ending stream. He finally zipped up after draining what he imagined was about a half-gallon of ammonia-wafting urine.

He needed water, but wasted no more time on physical issues. Servicing the pain and dehydration could wait. A check of the radar and the AIS tracker became the imperative. It was time to disappear.

The muscles in his legs had begun to warm as he walked and he sensed some recovery beginning to occur in his calves and quads. His entire back, however, from his upper glutes to his traps, were useless. Both biceps felt shredded and his hands were raw.

As expected, the ladder was agony and he reminded himself it was only soreness. Be that as it may, it took twenty seconds to summit ten steps.

Up to this point, everything had worked to plan. He had his vessel, completed a decent test of the instrument of his wrath——outside of the lab——and confirmed he was immune. While he was certain there would be attempts to stop him, he only needed a week to set his solution in motion.

He had the means to alter the world's current course. Acrimony aside, his curiosity, embedded in that dispassionate, analytical sector of his left hemisphere, made him wonder how fast his baby would spread in a population center. Any population center.

Computer modeling gave him some idea, but he often admitted the algorithms he used were a construct of wishful thinking. The nimrods at East Anglia and their global warming models were a perfect example. Those guys were an embarrassment to the scientific community.

Brody wanted to see the results in a real world setting; look at the stat lines live and compare them to what graphed on his laptop. There was also something else tickling his interest. He wanted to see who would eventually survive. *Wouldn't that be a fascinating review...*

Another spectacular day viewed in panorama from the bridge. *This is living.* He sucked in a cleansing breath, as he began to focus on the next task. The chartplotter verified his location and thinking about the next leg in his journey, he glanced at the radar monitor.

There was single blip, about three thousand meters to his six o'clock. The AIS tracker classified it as a motor yacht with Italian registry. He wouldn't have given it any further consideration except it was heading straight for him at more than thirty knots.

The psychological reaction to the possibility he was in danger didn't seem to translate to his physiological condition. The pain and stiffness still had him hobbled, but he had no intention of giving up.

He pushed the throttle full forward, set the chartplotter for a spot two hundred kilometers west, punched the autopilot and shambled out of the wheelhouse. If the people on the yacht were after him, he wasn't going to make it easy for them.

He'd found a Mauser bolt action rifle in the captain's quarters the night before, when he was moving the body. There was a box of 8mm ammunition next to it. He figured out how to put the bullets in, after messing with it for an hour. Brody never cared for guns, but his new life was bringing new experiences he found himself embracing.

The aerosol cans were in his backpack, which was in berthing. He wanted to keep them close, but had no interest now in wasting them on unwanted visitors. That was what the rifle was for. *Unless, of course, they make me.*

CHAPTER THIRTY-ONE

The Boarding

"The radios are charged." Rivka had moved to the flybridge and was sitting on the edge of the pilot seat, both hands on the helm.

Ruben had dropped the tank and respirator on the deck in the cockpit before joining her. It lay next to a brown canvas satchel containing a lightweight assault ladder that Demir had thrown in with the rest of the gear. An afterthought that had become an essential part of their plan.

"Where are they?"

"Yours is in the charger over there." She pointed with her chin. "We're on channel one."

Carver tucked the handheld in a pocket on his photographer's vest. He'd already removed the items he didn't want to lose, if he had to abandon the apparel in the water.

His partner glanced at him, and then peered back out to sea. "He's finally spotted us. He's making a run for it. Are you sure you're gonna do this without the suit?"

"Yeah, I'm sure. I can't move in that thing."

"I'm not arguing, luv. I didn't think they were practical when I checked them at Demir's. I didn't say anything at the time because of your mate, Henry. He was already in a snit. Imagine the twist in his knickers if we tossed the hazmat gear before we left."

The most efficient solution, in Ruben's mind, was to get in Javelin range and put the trawler on the seabed. It was obviously Moreau's plan and it didn't require special foresight to know Rivka wouldn't gripe about using the missile again.

The folks back home, however, wanted Carver to make a genuine attempt at recovering the doctor. It would be a bonus to safely obtain a sample of his wares.

"If this goes to plan, I think it would be a good idea for you to be in one of the suits on the receiving end. At least until we've cut his clothes off and thrown them overboard. We can even give him a salt water dip for good measure."

"I'll think about it."

"Now look..."

"We'll be on him shortly. Have you got that grappling ladder sorted out?"

"I'm on it."

"Do me a favor, pet. Bring me up one of the bullpups and a few extra magazines."

"You expectin' some resistance?"

"I don't know what to expect. That's why I want the bullpup."

He nodded, spun and slid down the ladder. In less than a minute he was back with the weapon and two extra magazines.

Rivka accepted them without looking up. She set the magazines on the console and bracing the wheel with her knees, checked for a chambered round and re-seated the magazine after giving it a gander. She then switched the firing mode to full auto, draped the sling over her head, and let the rifle dangle at her right side.

Ruben turned away, believing he'd never get tired of watching this woman go through her routines. Before descending to the cockpit, he inserted the earbud, confirmed channel one and twisted the power-volume knob.

At the ladder bag he keyed the mic. "Radio check, over."

"Loud and clear. I'm not sure what the signal will be like once you're inside. That trawler has a steel hull. Over."

"Roger that. Let's not stress about it now. Out."

The ladder was a piece of work. The grooved aluminum rungs were connected to quarter-inch woven stainless steel cables. The grappling hook was fastened to the ladder end with a screw lock carabiner. The back of the hook had a welded rod, which fit into a hinged pole with nineteen, twelve-inch sections.

Ruben snapped ten rods together and slipped the hook in the pole. He then put the tank on his back, adjusted the straps over his holster and fastened the waist belt. The pressure gauge drooped over his left shoulder. He'd turned the cylinder value on and holding the respirator to his face, took a few breaths to test the gas regulator.

He thought about an earplug, but decided to go naked. If he went below decks, he'd slot one then. He keyed his mic. "Rivka——how soon?"

"Hang on. I'm taking fire."

Hang on to what? The yacht was smacking the waves at full throttle when it swerved port with enough centripetal force to catapult him into and over the starboard side railing. He would have gone into the water if not for the pressure gauge catching on a gunnel cleat, arresting his fall.

For an instant he dangled, slapping against the hull; his feet skipping on the ocean surface. The boat then veered starboard and the impetus lifted him enough to wrap an arm over the gunwale.

He could hear Rivka saying something, but even if he understood, a reply was impossible. He had no way to key the mic. The tank weighed him down and he couldn't throw a leg up far enough to hook a heel over the taffrail.

Carver was stuck and he could feel his left shoulder weakening. If Rivka made another hard turn he was finished.

She'd kept the throttle forward and the boat began planing again—bouncing and slamming against swells. Each one further loosening his grip. After cutting through a high roller he held his breath. *This is it.*

Then gravity took over. For an instant, as the yacht dropped to the bottom of the swell, Carver felt weightless. He rose above the gunwale, with arms and legs flapping. When he began to fall, his left hand smacked on the railing. Screaming for energy, he clawed for a grip and pulled himself toward the deck.

The pressure gauge, still stuck in the cleat, jerked him to a stop in midair and flipped him. He fell to the deck, tank first. The impact centered on his spine, adjusting every vertebrae from T1 to T12. He went dishrag limp.

The fall also made the gauge come free and his horizontal momentum rolled him onto his stomach. As he lay, catching his breath, she was speaking to him again.

"Are you ready?"

With his thumb on the key, he said, "What?" He hadn't lost his voice but it was now deep and raspy.

"Aren't you listening? I said I'm going to make a pass on the left side of the boat, near its tail. Are you ready?"

"Give me a second!"

He could now hear her without the radio. As he pushed himself to his knees, her voice was coming from directly above him. When he stood, she was at the top of the ladder looking daggers.

"Would you *please* quit fucking around. The bloody nutter is shooting at us."

"You've got the machine gun...shoot back! Jesus, do I have to think of everything?"

"Oh, *you*! Get ready. I'm making the pass."

When Carver bent down to pick up the ladder pole, he brushed the pressure gauge and felt a stream of cold air blowing on his shirt sleeve. The hose had ruptured.

Rivka had made the turn and he could see the trawler's wake. There was no time to switch the tank. He squeezed the buckle on the waist strap and dropped the cylinder.

The speed came off the yacht's screws, on the trawler's port side stern. The yacht was caught in the trawler's wake and Carver, doing his best to maintain some balance, discovered he didn't have enough length on the ladder pole to set the hook.

Reminding himself to breathe, he laid the pole across the yacht's taffrail to snap five more rods in place. When Rivka started yelling in his ear, he took the time to twist the volume knob to off.

Back on his feet he braced the bottom of the pole against his instep and thrust the hook toward the trawler's hull. As soon as he felt the pole strike, he snatched the end above his head and took four staggered steps backward, looking for the hook's position. Perfect. At four-inches above the gunwale, he yanked the pole and set the hook in the coaming bolster.

He had a hand on a ladder rung, which was more luck than savvy. When the hook caught, the pole came off and Ruben couldn't haul it in. It went in the water and was sucked under the trawler's transom from the screw cavitation. *Oh, man...I don't know if I wanted to do that.*

With both hands on the ladder, he was gazing up at the hook wondering how he was going to make the jump. Rivka resolved that incertitude with a radical turn port. Ruben was in the air again. When he smashed into the side of the trawler, the shock rippled to his backbone. It was only the sticky grip afforded by the nitrile gloves, that kept him from going the way of the pole.

As he banged against the steel hull, his right foot found purchase on a rung. It stabilized him enough to get his left foot in play, and he was climbing. When he reached the top, he wanted to peer over the gunwale and look first for the scientist and then for cover points.

The effort of the climb, and movement of the ladder, however, made him rethink that approach. If he was spotted taking a peek, the nutty professor would be on him before he could pull himself onto the weather deck. He'd be processed into chum by the prop.

He threw one arm over the gunwale, then the other. While gripping the coaming bolster, he pumped his legs up the remaining few rungs, until he could do a dive and roll on the wood planks covering the stern.

Pistol out and in a crouch, Carver surveyed his surroundings. The trawler had the mast centerline aft of the superstructure, with two outriggers connected. Just forward of the mast were two loaded net drums. The warp winches and capstans were port and starboard under the outriggers. Between the mast and taffrail was what Carver thought must be the fish hold.

He had plenty of spots to hide behind.

The soft pops of gunfire confirmed Rivka had Bennet distracted. Carver made it onto the boat without being seen.

The ambient noise made it difficult to determine where the doctor was shooting from, but Carver assumed it was on the port side. He was standing erect now and could see the yacht on his left, paralleling the trawler. Rivka was returning fire from the flybridge. *Goddamn, she's sexy.*

290

The starboard weather deck passageway was clear to the forecastle. There was one hatch halfway down the superstructure, and beyond that, a ladder he assumed went to the bridge.

The run down the passageway convinced Carver the shooting was indeed coming from a port side weather deck. The only sounds he heard were the wind and sea. He moved past the hatch, going directly to the ladder. He reckoned he could get behind or above Bennet by crossing the bridge.

Carver needed to get to the bastard while Rivka had him occupied. He knew he could manage the rifle, but facing a case of the killer flu creeped him out.

The climb this time was easy. His legs were holding up and he felt pretty good about himself. In a crouch at the wheelhouse door, he did a quick peek through a window. The space was empty.

Just the same, he entered in a crouch, pistol up, and closed the door with a gentle push. The port side entrance was directly in front of him. As he waddled toward it, he heard the distinct report of a rifle. *That sounds familiar.* Carver had a .30-06 in a bag back home.

The notion of Bennet with a hunting rifle made him hesitate long enough to look around. He wondered if he could spot the dude through a window. What caught his eye, though, sitting atop the radar screen next to the helm, were two cans of deodorant spray. *Oh, yeah—raise your hand if you're sure.*

Unless the guy was an obsessive compulsive about perspiration, Ruben was staring at Dr. Devil-may-care's handiwork. For sure, their appearance made them seem less threatening. Other taglines like "Cute and Girlie" and "Total defense", popped into his head.

The pistol went in the holster. He then examined his gloves for any tears and satisfied, scooted to the base of the instrument panel. He reached for them in the same way he would an old blasting cap—with complete deference. The idiot savant would have made them safe to handle but it didn't hurt to be careful.

He wasn't going to stick them in his pockets. The crazy man had a one-hole punch that could bring down a mountain goat. The cabinet below the coffee pot was at eye level and struck him as good a place as any to hide them.

Ten seconds later they were covered with a tea cozy, pushed all the way to the rear of the cupboard. He went back to the door he'd come through, peeled the gloves off, rolling one inside the other, and tossed them out, hoping they'd gone over the side.

A second pair came out of a hip pocket and he was ready to join Rivka's attempt at communication. *She's such a people person.*

The wheelhouse windows didn't provide a view of where Ruben believed the doctor had set up. He could hear the shots: one every five or ten seconds and a lull while he reloaded. *I guess I could just go kill the guy.*

The sound of Rivka's errant rounds peppering the bridge made him a little nervous. He didn't want to be greeted by one of her bullets, as he opened the port side door. The idea of asking her to cease fire bubbled up and he suddenly remembered the radio he'd turned off.

"Hey, darlin'. Are you still on?"

The crackle in reception didn't mask the irritation. "Where have you been?"

He lied. "You were right about the hull interference. Do me a favor and stop shooting. I've got the helm controls. Over."

"What are you going to do? Over."

"I thought I'd put the brakes on and have the doctor come by for a cuppa coffee. Over."

"Are you sure you know what you're doing? Over."

"Rivka...baby, if this relationship is gonna work, you gotta, like, quit with the negativity. Out."

No longer in a crouch, Carver walked to the helm and taking a second to determine which was the throttle control, yanked it back. He waited a few seconds and put the screw in neutral before punching what he believed was the engine's kill switch.

Everything went silent.

Carver positioned himself behind the helm, and fingered the snap on his holster's retaining strap. The H&K dropped neatly in his hand. He held it at his hip, barrel down. The helm cabinet hid it from sight. He didn't want to give the doctor the wrong idea when he came through the door.

Rivka had stopped shooting and she came on the radio. "He's coming, luv, but there seems to be something wrong with him."

"Did you hit him?"

"That's a negative."

Ruben's sudden concern: Bennet was sick. The deodorant was out of reach, but if the shitbird was contagious...

He keyed the mic. "Tell me when he's at the door." *I've gotta think.*

Thirty long seconds later. "He's at the door."

It slowly opened and Ruben, ready to drop for cover, yelled, "Dr. Bennet—James—it's Moses Horwitz. Please don't shoot."

"What...I don't...how?"

"Yeah, I know, it's freaky, but don't shoot. Are you sick? If you're sick please don't come in here."

"Why were you trying to kill me?"

"I wasn't, but my friend on that boat didn't know what else to do, but shoot back. She wasn't actually trying to hit you."

"I don't believe you."

293

"No, no, seriously. Let's talk."

"I don't want to talk, I want you off my boat!"

"Okay, okay, but I need to know if you've made yourself sick."

"*I'm not sick!* Stop asking me that. I'm *sore*."

The relief was indescribable. "Okay, Jimmy. Come on in."

The rifle was at Bennet's waist, barrel up. Ruben recognized the make. "Please don't point that thing at me."

"Why are you here?" The barrel dropped a fraction.

"Jimmy, you already know the answer to that."

The barrel came up and Ruben raised his empty hand. "Whoa! Take it easy. The whole world knows about you. I had a helluva time gettin' that yacht away from the French dude. That was the guy who wanted you dead. Not me."

"He's Algerian and I figured as much."

"Yeah, well, now he's dead."

Bennet adjusted the rifle butt, his finger inside the trigger guard. "What do you want?"

"There's no way you're gonna survive. Not without my help. The President of the United States knows about you. The Turkey authorities know about you. The frickin' Israelis know about you. They've have your picture, copies of your passports..."

Bennet cut him off. "They don't have everything."

"They've got your DNA. What else do they need?"

"You haven't told me what you want."

"I want you to come with me. I'll get you out safe. You can't stay on this tug. They'll never let it, or you reach land."

"You're lying!"

"Jimmy, please...if you kill me, she leaves and an F-16 will show up and that'll be it for you and our plan."

"What do you mean *our* plan?"

Ruben, watching Bennet's body language, saw it register the deodorant cans were missing.

"Where are they? Give them to me or I'll kill you."

"I can't do that. Not right now."

"*Give them to me!*"

"Not gonna happen."

Ruben knew the look. He saw the grip change and the finger twitch. He dropped just as the gun went off. Without waiting to continue this part of their conversation, Ruben went low around the helm.

Bennet, struggling to chamber a round, stood stock-still. Ruben could see the dipshit's eyes cross, as they followed the slide-covered barrel of the Heckler & Koch come down on his forehead. A groan and gush of air emanated from the feckless dope, as he hit the deck face first—the rifle still in his hands.

Radio up, Ruben's voice was a grated whisper. "Hey, doll."

"*What?*"

"You think you can fish this guy outta the water before he drowns?"

CHAPTER THIRTY-TWO
February 14, 2006

Valentine's Day. The bar on the second floor of Madam's Organ was packed. Ruben, alone as usual, was on his third Tanqueray martini. He'd been on a diet for a few weeks and had the bartender hold the olives.

The band wasn't going on for another thirty minutes, but Gary Clark Jr.'s latest CD was cranked up and the crowd, composed mostly of couples in every gender combination, were enjoying themselves.

His only offer so far came from a couple of queens looking for a little strange. It gave Ruben a whole new meaning to the lyric *looking for love in all the wrong places*. After graciously declining, he sat wondering what happened to Rivka. It'd been six months, but for Carver, she was definitely the one.

They'd dumped the Javelin and other paraphernalia overboard, before beaching the yacht, after dark, at Kumköy. Demir had the Ford waiting for them and they were taken directly to the U.S. Consulate. There they transferred the errant scientist to the waiting arms of Art Sheppard and Henry Dever.

The husbanding agent told the pair the Turkish government was willing to continue pretending not to know anything, as long as a generous compensation went to the families of the dead fishermen. Ruben got the feeling there were other more significant concessions made, but nothing was said. Demir had also declined to reveal what his cut was in the process.

Art was even less forthcoming. As soon as he got his hands on Bennet and the deodorant cans Ruben had wrapped in an inch of duct tape, he disappeared. Several weeks later, a letter of appreciation went to the Director of NCIS for Ruben's and Henry's participation in a successful training exercise.

It wasn't exactly a tearful reunion with Henry, but bringing Bennet back alive seemed to go a long way in mending their relationship. His old friend was back in Mexico City, doing whatever it was that continued to impress the Agency. Their only contact was a Christmas card Henry sent with a picture of him and his family.

The last he saw of Rivka was when he went with her to the American Hospital, about thirty minutes from the Consulate. She'd come down with a fever on the yacht. The knife wounds had gone septic and she was admitted into intensive care for treatment and observation.

He went back two days later to see how she was doing, only to find she'd discharged herself. Apparently, she had a couple of churlish visitors. The hospital staff were still cleaning up when he walked in.

Adan had fully recovered and was transferred to headquarters to sit at a desk two cubicles down from Carver. They ate lunch together two or three times a week and bitched about the job. The former devil-dog was good company.

The tiny puddle at the bottom of his glass alerted the bartender to step over. Ruben waved him off, contemplating a taxi ride home.

He pulled a few crumpled twenties from his front pants pocket. As he smoothed them out on the hardwood, he was jostled a bit. He didn't look around.

The place had started jumping with a party atmosphere.

When an arm fell over his shoulder, he looked down to see a hand with freshly manicured nails giving his peck a squeeze. Ruben signaled the bartender pointing at his glass and then held up two fingers. *I love that smell...*

The whisper in his ear went straight to his groin. "Aren't you a luv."

When he spun on the barstool to face her, she smiled and gave him a wet kiss on the mouth, sucking his lips into a pucker. When she pulled away a few inches, her bottom lip protruded into a small pout. "Ruben...I need your help."

Thanks for reading *The Istanbul Agent*. I hope you enjoyed it. The fourth book in the series, *The Jihadist List*, will be out in winter 2016.

If you'd like to hear about news, giveaways, and other new releases, please sign up for my email newsletter. I'll never sell or abuse your information and you can unsubscribe any time. The form is on my website: http://www.jeffreyseay.com/#!contact/c1kcz

Printed in Great Britain
by Amazon